ILIYA ENGLIN

TRAIL OF AN INCUBUS

A NOVEL

ISBN 0-9582711-0-0

Distributed in association with www.amazon.com
Cover Art: "Seated Demon" Mikhail Vrubel (1901)

THIS BOOK, MY FIRST,
HONOURS A NOBLE MAN
WHO TAUGHT ME TO
NEVER SURRENDER.

I SALUTE MY
FATHER'S SPIRIT.

Prologue

A long army truck slowly negotiated the winding road under watchful eyes of the guards and rumbled to a stop in front of the steel boom gate.

The driver was alone, but guards froze at the sight of his uniform. His arm, casually dropped overboard to proffer his documents, was clad in "frog" camouflage of Waffen SS, a much feared and admired commando corps – combat arm of the SS empire.

The appearance of such men was feared for two reasons. First, they were superbly trained killers whose prowess merged into legend, and whose behaviour at this uncertain time was not at all predictable. Second, they only appeared where the rearguard action of the Third Reich was likely to be at its most desperate, much so by virtue of their presence.

The sergeant quickly rifled through the papers and returned them to a powerful hand that hung carelessly in the air. Its graceful fingers closed around the bundle of documents and the head, clad in a scarred helmet, nodded imperiously.

Gears were ground as the boom gate was raised, and the truck laboured up the mountain, stopping at the mine's entrance.

The driver cut the engine and jumped down, landing with a nimble crouch of a hunting cat. He was not a tall man, but very muscular and barrel-chested, something not even a bulky combat jacket could conceal.

He walked briskly to the entrance, where the commandant was hurriedly straightening his tunic. By the time he was approached, he stood at rigid attention, his right arm quivering in the air.

"Heil Hitler!"

The SS officer nodded, throwing up his hand in a short, careless gesture of return salute. He handed the commandant an envelope and stood stock-still.

Shivering slightly in the rising wind, the commandant removed a single sheet of stiff letterhead and studied the few lines it contained.

"By order of Himmler, no less," he commented as he scanned its lines. "All assistance to be rendered without question."

He returned the paper to the envelope and handed it back. The SS officer took it from him and neatly replaced the entire bundle in his breast pocket.

"It seems that I am at your service," said the commandant with an acrid undertone. It was, after all, almost the end. In less than a week neither he nor this elite psychopath would be in uniform.

"I need twenty of your youngest female prisoners," replied the SS officer in a totally neutral tone, his deep melodious voice seeming to counter the insult with its very calm.

"Indeed?" asked the commandant with a grimly lascivious chuckle. "Anything else?"

"And two guards, of course," replied the SS officer. "It's an urgent assignment."

"Of course," replied the commandant with a leery smile. "May I ask what sort of a brothel you are running, Kamarad?"

There was no reply as such, but the large head clad in steel swivelled slightly, deep-seated eyes boring a hole in the commandant's forehead.

It radiated danger, that long, heavily ridged face with a lantern jaw and dense eyebrows. Its expression was a dispassionate menace of one who makes a living out of death and chaos – inflicted thoroughly and completely, unhurriedly and without fear, doubt or emotion.

Not being a man of combat experience, the commandant felt ice spread from the pit of his stomach, as if staring down a rifle barrel or standing close to a live wire. He backed away slightly, smiling hastily to cover his gaffe.

"I will see to it," he said shortly, his throat in spasm. He turned on his heel formally and disappeared inside.

Twenty minutes later a straggly line of women clad in heavy work clothing was marched and loaded into the truck as the SS officer stood aside, staring impassively. He watched the prisoners clamber into the truck. One slipped and was roughly pulled up by the guard, who kicked her for good measure as she began to climb again. She crawled inside on all fours without a sound.

The SS officer jerked his chin for the guards to join the prisoners inside and locked the tailgate behind them without saying a word. The truck rumbled past the boom gate and was out of the camp.

An hour of slow driving later, they negotiated a steep drop into the valley and accelerated along a flat stretch which followed a mountain stream. The driver seldom slowed down, using the entire road surface to take corners.
With little warning he turned off into a lane into tall pine forest, then rattled along the uneven track for a few more minutes. He pulled onto the grass in a forest glade, where the engine died. The passengers heard the door open, then the driver emerged at the tailgate to unlock it.

"I will question prisoners over there," he pointed to the far side of the glade. "Each will wait for the previous prisoner to return and come over one at a time."

He marched to the far side of the glade and motioned with his hand.

A guard jerked his rifle for the first prisoner to come out. She stepped gingerly between the two soldiers and dropped heavily from the truck. They watched her level with the officer and saw him smile as he asked her something.

She shook her head briefly, and he nodded formally in reply. She returned to the truck and started climbing inside. The next rose to follow.

One dark haired girl was seen to nod affirmatively. He motioned her to stand aside rather than return to the truck. She turned out to be the only one to satisfy his inquiry, and when no more interviewees were left, he turned and nodded for her to approach.

"What is your name?" he asked softly.

"Hannah," she replied tonelessly, staring into his eyes without fear.

"Are you a Jew, Hannah?" he asked in the same kindly tone.

She nodded.

"Excellent," he replied, his posture relaxing. "I wish to make you an offer."

She listened intently, standing stock-still until he finished.

'Think about it for a while," he said.

"No," she said quickly.
He leaned close and studied her face intently.

"You haven't thought about it," he said, his voice still level.

"I don't need to," said Hannah with a short shake of her head.

"You are not afraid of me?" he asked with some surprise.

"I am," said Hannah. "I know this uniform. But you can only kill me, and I would rather die than help something like this come about."

"But don't you want revenge?" he asked with amazement. "For you? For your family? For your people?"

She thought for a while.

"Possibly," she replied. "But not like that. What you

are suggesting is even worse than what happened."

They stared at each other in silence. A breeze caressed Hannah's short, unevenly cut brown hair. There was a distant sound of a warplane diving into a bombing run, followed by dull thuds of faraway explosions.

You see," said Hannah suddenly and forcefully. "Only five years ago, I would have said you are mad. Today I believe everything you just told me. I have no idea who you really are, and maybe what you plan to do is for the best – but I don't think so. A thing like that cannot be righteous."

"Very well then, Hannah," he replied calmly. "Walk back with me and don't be afraid."

She nodded, her eyes calm with resignation, and turned towards the truck, the officer following a few steps behind. When they were nearing the vehicle, he drew his service pistol, cocked it and pointed the barrel at the back of Hannah's head.

They were stood next to the truck. Guards stared expressionlessly, their eyes filled with total indifference. As the girl approached, they merely leaned back to avoid being spattered by brain and bone.

One second and two masterful shots later they both slumped into the tailgate, blood dripping from holes drilled perfectly through the centre of each forehead.

The prisoners shrank back in abject fear, but the officer smiled and replaced the gun in its holster.

"Come out," he called, waving them over the tailgate. He held it at an angle motioning them to slide down to the ground.

They stared at him motionlessly.

"Out," he called more curtly. "There isn't a lot of time."

They hurried down, clambering to the ground awkwardly. When the truck was empty, he nodded, replaced the tailgate and turned to face them.

"Hannah is in command," said the officer, speaking clear, simple German. "I am setting you free, but you must hide in the forest for a few days. If the soldiers see you, you will be shot for escaping."

They stared at him with little understanding.

"Go," he repeated, a note of irritation creeping into his voice. "I have to leave. You can walk down to the stream and live on berries. Surrender yourselves to the English. They should be here in a few days."

They turned to follow Hannah, who led them in the direction he indicated.

He easily threw two bodies into the truck as if they were sacks of hay, closed the tailgate and ran towards the cabin. He drove out of the forest quickly and maintained that speed until the road came to a bridge spanning two near-vertical sides of a steep gorge.

The SS officer paused in the middle of the bridge to toss the bodies into bushes far below and drove on, passing the town of Wödden and using side roads to avoid it. The roads were largely deserted apart from a few civilians pushing their pathetic loads away from what was likely to be a savage fight for the home soil.

Fifteen kilometres from the Swiss border he pulled over to the side of the road, tossing his helmet onto the seat. His war had ended.

The officer jumped out and walked into a forest, pulling an old field compass from his breast pocket. He stopped to take a bearing, aiming at a towering peak, rising some distance across the border, and walked on, making leisurely progress towards the mountain.

He walked at a steady pace, unhurriedly, occasionally consulting his compass and moving easily despite his build. It was only when he crossed the river that marked the border and commenced a hard climb up the opposite bank that his breathing deepened.

By day's end he stood at the foot of the tall peak, looking around for familiar landmarks. He started moving in circles until he found what he sought – a small entrance to a cave, hidden by rocks and a fallen pine tree. Breaking dry branches in his way, he entered the cave and waited for his eyes to adjust to the dark, listening to the murmur of water running in darkness.

Once his vision became clear, he located a large flat rock and exerted all of his enormous strength to move it aside. Underneath was a metal box buried level with the ground.

The SS officer extracted a suit of sensible civilian clothes and a pair of light walking boots, favoured by the middle class of that region. He stepped out of his uniform and walked naked into the depth of the cave, plunging into an icy cold stream where he lay still in rushing water until quite cleansed. He emerged, steam coming off the skin and droplets rolling down his massive physique.

Having changed into civilian clothes, he rolled the uniform into a ball and placed it inside the box, pushing the rock back over it.

He then curled up on hard ground, thinking about the phase of his life which just ended, to join many other stretches of time spent in the relentless pursuit of his goal.

He marvelled at Hannah, the girl he released in the pine forest beneath the stinking concentration camp, where she spent five years of her life making poisonous ingredients for artillery fuses inside an old mineshaft.

For as long as she was in that camp, she risked her life with every leakage of some toxic filth – the prisoners would have been sealed inside. Yet she continued to be a moral being, making moral choices and refusing to turn on her kind.

He knew this to be the highest form of courage, and mentally saluted her inside his cave, much as he knew such bravery to be a major obstacle in his quest.

He decided to rest a few years and wait for the world to stultify. There were too many people about with the experience of absolutes.

Time to play tourist for a while, he thought as sleep descended upon him, a silky fog in which his tired body soon dissolved.

The underground stream murmured in total darkness.

**

Nearly seventy years later and on the other side of the world, Martie Stanes groaned and hauled himself to his feet from damp ground. On second thoughts, sinking back onto his knees was fine for the time being.

Martie's torso swayed unsteadily, watching his father's station wagon disappear in the undergrowth towards the road. He groaned again and drew a long, slow breath to counteract the numbing agony spreading from his groin.

For the parent of any daughter, Martie was the worst nightmare incarnate – a well-built teenager with even teeth and a clean appearance, which concealed a testosterone-crazed marauder. In his capacity as local heart-throb, tennis ace and only male aware of female orgasm, Martie deflowered much more than his share of classmates.

It didn't hurt that his father was the local bank manager, nearest a rural town comes to having a feudal lord. Had Martie known about mediaeval history, which he did very little, he would have approved of droit de seigneur and would have striven to uphold it at every opportunity.

Tonight things went wrong. Maggie was a magnet to Martie and his erstwhile competitors for three reasons. First, she was both pretty and intelligent. Second, she was presumed to be a virgin since nobody had the slightest grounds to claim otherwise. Third, she was the district's karate champion, which somehow made seducing her more of a challenge.

For Martie, the latter proved his undoing. After an evening of reasonably pleasant conversation and marijuana they drove back the scenic way, stopping to sample cosmic sounds of the river running through the old forest in dim moonlight.

This is where Martie made a rash move, which resulted in a polite laugh. A repetition earned him a wrist twisted back blindingly fast. Whilst he was trying to recover from an imminent fall backwards, a half-hearted kick was flung into the groin. That left him totally paralysed whilst Maggie calmly started his father's car and disappeared towards what he hoped was her home.

Martie got up and staggered after her. He blundered back to the road and started walking along its middle, his sandal-clad toes curling at the thought of tiger snakes taking advantage of the still-warm bitumen. The only source of light was a clouded moon, and he guessed, more than saw, where the road went.

He was making steady progress in the cool air, groin throbbing dully. His breath now returned to normal, and nausea abated. Marty was about a third of the way along when his prayers were answered, cones of light slicing the forest behind him.

He hailed the car and was surprised to see a late-model Mercedes 4WD, its coal-black coat gleaming in the reflections hurled by powerful lights. It travelled slowly, engine barely registering above the rumble of tyres. When its driver saw Martie, he pulled over in a graceful arc, and Martie ran to its side. The passenger window slid down, and Martie leaned against the door to inhale the smell of expensive leather.

The driver was a youthful-looking man with a mane of dark hair. Martie saw little of his face except a proud leonine profile with a powerful cleft chin jutting out above what looked like a dark turtle-neck inside a sports jacket of similar colour. He noticed the hands resting on top of the steering wheel – large, heavy knuckles over long graceful fingers, lightly gripping the leather.

"How's your walk?" asked the stranger.

"Um," said Martie with failure of eloquence that so often destroys a teenager's self-esteem. "Would you be able to give me a lift?"

The dark head nodded obliquely, indicating that he saw no possible reason to refuse.

"Get in."

Grateful, Martie slid into the front seat after winning a struggle with a recessed door handle. He and started pulling at his belt as the car rolled away with fluid grace.

"What is your name?" asked the stranger in a deep, melodious voice. British intonations, but a tiny

European accent – vowels are too short, thought Martie who had a flair for languages.

"Stanes, sir," Martie did not know why he added "sir", but felt much better for doing it. "I live in Cranville."

"That's the other way, Master Stanes," said the stranger, looking at him intently. "Are you lost?"
Martie launched into a sanitized version of the night's events, managing to emerge as a wounded and scorned lover. The stranger chuckled appreciatively.

"Youth," he said after a little thought. "You know, this is the best time of your life."

"Not tonight, sir," returned Martie gloomily.

"What's so damn good about this girl?" demanded the stranger with a smile. "What – a stunner?"

"Not exactly," answered Martie. "Good-looking, sure - a redhead. But..."

"Not unique," the driver finished Martie's sentence. "Wonderful companion?"

Martie shrugged his shoulders in genuine puzzlement. The stranger laughed.

"Easy manners? No, I doubt a lad like you would need to be after that. Ah! Is she a..."

"Virgin!" blurted out Martie. "Yeah."

"Of your age?"

"I think so."

The car pulled over to the side abruptly. The stranger stared at Martie intently and shook his head.

"Amazing what you find when you stop looking," he said. "Here and now, of all times and places! No, my young friend – there's something she's not telling you."

"We reckon not," replied Martie with expert confidence.

"Who constitutes 'we'?"

"You know," Martie blushed slightly. "The boys."

"Ah, the local dick squad. What if she is isn't into men?"

"Oh," the possibility never occurred to Martie. He thought a while with an air of an expert studying a challenging dilemma.

"No."

"Why not?"

"She likes boys. Just won't... You know."

"Did you ask her why?"

"Lukie did. He is the best looking of the lot. She said she didn't want his you-know-what after where it's been."

The stranger laughed and put the car back into gear. "Is that what she said? Well, good for her."

"Oh, we all heard it," said Martie, shaking his head. "At the school dance and all."

The stranger laughed again. "I tell you what, young man."

Martie looked at him eagerly. They approached the gates, and the car stopped. Martie opened his mouth, then realized that he was delivered to Maggie's property without a slightest hint of directions by a man he has never seen in the area.

"I think you should leave her alone from now on," said the stranger gravely.

Martie instinctively leaned against the door, his fingers finding the door handle. He pulled at it, but the lock failed to give way.

"Do you understand me?" asked the driver, his black eyes boring into Martie in the moonlight.

"Yes. Yes," whispered Martie hastily. "I got it."

The driver moved his right elbow slightly, and Martie felt more than heard a click in the passenger door. The handle gave way, and for the second time that night he found himself falling onto damp ground.

The Mercedes towered over him motionlessly, its exhaust rumbling to the sound of eight cylinders. Panicking, Martie backed away from the open door, gazing at the stranger's face in terror. They continued to lock eyes as the driver leaned over, reached for the door and pulled it shut.

The car rolled back onto the road and suddenly accelerated, tyres squealing slightly. Martie remained dead-still, watching its tail lights disappear into the forest – two demon eyes staring at him through darkness.

Part I:
The Disciple

His car rattled over the shingle road, the day's heat shimmering around distant horizon. Rick Charlton slid a cigarette from his crumpled pack on the dusty dashboard and pushed in a well-worn lighter, chewing on the filter.

He touched its glowing centre to the tip and inhaled deeply, continuing his progress towards distant hills across the flat plain. The road was surrounded by sagging wire fencing, which kept despondent sheep from wandering into occasional traffic. There was nothing else.

Rick was driving through a part of the world once made wealthy by the ancestors of these sheep – but that time had long passed. A few families still clung to the ravaged valley, mostly for lack of better things to do and nicer places to be.

Grocery samples rattled in the back. Rick worked for a shady outfit that supplied mangy country stores, whose high prices were sustained by inability of local inhabitants to buy the fuel required to reach more competitive emporia. He worked largely on commission, which made living difficult, and he was looking for other work, but not vigorously. It had to be admitted that he enjoyed driving all day and wasn't in a hurry to turn over a larger amount of tax in exchange for losing his freedom.

He suddenly straightened in his seat and touched the brakes, bringing the car to legal speed. He was evidently too late - a solitary white sedan shot out of the roadside bushes to fall in behind him. He could see uniform blue of the driver's shirt and pulled over obediently once the white car flashed its lights, driver impatiently stabbing his index finger towards the side of the road.

Rick sat still for a while, then shook his head and pulled his licence from the wallet. A tall slim figure got out and ambled towards him slowly. The policeman was wearing a leather jacket, a bulge evident at the right hip.

Rick rolled down his window and looked up into the mirror sunglasses.

"Please step out of the car, sir," said a pleasant baritone. The policeman stepped aside to allow the door to swing its full range.

"Ah, what's the story, officer?" asked Rick, not a stranger to encounters with traffic patrols and sensing that something was different.

"We are checking all similar vehicles in this area," replied the patrolman, glaring at Rick's goods intently. "What do you have in the back, please?"

"Biscuits," chuckled Rick. "Chocolate hearts. Marsh mellows. Like one?"

"I need to have a look, sir."

"Sure," Rick pulled the handle that sprang the lock

on the rear door. He walked around the back and bent down to pull the nearest box to the edge of the cargo area.

He never saw the knuckle duster flash in bright afternoon sunshine as it crashed into the back of his skull, felling him with a sickening crunch of bone. His body stiffened and slid down the tailgate, trailing a small trickle of blood over grocery samples.

***

Jack Turner shifted his weight on the cheap carpet. He was lying behind a faded couch with a thick steel plate covering its back. It was two in the morning.

A proud member of the SAS, he once volunteered to serve on a Pacific island, mopping up after a spree of crimes against humanity. He served with distinction, but the sight of what fellow humans with guns could do to those without sickened him and changed him forever.

He left the army and spent some time as an officer in a maximum-security prison until a former drug dealer held a home-made knife to his throat.

The prisoner was screaming numerous demands, and for a few minutes Turner listened, more out of disbelief than confusion. After he had enough, he grasped the knife hand and dropped his chin to the chest, feeling the blunt blade rasp his face, then twisted on his feet, throwing the prisoner off-balance and slammed a knee into his groin. The culprit was carted off to hospital for removal of a ruptured testicle, and Turner faced a disciplinary committee.

He was told that he violated every rule in the book by acting before the negotiators arrived. He resigned on the spot, silencing the bureaucrats in mid-sentence.
But he was too special to waste, and police had him a week later. He was promoted to a detective after a year, but spent little of his time detecting anything except targets. He was the star of protection squad, who prevented unspeakable things from happening to people who mostly deserved them, but turned state's witness, which made their maggot-ridden souls worthy of protection.

Turner was currently plying his trade by sleeping outside the bedroom occupied by an older Vietnamese man who fell out with his extended family, prolific smugglers of heroin by sea. A van was backed up against the front of the dreary suburban home. Two more men were camped in it with submachine guns, and an occupant of an armour-plated cubby house in the back yard covered the rear with a sniper rifle.

The street in an ageing beachside suburb was totally silent. Turner rubbed a cramp out of his leg, feeling the shotgun dig into his side. He heard Mr Tran snore quietly in the windowless bedroom and glared at his luminous watch for the fourth time that hour. Sleep did not come easy when he was deprived of exercise. Damn it, they expected him to be bright-eyed in the morning.

Nobody heard a muffled whirr on the gravel driveway. Later it was determined that a toy radio-controlled truck laden with C4 was manoeuvred underneath the van, then the toy's own batteries were used to activate explosives in its tray.

Nothing much was left of the van or the occupants.

Then they came through the demolished window, very professional and calm. Turner saw three figures in black criss-cross the room with pencil torches taped to rifle barrels.

They nearly made it into the bedroom when a shotgun blast took out the front two assailants, the third diving to the carpet and firing into the couch. Turner felt more than heard the steel plate inside the couch vibrate with the force of 7.56 mm rounds as he pumped the shotgun and fired it over the back of the couch, his cocked wrist nearly breaking from the force of the recoil.

He heard the third man gurgle out his last breath and waited a few seconds in total silence. He left the safety of the couch just in time to see the squat figure of Mr Tran vault easily over the remains of the windowsill and disappear in the dancing shadows of the flames licking the remains of the van.

Turner ran out onto the street eventually, but checking to see whether anyone around was still alive

– in vain – cost time, which compensated Tran for his formidable age.

**

Constable Crain drove along the dirt road slowly. In truth, there was little purpose to his movement, and he edged the diesel 4WD through the hills slowly because after checking the fire track he needed to do his own weight in paperwork, a curse of running a station in a tiny country town.

He saw a glint of metal in the vegetation and accelerated to draw level with the ruined station wagon. He put his hand to the holster as he rounded his bonnet, then backed away and grabbed the microphone.

**

The street was now cordoned off and shuddered to the flashing of blue and red lights. Turner was drinking rancid coffee from someone's thermos with a blanket around his shoulders. He sat in the back seat of his chief's car, watching the big man walk around the ruined safe house, shaking his head ruefully and barking orders into his mobile phone.

Garrison made it back to his car and sat in the front seat motionlessly, staring at the flashing lights. Turner didn't visibly react to his arrival.

"It's bad, Jack," said Garrison without turning

around. "The slant-eye is gone. The Attorney-General is screaming his head off."

Turner said nothing.

"I know it's not your fault," said the inspector. "But you are in a lot of trouble, you know. That's the problem with being commanding officer."

"Fuck it," said Turner, trying to control the trembling voice. "I am alive."

Garrison merely shook his head.

***

The next day was Sunday, and the Stewart household slept in – that is to say it awoke after dawn.

Maggie was up only a few hours after creeping into bed. She parked Martie's car half way between the farmhouse and the gate, reversing it with the least noise possible, so that her hapless suitor could retrieve his steed without waking everyone up. She closed the door, but left the keys in the ignition. The car was now gone.

As she looked out at the road, her throat tightened, and she found herself breathing heavily and breaking out in sweat, even though a cool eucalyptus-scented morning breeze drifted through the flyscreen. She felt dizzy and heard her heart thump rapidly against her ribs, clutching the windowsill to remain upright.

The feeling wore off slowly, leaving her exhausted and frightened.

She put it down to what Martie's clumsy efforts signified. They were a blunt reminder that one day she will have to leave her home and blunder around an ugly, frightening world, looking for a man who would return her feelings. She knew for some time that this commodity was not available locally, and the knowledge of having to seek it somewhere at large was one of those weary dreads, a distant but awful reality of her life along with bush fires, droughts and farm repossessions.

She crept to the bathroom and gave her hair a damn good wash because Dad hated marijuana, smelled a lifetime's worth of it in Vietnam and went berserk at any suggestion that the drug is harmless. In any case, this was one wholesome product of the local hills whose scent one did not wear to church, which is where they were headed next.

Her following move was even less conducive to worship – she put on a tight black dress and patterned black stockings, which made her father shake his head in resignation when he emerged from his bedroom dressed in his ancient blue suit.

The dress was particularly devastating since Martie was standing outside the church looking very chaste and modest in a clean pair of designer jeans and a simple white shirt.

His father was exchanging platitudes with the Reverend, Martie's mother drinking in their conversation from the side. Martie barely looked up when Maggie slid past him, but a little shudder of his shoulders gave him away. Maggie sat next to her father with a hint of a smile on her shapely lips.

***

The forensic people lifted the bloated body of Rick Charlton out of the crumpled station wagon.

"Do you need anything else?" asked Crain in the general direction of the two city detectives.

The tall woman swept her eyes over him without pausing her conversation on the mobile handset and turned away.

"I suppose not," said Crain and walked back to his 4WD.

He swung into the highway without braking, letting his heavy diesel smooth the steep curve. Crain accelerated with annoyance, burning the distance to town with scant respect for the law. He slowed down only as he drew near the pub, pulling up, in a practised gesture, inches short of the ancient horse trough dating back from the gold bonanza for which the pub was erected.

The regulars were well into morning session, acrid

tobacco smoke mingling with clinging odour of stale beer. This was the best place to be in a town whose produce was barely worth transporting to markets, and most of the locals were ageing farmers whose offspring long fled to the big smoke.

After eyeing the scene, Crain expertly pocketed the keys from Pete's table. Pete was one of the wealthier local residents because he sold flowers by the side of the highway. He was ashamed of this unmanly manner of making a living and spent his spare time drowning this fact in beer.

A little later, Crain was very pleased with himself as he trudged towards his car, burping from a hefty dose of lemon squash. He ascertained that nothing unusual had been reported in the pub, which made it very unlikely that anything unusual, had, in fact, taken place in a small town.

Crain drove to the station, switched off the engine and rolled to a stop without bothering with a handbrake. He was unlocking the door when he heard the smooth growl of a powerful sedan and turned to see the city detectives pull up behind him.
He walked through the door and sat down at the counter, greeting them with the smile he reserved for a startled senior citizen reporting indecent exposure. Their faces did not change.

"Where were you last night, Constable?" asked the woman without a preamble.

The smile slid off Crain's pudgy face, leaving one very irate policeman.

"In the fucking pub, love," he replied, leaning his powerful bulk across the counter. "All fucking night, along with the whole fucking town. You gonna tell me why you asked?"

"I resent your attitude," she replied without missing a beat.

"Good," said Crain, nodding approvingly. "One thing I don't have to explain further."

"What were you doing there?" asked the male, who appeared more junior and polite. "I mean, it's the middle of the week, isn't it?"

"You never lived in the country, have you son?" asked Crain incredulously.

"No."

"Well, let me educate you. The pub is where everyone goes after dark. Including myself. And in case you are hoping, I drink ginger beer: the barman and I have an arrangement. I ask for lager, and he serves me lolly water. I hold the glass, I sip, I listen, I keep an eye out for trouble and I hear what I need to know without a single drop of booze passing my lips. I don't like alcohol. Okay?"

The kid didn't answer and looked to his partner for

the next volley.

"Do you drive any other vehicle apart from the one outside?" she asked.

"No," said Crain. "Why would I?"

"Are you certain? Like, if we dust any other local vehicle, could we find your prints?

"Well..." Crain pretended to think. "There was old Jim's tractor. I got it out of the bog for him when he burst a tyre. It was after lunch, and Jim was too pissed to do the honours. That help?"

She made a note in her black book.

"Any other questions?" asked Crain. They both shook their heads.

"All right. So what the fuck is this about? I've been on the Force before you shits were born. How dare you?"

"We are conducting an investigation into a multiple homicide," said the woman importantly.

"And I am the local copper. I might know the suspect, for Christ's sake. I might pass him every day. He could be selling me groceries. I might know the last time he had a crap. Why are you holding out on me?"

"Please wait here, Constable," said the woman without a hint of emotion and walked outside. Crain watched her make a phone call with her back to the open door, standing some distance away. She shut the phone abruptly and came back.

"Okay, we had to ask," she said, sitting down next to the counter. "I spoke to the boss, and he said to give you what we have."

"Oh, a team player," said Crain, still seething. "How nice."
"We think it could be a cop," she said, ignoring him entirely. "Or someone impersonating a cop."

"Super," said Crain. "Now can you tell me why?"

"The last victim left his wallet in the glove box. But his licence was in his pocket, as if he removed it to show someone. The licence was issued recently, and we didn't find any prints on it except his. Looked like he got it ready, then just shoved it in his pocket."

"Anything else?"

"Yeah. It's unusual – four killings, but all very different. Methods, places, victims – nothing in common except they are all dead. But he is good."

"At what?" asked Crain quickly, his professional habits in charge and insults forgotten.

"He is an expert killer," said the woman curtly. "A

broken neck with the first woman and a crushed carotid with the first man. With the second he smashed the back of the head with a blunt object – a fatal blow that broke the hardest part of the skull. The third man he knocked out with a punch to the side of the jaw, then stabbed him in the heart. Not your standard domestic stab, either. Went in under the diaphragm and pierced the left ventricle with a thin but very sharp blade."

"Not a local, then," said Crain conclusively. "There's only Charlie Snyde. He's ex-Vietnam, and he doesn't like to talk about it, so I think he's seen a thing or two. But there's no way he could dress up as a cop. He is short and fat and I've never seen him cleanly shaven. Besides, his breath would kill you before he could get his knuckles anywhere near you."

**

Turner gradually woke up in the middle of the afternoon, his mouth all lead and skin covered in a film of sweat. Warm humid smog had long since replaced the crystal air of the dawn, drifting into the open window with muffled traffic noises.

He was stiff from an unusually long and comfortable sleep and began to do a few stretches to loosen up on the balcony overlooking the opaque waters of the bay when his phone chirped. He ambled into the kitchen and removed it from the cradle.

"Jack," Garrison sounded tired and defeated. "They

found Tran."

"Yeah," echoed Turner gloomily, the implications immediately obvious.

"They tightened a wire around his neck and cracked his larynx," said Garrison. "So he opened his mouth, and they cut out his tongue with bolt cutters. Then he bled out."

Turner stood in the kitchen silently, looking at the calendar still showing the previous month.

"I am briefing Farrell tomorrow. He'll need you to do some paperwork today. Don't talk to anyone else. Better still, get lost for a few days. I don't want you in town."

Without warning, Garrison hung up.

Farrell was a very unpleasant barrister, his arrival good news all by itself. Just the very fact of his representation meant that things would eventually level out. He began life as a cop, but left after refusing to cover up a convenient death during a violent arrest. He occasionally took the cases of cops he considered wronged free of charge.

Turner poured himself some water from the fridge and toasted his boss silently. He reasoned that there was nothing wrong with exhausting and deadly combat so long as your comrades took the trouble to return your loyalty.

He considered going for a long drive but decided to leave that instruction unfulfilled. The fact was, he had nowhere to go. His father died in a mine collapse when Jack was small, and his mother followed a string of losers around the outback until her death a few years ago.

Stroke, they told him. Jack flew to the outback town from the army base and sweated in the vicious November sun in his dress uniform. The minister was almost embarrassed to give the eulogy, and afterwards the locals said that he knew her least of all the service providers in town. The publican would have been better placed to talk about the deceased, albeit with few facts proper to mention.

There were virtually no personal effects, and he left the minister in charge of her meagre property. There wasn't even a wallet – she kept her Social Security regalia in a shopping bag with a few coins. He left the outback town and her grave, clawed from hard red soil, and he never returned.

***

The V8 was purring just right at one-twenty, stiff suspension taking the highway curves through the rainforest in its stride. He drove with all perfection of his training, gloved hands lightly gripping the steering wheel.

Behind mirrored sunglasses his eyes took in the

shadows cast by vegetation onto bitumen. There was no traffic this early, and he drove along the empty road, savouring solitude.

He saw her far in the distance, blue dress a bright blur against the dusty cream of her ageing sedan. She was trying, in vain, to change her right rear wheel, straining at the tyre lever to budge the rusting wheel nuts.

Alma Walters was not exactly young, but she knew a well-built man when she finally saw one. A divorcee in a regional centre, she was pretty much going to waste. It was a fact she acknowledged too late, after her ungrateful children grew up and fled north in pursuit of greener grass – or, more precisely, its cannabinoid-laden seeds.

She pushed out her chest and put on her most youthful smile, watching him approach slowly. He pulled up behind her and walked out, taking care to zip the black leather jacket over his blue shirt.

"Permit me, madam," he said gallantly, placing his boot on the tyre lever. He slightly tensed his thigh, and the lever creaked down.

"That's really good of you, officer," she said. "Thank you."

***

Crain spat, something he needed to do ever since his conversation with the overdressed fools from headquarters.

What hurt was how little they thought of his intelligence and experience, interrogating him with all the finesse of rookies shaking the home address out of a drunken teen. After a quarter of a century of unblemished service, he was entitled to be considered a harder target.

He now sat on the side of the highway in his favourite lair, a heap of earth thoughtfully left by the road engineers, which concealed his 4WD from either direction. The working end of the speed camera was resting on the roof, visible only to the sharpest of eyes.

It was a pleasant balmy day, and motorists defied traffic regulations in huge numbers. The hard drive of the camera was sounding increasingly laboured after the second hour, miscreants flying past without the finest idea of how unpleasant the day would turn out to be.

Crain was relieving himself on the blind side of the car when he felt a deep rumble under his feet. He saw a giant rig rush by and felt its slipstream lash his face. As the thunder of its passage died down, he heard a loud squeal of the speed camera console and rushed back to the driver's seat.

The figure displayed on the console compelled him to

leave his hiding place, the rig being clocked at over thirty above the speed limit – enough to land the driver in jail not only for speeding, but also for dismantling the engine governor, which kept speed under the limit even if the driver tried to exceed it.

Crain tore the speed camera sensor off its suction cup on the roof and tossed it into the passenger leg well, starting the engine. He skidded onto the road in a cloud of unburnt diesel, distant cars shifting to the centre lane out of his way.

He cursed as he accelerated slowly, the emergency lights slashing the soft daylight. He had to get the Toyota into fourth gear before the turbine cut in, propelling him over the speed limit and into realistic pursuit of the disappearing truck.
He caught it on a steep climb, the rig's giant engine labouring against slope in the slow lane. Without bothering with the siren, Crain drove alongside and furiously pointed to the side of the road. The driver complied sullenly.

Crain parked behind him – there was little point parking in front of something this size to stop it from leaving – and walked around the rig, his hand within working distance of the Glöck. He had seen plenty of amphetamine-crazed drivers on this stretch of road. The driver clambered down from his cabin.

Crain saw a lean middle-aged man in soiled jeans and the obligatory blue singlet, whose pale green eyes stared with resignation.

He did not look at all stoned and proffered the paperwork sullenly. His weather-beaten face was creased in a miserable expression very appropriate to the likely outcome of what had just occurred – and its impact on his family's diet.

"Do you know what you were doing back there?" asked Crain angrily. He felt no sympathy at all, having seen his share of road carnage.

"Ah, about one-ten?"

Crain shook his head in disgust and laid out the paperwork on the prime mover's running board. He didn't radio for checks because, technically, the man was under arrest and would be spending many hours in Crain's town waiting for the rig to be picked up by another driver. There was plenty of time to unearth any hidden truths.

"One-thirty-nine, mate" said Crain curtly, pointing to the speed camera console. He started filling out the form.

"You must have a blitz on," said the man irrelevantly, to pass the time. The consequences were clear, and he knew better than protest.

After a few seconds Crain stopped writing and looked up, his face tightening.

***

The service was mercifully short, and Maggie was highly bemused by the sermon. As if to tweak Martie's bruised private parts, the Rev chose to remind his audience about the ungodliness of local promiscuity. The youths heard the reasons to refrain from their favourite past time with baited breath and smiles composed of guilt, envy and pride, but Martie sat motionless, his head slightly bowed and turned away from Maggie. She felt a million dollars.

It was a different day that confronted them outside. The earlier warmth had gone, and ragged dark clouds flew overhead, savaged by a gusting wind. Maggie held onto her very short skirt, taking care not to lose the footing in front of the lascivious congregation as she walked with her father to the car.

They passed a few of their neighbours, but Maggie suddenly noticed that little conversation took place. She looked up and followed turned heads to the picket fence, where a powerfully built man with a mane of black curly hair stood still, staring at them motionlessly. His arms hung freely by the side of the barrel chest, clad in a black sweater.

His deep-set eyes, wells of darkness in his regal face, locked with Maggie's, and she felt her throat tighten for the second time that day. After an eternity of silence the man put his hand to his chest and bowed slightly. Maggie did not react.

He turned and slipped into his car, a dark vehicle with

sweeping lines. Its powerful engine throbbed in the sudden silence, then the vehicle sliced a circle in the gravel car park and shot off down the road.

Maggie clutched her father with all her strength to avoid folding over onto the grass, a fate worse than death for someone in her attire. She felt her father's powerful biceps tense to support her, his gnarled hand clutching hers.

"What is it?" he asked curtly, in his army voice, the one that demanded immediate and precise answers.

"I...don't know, Dad," she whispered. "I think I'm okay."

"It's the late bloody nights," rumbled her father. "And the bloody dope. Silly kids."

He led her to the car, where she caught her breath and smiled at him. He shook his head in disapproval and started the engine.

A trickle of blood emerged from Martie's mouth, and he became aware of the stinging pain of a bitten upper lip. He wiped the blood with the back of his hand, but couldn't take his eyes off the dark car disappearing down a road between the corn fields, their golden husks flailed by gusts of cold wind.

***

Crain looked at the truckie with gathering horror.

"Well," drawled the man. "I saw a cop stop someone, so I thought, well, I've passed the local fuzz and I have two hours to catch up. So I..."

"How far?"

"Dunno now," said the truckie, losing interest. "You booking me or what?"

Crain leaned to within inches of the man's face. "How fucking far?"

"Lay off, will ya?" The driver stepped back. "About twenty clicks, okay? Just after the last ramp."

He stared at astonishment as his licence was thrown at his feet, the cop suddenly racing back to his car empty-handed.

"Your lucky day, dickhead!" yelled Crain over his shoulder. "Don't come back, will you?"

Then the puzzled truckie saw the police 4WD skid a U-turn and roar down the hill. He shrugged and picked up his licence indifferently. Now hours behind schedule, he didn't expect to keep the job anyway.

Crain drove very fast, but his head was remarkably cool for a man racing a glorified tractor down a winding road at nearly double the sensible speed. He extracted his pistol, cocked it, briefly taking both hands off the wheel, and placed in the crevice in the dashboard before getting to the next bend.

He eyed the microphone, torn between the fear of inevitable ridicule and the consequences of muffing an incident of this importance. Either way, his arse could be up for grabs. He wrestled with himself a little, then picked up the headset.

"Central, car eleven-three-two-five," he said into the mike.

"This is Central," it crackled back..

"In pursuit of a possible murder suspect at..." he stared at the GPS screen. "One three five oh dash forty-three nine one, in the Southerly direction on Highway One.

"Acknowledged. What speed are you at, Constable Crain?"

"Hang on," he said shortly. He dropped some speed and set the vehicle into lower gear for a particularly tricky bend. He was nearly at the location mentioned by the truckie.

As he came around the corner, he saw a faded station wagon on the opposite side of the road, a tall blond man dragging an unconscious girl away from it towards the undergrowth. He wore what looked like a genuine police uniform, but his leather jacket was wrong, a shade darker than regulation blue, and his boots were ankle-high, army style, instead of elastic sides.

His car was parked behind the station wagon, a gleaming white V8 just like the recently issued cruisers, but the upholstery was wrong too, civilian crushed velvet instead of police-issue vinyl.

"Give me everything!" screamed Crain into the mike. "It's him! I've got the bastard! Fuck! Get everyone down here!"

The terse reply was drowned in a squeal of his brakes as he skidded into a vicious turn. Crain was moving at just under the legal limit as he piloted the nose of his 4WD into the side of the fake police cruiser, just in front of the driver's door.

Searing pain flaring between his shoulder blades, Crain grabbed the Glöck and fired through his shattered windscreen, but the blond man dropped his load, rolled expertly into the ferns and disappeared from view, bullets flying harmlessly over his head. Crain's vision grew dimmer as the pain grew hotter. Then it faded altogether.

***

Turner sat in Jeff Farrell's waiting room, helping himself to eyefuls of the secretary as she went about her duties. She in turn appreciated being mauled by the glances of a handsome man, still young and obviously very fit. She liked the warm hazel eyes too – a little tired, but warm and intelligent.

Farrell was unfashionably prompt. A short, stocky man with a buzz haircut over a tanned scalp and a drooping black moustache, he marched towards Turner and shook his hand. He had rough, powerful spades for palms, with stubby fingers jutting from a very white shirt.

His chambers were Spartan for a man of his reputation and income – a veneer desk, some shelves in what looked like worn ash crammed with tomes and a soft green light glowing on the desk. He indicated where Turner could sit and lowered his stocky body into a leather-upholstered chair.

"There is not too much to do, Detective Turner," he said reassuringly. "This is a witch hunt. You are the most senior officer left alive after a flop, so you can expect them to pin it on you. Or try. I intend to block any attempts at laying the blame on you through improper questioning. Is there anything you want to tell me?"

Turner first shook his head, but then gave Farrell a brief account of his last assignment. Farrell listened without a single movement – it even looked like he stopped breathing.

"Is that what happened?" he said to Turner.

"Yeah," said Turner thinking. "I think our location was leaked."

"Sold, you mean," corrected Farrell with his brows creasing in anger. "You go home, Detective. You get pissed and get some sleep in the next few days. Let me do the rest."

***

He came to on an ambulance stretcher, the flashes of emergency vehicles now obliterating daylight. A steady thump of rotor blades reverberated in his head. As he regained focus, he saw that the Commissioner of Police was standing next to him in person, barking into a phone set.

"Oh, you are with us," he said, smiling at Crain broadly.

"Did you get him?" rasped Crain through the parched throat.

"Not yet," replied the Commissioner. "What did the cunt look like?"

"E-fit," said Crain tersely. The Commissioner snapped his fingers at his assistant, who ran away to come back with a laptop. The Commissioner and a medic held the computer above Crain's head, immobilized by a sturdy collar around his neck whilst the assailant's features slowly emerged on the screen.

"That's pretty much it," said Crain after twenty minutes. His pain glowed dull, a pile of hot charcoal somewhere between his shoulder blades, and he was starting to feel wavy again. But he was pleased with the fit – the picture even picked out those shiny, empty eyes and the short, curly hair.

But the Commissioner didn't share his fulfilment. As he looked at the picture, his facial expression darkened into a storm cloud. He snatched a handset.
"Hughie!" he shouted into the radio. "Come in, this is Commissioner Arnold! Now, fuck it, now!"

"Yes sir," Hughie sounded surprised, thought Crain as his consciousness started to dwindle.

"Pull your men back to the edge of the forest," ordered the Commissioner. "Do it this second and report back."

There were a lot of crackles and gurgles as different encrypted channels came alive with urgent orders. Crain couldn't turn his head to see the men, but he heard them trampling back through the forest.

"Sir," he said weakly. The Commissioner turned and leaned towards him.

"Who is it?"

"I'll tell you, Constable, you deserve that. The chap whose car you smashed is an old acquaintance. Mark Fraser – know the name?"

Crain nodded in realization, even as the haze was now solid in his head, preventing him from concentrating. Crain pursed his lips, dimly realizing why the search was rapidly called off.

"Oh yeah," said the Commissioner, reading his thoughts. "Expert with every type of small arms, marksmanship, explosive expertise, instructor in hand combat, survival techniques and tough as a goat. Also, in my estimation, completely mad but clever enough for us not to know until too late. Anyway, here's your ride, Constable. You did good."
Crain fell asleep more than passed out when they lifted his stretcher into the ambulance.

The Commissioner raced back to his vehicle, shouting into the radio. A police helicopter appeared above the nearby hill.

The Commissioner switched channels to make himself heard by every unit on the ground.

"This is the story," he said curtly. "The guy in the woods is a very bad fellow by the name of Mark Fraser. Kicked out of the tactical response group a year ago. Likes violence, very good at it, will kill with pleasure and not to be approached. We don't know what he's armed with, and I don't want anyone finding it out the hard way."

"We pull back to the edge of the State Forest and wait until dark. There's nothing but bush on the other side for forty miles. No way he can make it in one night. We will get the helicopter with thermal gear up as soon as it gets cooler. There is a little rain on the way, so we should get a perfect image within a couple of hours."

"If you have any questions, ask someone smarter. Out."

***

The black Mercedes was parked at the edge of a scenic platform, lights of the distant city a sparkling sea that blended with the unusually starry sky.

The driver stood next to the open door, the heavy features of his face awash in the stiff breeze travelling from the ocean through the darkness. He stood absolutely still, heavy head slightly bowed against the wind, and listened to the evening news, the burning gaze of his deep-set eyes piercing the star-lit horizon.

Without waiting for the weather report he turned and started his vehicle, driving until his mobile phone chirped, indicating a return to an area with adequate signal. He pulled over and sat in the back seat, where he set up a laptop with a mobile modem.

He dialled a number and ran a port sniffer, which quickly found a hole in the firewall of the police network. He was logged on as a privileged user within minutes.

He hacked into the payroll database and saved a list of names, addresses and badge numbers on his machine. His next move was to access a large web page cache, a collection of downloaded pages sought by the users of the police network from the Internet.

He copied its lengthy contents into a single text file on his machine and switched off the mobile phone, terminating the connection.

As the night breeze blew into the open doors of the Mercedes, he found what he was after and noted the badge numbers.

He picked one that suited his purpose precisely – as if he ordered it himself, he chuckled, wrote out the address on a piece of paper with a gold fountain pen and packed up his gear.

It was a long way, he noted, but then he wasn't ready to act just yet. Even he needed more information as it came to hand.

***

Maggie awoke the next day, and her first sensations of the morning were not pleasant. Apart from undeservedly feeling very hung over, she was feeling the beginnings of a really awful period, complete with headache, nausea and an overwhelming desire to hide her head under the blanket and stay still.

As any good dairy man, her father was now awake many more hours than his precious offspring cared to contemplate, and Maggie trudged to the shower in the dank silence of the farmhouse. Her mother was killed in a road accident by a drunk years ago, when drunk driving was condoned, never mind possible.

By and large, the Stewarts did a good job of maintaining a home where most would be barely able to run a house – but Maggie wasn't yet a sufficient counterweight to her father's infantry ways, and she never allowed her eye to dwell on the details of their home making.

By the time she finished her shower and choked down a small amount of breakfast, it was clear that her day was not going to improve, but there was no question of alerting her father to what he would immediately label as drug-related malaise. She swallowed some Panadol and walked the long path to the gate. She awaited her school bus, the crisp morning air caressing away her nausea and headache.

She swore she would never use drugs again as long she lived, knowing this promise to be futile. At least she would stick to the clean stuff, she vowed, not the crud she and her classmates could afford. Maybe grow a few plants some place, she thought idly. Dad's old Land Rover could reach places few wheeled vehicles dared even approach, and maybe it was healthier to eat the seeds instead of smoking.

Maggie didn't really like dope that much, but her friends never socialized without it, and whilst their company was a deeply flawed offering, it was better than a dank house and the crushing weight of her father's memories. Those were a poisonous blend of cordite-stained carnage of Vietnamese jungle and the booze-sodden carnage by the side of an Australian highway on a stretch which wound its way through the most beautiful temperate rainforest on earth.

***

Turner went to the gym at dawn, and the heavy, ceiling-tall punching bags paid the full price of recent events. The recreational users first shied away from his broad-shouldered frame slamming into leather, then flocked to watch. Other activity in the gym slowly died away as he graduated towards serial spin-kicks, never allowing the bag to come to a halt between swinging on his toes, much like a ballet dancer, crashing his foot into the bag, then quickly withdrawing and kicking again from the inside of his knee.

His energy ran out long after most spectators drifted away to their jobs. Turner sank to the bench, feeling rivulets of sweat run down his naked torso to the tiles. Smoko, the owner of the gym, came over with a bottle of Gatorade. He was drinking beer.

Smoko's real name was Yannis, and he came from a traditional Greek family. His parents were peasants from Crete who worked themselves to death in the new country, but not before they populated it with a brood of hardy children.

Their offspring were also prolific breeders, but their work ethic was rather less uniform. Smoko's brother was an eye specialist somewhere in the leafy suburbs and made a packet. The rest started off in factories and drifted into service industries, as is custom in impoverished industrial countries, whose once productive workforce ends up driving, feeding and whoring tourists from industrial countries not yet so impoverished.

Yannis was his family's black sheep. In youth he used his natural bulk to persuade the customers of a certain unlicensed lender to be timely with their payments. This occupation put him on a collision course with respectability, and he was soon ruling a small clan inside a maximum-security jail after one of his persuasions went wrong. He laughed when offered to have his sentence halved for information about his employer.

The loan shark was neither ungrateful nor dumb enough to expect that kind of loyalty for nothing. Yannis was picked up from jail in style, in a hot rod whose keys he was handed on arrival to an old terrace house, where his family threw a very noisy party. Included amongst the keys was a large bronze implement that opened a run-down warehouse, rent-free to the loyal enforcer until he managed to make it pay as a gym.

It was a strange friendship, an elite policeman and an ex-thug, but it worked better than most relationships Turner struck up in his rapidly lengthening life. Both men saw too much of violence and neither wished to see any more. They both loved and cared for less resourceful denizens of their nasty reality, and neither wanted to make it an uglier place than it was already.

They sipped their drinks in silence until Smoko finished his beer and blew out a gargantuan burp, throwing the bottle into a metal drum at the entrance to his office. It was a long throw, but he never missed.

"So what you do, Jack?" he asked casually.
"Lost a canary," replied Jack tersely. He didn't really want to discuss the failure of a classified operation with a convicted criminal, but there was no point hiding from Smoko, who was nodding wisely.

"In trouble?"

"Maybe."

"Need anything?"

"Hopefully not," answered Turner carefully and not

at all in dismissal. "I'll know in a few days."

Smoko nodded. "Well, let me know if you do," he said, lumbering away.
"Thanks, man," said Turner meaning it. He knew it was the most solid promise he heard this week.

***

The temperature dropped abruptly as the cold air drifted in from the nearby ocean, and the helicopter went up bearing Arnold next to the pilot and four snipers with thermal scopes strapped to the machine's skids.

They had their quarry after an hour of sweeping the grid, just visible to naked eye in the dwindling light, but very obvious on the infrared gear. Fraser was halfway up a tall gum and almost totally blended in until the wash from the rotors stirred the branches away from him.

"Attention Mark Fraser!" boomed Arnold into the mike. "Acknowledge immediately by raising your right hand."

The figure didn't stir. The Commissioner switched channels on his mike to the helicopter's intercom.

"Put a few into the trunk just below him," he ordered one of the snipers. The man barely seemed to aim, but the bullets tore into the tree with absolute precision, leaving a ragged line of large holes. Bark chips sprayed the figure hugging the trunk just below.

"We are serious, Fraser!" boomed the loudspeaker. "Raise your hand right now!"

The figure remained still for a short time, then raised the right hand slowly.
"Now climb down. Make no sudden moves. I am authorized to use deadly force, and..."
The speaker died as the Commissioner flicked the switch.

"...Believe me, I'd like to use it." he said into the din of the helicopter. He watched as Fraser climbed down very deliberately and stood still at the trunk of the tree.

An hour later a tall figure broke through the bushes near the highway, trapped in the cone of the helicopter spotlight. Clearly out of ideas, Fraser stepped into open space and lay on the ground with his arms and legs outstretched away from his body. Only then did a very large number of men with drawn automatics approach.

**

The Mercedes pulled into the drive of a mediocre-looking clapboard house in a row of other houses just like it, barren kennels of post-war settlers who had since done better and moved on, leaving behind barren gardens and decrepit hardwood fences.

The driver marched to the door, a laptop slung over his shoulder in a carry bag. He knocked twice, the contact of his knuckles with plywood resounding through the house.

The door was opened casually by a tall man who clearly feared nothing, a fact underscored not only by his creased police uniform but also confident bulk. He stood still, long arms hanging by his sides in a posture of practised indifference.
"Sergeant Bristow?" inquired the driver.

"Yeah. Who are you?"

The driver smiled.

"That is a question I have no time to answer fully," he replied. "But the bottom line is this. Not only are you a connoisseur of child pornography, but you are also stupid enough to browse it on your work computer."

Bristow's belligerent appearance deflated as if punctured by an invisible needle.

"I think I should come in," said the driver in a neutral tone. Bristow stepped aside, moving like an automaton. The driver walked in. He stared at Bristow for a few seconds, then sharply retracted his elbow to slam the door behind him.

"Call me..." he stopped, then suddenly smiled. "Darius. Yes. He was the last of your kind I truly admired. Now let's sit down some place clean."

Bristow backed away from him until they ended up in the kitchen, where Darius gingerly removed the remains of a take-away from the table and deposited them in the sink. After pausing, he flicked open a grimy window and inhaled fresh air with appreciation.

Bristow stood in the middle of the kitchen staring in silence as Darius sat down at the table and placed his bag on the cleanest part of its surface.

"I want to see your badge," said Bristow hoarsely. Darius laughed.

"You poor drone," he said shaking his head. "It's not like that at all. I am not a policeman – I want something from you."

Bristow sat down opposite him, the colour slowly returning to his face.

"What you should have known," said Darius opening his bag. "Is that when you surf the Net, a copy of everything you browse ends up on your computer. Now, slow government networks like the one that is supposed to help you catch criminals, can't accommodate people just downloading the same pages every time. So they cache them."

He caught a look of incomprehension in Bristow's eyes.

"Yes, French wouldn't be your forte, if you pardon the pun. Caching means you store a copy of the page in a special store on your own network unless you specifically ask to reload it from the Internet."

"Now, cache systems track who cached what and when, precisely to catch perverts like you who abuse their workplace computers. Just for the record, not even I approve of your ilk."

Bristow shook his head.

"All system logs are wiped after two weeks," he said hoarsely. "Nobody has looked at them in three years I've worked there."

"Yes. But, of course, there is one permanent backup. Every Internet provider must keep one, and guess what's in it."

"The backup is mainly gibberish," said Bristow triumphantly. "The burner they use to cut it on disc is stuffed. They bought it for the firearms register, but what it burned used to fade after a few months. They don't really care if they lose our data, so they gave it to us."

"True again. But the fade takes a few months, do we agree? So if I called the duty manager right now and asked him to check, would that be a problem for you?"

"I hope you know what you are doing," said Bristow

hoarsely, wiping away beads of sweat from his forehead. "You just don't fuck with people like me unless you know what you are doing."

Darius leaned forward and held Bristow's stare.

"If I walk out of that door and leave you the way I found you, you will never know how lucky you have been," he said quietly and slowly. "This is not about petty thuggery, my friend. Yes, I know what I am doing."

Bristow said nothing.

"Here's my proposal. I need you to alter some data in the fine files and then I will upload a virus, which will wipe the cache from here. You have to take your chances with the backup, I am afraid, but it should be safe enough."

"Is that what this is about?" asked Bristow incredulously. "You want to wipe some fucking fine?"

"Not quite. I would actually like to create one."

"Why?"

"As of this point, the less you know the longer you will live."

"Don't threaten me," said Bristow easily. He had well over a foot of height over Darius, and his long arms flexed by his sides. "I can bite you in half."

Darius smiled and held his stare. "Promise?"

The kitchen table flew into a corner as Bristow got up. He retracted his leg and jumped into the space between him and Darius, left fist aiming a hay maker right in the middle of Darius' face. Then his world turned upside down and faded.

When he came to, he was lying on the kitchen floor, his shoulder an agonizing cauldron of pain. Darius sat on the small of his back and easily held Bristow's right arm behind his back, applying just enough pressure to irritate the torn muscles. Any movement was out of the question.

The laptop was safe in Darius' other arm.

"Are you awake, Mr Bristow?" asked Darius in a neutral tone. Receiving no answer, he tugged on the arm slightly. Bristow screamed in agony.

"I thought so. I repeat the question – is it a deal?"

"Yes!" moaned Bristow. "Yes, stop!"

Darius gently untwisted Bristow's arm and laid it by the man's side. He started up the laptop and placed it on his knees, sitting next to Bristow on the floor. Bristow panted but lay still, experiencing pain the like of which he never felt from his shoulder every time he tried to move.

"I am accessing the police frame," said Darius in a businesslike voice. "Name and password."

"Jay-Bristow," Bristow whispered. "Eight one nine, a-for-apple, gee-for-George, vee-for-Victor, seven, three, five."

"Right," said Darius after a few minutes. "I need to create a record of an offence on the Hume Highway three days ago."

"Press F5, then do a search for all files with 'Hume Highway'."

"Done," said Darius after a few minutes.

"Copy one and paste into the same directory, then rename it with a different date and time."
"Done."

"Now open the copy and change the licence plate, and time details. Can't change the location."

"Done. How do I change the picture?"

"You can't without it being detected. And you can't use one of your own – the angle won't be right. Just delete it, the traffic people will write it up as data corruption."

"What about the original?"

"They only keep it on file for a week."

"I am now logging out," said Darius. "Give me your supervisor's user name and password."

After a moment's hesitation, Bristow complied.

"I am now uploading the virus into the cache," said Darius. "It'll wipe everything at midnight. I am doing the same with the access log. You are now innocent once more. Keep your mouth shut, and nothing will happen to you any time soon. Unfortunately."

Still sprawled on the floor, Bristow heard the heavy footsteps echo in the cheap frame of his house as Darius left, leaving the front door wide open.

***

They wheeled Fraser into the interview room in a special device – a wheelchair with a solid frame with straps for wrists and ankles. The head wasn't restrained, but the handles at the back were a few feet long, allowing the chair to be wheeled out of reach of biting.

The Commissioner sat on the cheap plastic chair with his head slightly bowed and jaw thrust forward, as if about to inhale Fraser whole. He stared as the prisoner was positioned opposite him and locked to a metal bar on the wall with handcuffs.

Two men stared at each other for a while.

"Well?" asked Fraser lightly.

"This is a formality, Fraser," replied the Commissioner choking his anger. "We both know that. We both know you are not going anywhere, except, perhaps, to hell, if your fellow prisoners care to arrange it."

"They will have to plan it well," said Fraser in the same conversational tone.

"And I wish them success," replied the Commissioner. "I would get myself arrested just to help out."

"Is this what you came to tell me?"

"No. Yes. Fuck you, Fraser. I should have charged you last year."
"I am completely innocent."

"You are completely insane!" shouted Arnold, the huge veined fists balling up at his sides. "A fucking serial killer! In my uniform!"

"Don't know what you are talking about."

"You were seen dragging the last victim into the bush, you scum!"

"No. I stopped to help an unconscious person, then some maniac country cop smashes into my car and pulls a gun on me."

The Commissioner nodded in amusement. "Are you hoping to get away with this story?"

"I want to speak to a lawyer."

"Oho! He wants a lawyer!" said the Commissioner to the men flanking him. "In my own good time, bastard. We haven't completed our investigations."

"I still want to speak to a lawyer."

"Well, you are a little behind the times. By the special powers vested in me – last year, actually, whilst you seemed to have been out of town – I deem it necessary to hold you in custody for one week pending collection of evidence concerning certain serial crimes."

Fraser's facial expression hadn't changed.

"So fuck you dead," said the Commissioner, already walking out of the room. "That's what I really came to tell you."

***

Darius parked his Mercedes in the prison car park and walked into reception, carrying a cheap vinyl folder full of blank paper. He was allowed to take that with him, but his gold Montblanc was taken away with his car keys, watch, wallet and telephone. In its place he was given a biro made out of soft plastic with a blunt stylus. He tried it on the back of his hand, failed to make it work and obtained another.

Having thus passed the metal detector, he sat in the interrogation room, watching silently as Fraser was wheeled in and his chair locked to the wall.

"Good morning, Mr Fraser," he said in deep gravel voice. "Darius is the name, and I am here to get you out."

"Oh," chuckled Fraser with a trace of contempt. "Legal Aid, right?"

"No."

The arrogance momentarily slid away from Fraser's mouth. "Then who appointed you?"

"You did, Mr Fraser. Some time ago, in fact. I am disappointed you don't remember – or maybe you don't associate your past with my desire to represent you."

"I don't think I understand," said Fraser.

"It's not important to the job at hand," replied Darius.

"Let's concentrate on what we need to do."

"Do you know why I am here?" asked Fraser with mockery returning to his voice. "You are wasting your time."

"I will be the judge of that, Mr Fraser. As luck has it, I am quite aware of your situation," Darius said with a terse smile. "Now, the sole witness to your alleged handling of the last victim is being treated for a major head injury in hospital, his state being described as serious. He may not come out of coma for a very long time, and his recollection of what he saw will never stand up in court. There is no other material evidence to link you to the highway murders. Not only that, but you have an alibi for one of them..."

"Oh yes," said Fraser in a totally neutral tone, his eyes flickering towards the wall.

Darius turned his head and stared at the brickwork. It took him a while to notice what Fraser's sniper eyes picked out a long time before. There was at least one smudge of fresh paint where fibreoptic cameras and microphones were installed to record their conversation on digital videotape.

"...As you would well know if you were told the specific times and places of alleged offences," Darius continued.

**

Farrell sat at his desk wearily and stared at the powerful man dressed entirely in black, his dark curly hair flowing down from his shoulders – only the face protruding from the blackness. This didn't feel right from the start, he told himself. I really should have asked for everything in writing.

But his recent divorce was a festering thorn in his side. Few people realize that there is no escape from the clutches of family law for productive people, even top-notch barristers. Farrell was crippled by a recent property settlement, and money was precious until the land value picked up and allowed him to withdraw his charred fingers from some investments.

So he accepted this strange appointment, although he had never heard of a solicitor called Darius. It was now well past seven at night, but his bank never slept either.

"At your service, Mr Darius," he said with false joviality. The contrived smile underscored the fact that few of his clients found the circumstances of his service pleasurable.

Darius briefly bowed his head and slid across a relatively thin file. Farrell opened it and swung his chair towards the light, a tactic he used to hide his involuntarily revealing facial expressions from clients.

Ten minutes later he put the file down and faced Darius.

"This has to be bullshit," he said uncertainly.

"Why?"

"Don't ask me what, but something bloody smells. Okay, let's start from the beginning. Are you a solicitor?"

"Oh yes," replied Darius with a curved smile. "I just don't practise in this jurisdiction. As a legal practitioner, that is."

"I normally accept briefings only from practising solicitors, Mr Darius."

"As you are entitled to do. But you are also a man of principle, known to exert himself to right wrongs lesser men connive at. You and I do agree that this is a wrong," Darius placed a heavy hand on the file. "This man could not have committed at least some of the crimes he is accused of."

"Hell, the cops themselves took the trouble to provide him with an alibi on the other side of the state. But that doesn't stop them from holding him in jail – without charges – just because a man of his skills happens to be in a convenient location. Is this the kind of event you normally turn your back on, Mr Farrell?"

Farrell stared at him for a few moments, then shook his head decisively.

"Are you aware of my fees?"

Darius snapped open the briefcase and retrieved a chequebook. "I am now going to write a cheque for your trust fund as a retainer. I can assure you it will be cleared."

"All right," said Farrell reluctantly. He palmed the file. "I have to show this to the Attorney-General. Leave this with me, Mr Darius."

Darius stood, bowed his head curtly then left, his cheque a bright yellow stain amid an empty desk. Farrell sank back into the chair to clear his head for the last appointment.

As Darius traversed the reception, his eyes slid over a tall man with a gaunt, unshaven face that belied his short haircut. The man stared back pointedly, replying to Darius' curt nod with an upward flicker of his eyebrows. His body remained slouched lazily in his chair, but the eyes were suddenly bright with alert. He bored into Darius, and his stare escorted the dark figure to the door.

Jack Turner had seen enough killers to recognize one on sight.

***

They sat in the Attorney General's office overlooking the river bank, coffee-coloured water making its way past lush emerald grass flanked with yellowing trees. Irish whiskey was being drunk out of coffee mugs in a blatant violation of the Public Service Code of Conduct.

"I don't fucking believe it," said the A-G, shaking his narrow head. He slumped in his chair, the yellow silk tie loosened and hanging limply from his collar like a cut noose on a corpse. "We nab the mongrel in the act – and he has an alibi? A speed camera?"

"Yes, sir," confirmed the Commissioner grimly. "Four hundred kilometres away, almost exactly at the time of the third murder."

They sat in silence for a while, absorbing the infamy of it.

"How is this possible?" asked the police minister. "Could this be a computer fuck-up?"

"Not likely," replied Parkwood, a short man in denim jeans with a shaggy grey beard. He was an IT magician lured to run the police network some years ago. "The time and location check out. The picture hadn't come out – but, I am afraid, that's not uncommon."

"Why?" asked the police minister.

"After the speed camera is returned to the station, it's

plugged into the station computer, and the files are uploaded to the station network. Then we transmit those files down ordinary phone lines. One crackle of static, and pop goes the image. It doesn't affect the rest of the information, but the kind of picture format we use is very sensitive to corruption."

"Who dreamed that up?"

"The contractor," replied Parkwood with the roll of the eyes. "They use a proprietary image format because they consider it better for enhancement. Bullshit, I think myself, but not strongly enough to recommend an overhaul of the entire system, which is what a change of contractors would require."

"Is the original saved anywhere?"

"Not for long, I'm afraid. Since the speed limits were lowered, the system had been swamped. Unfortunately, the originals on both the camera and the station computer are long gone. We have to clean the files every few days. The only version we keep is in headquarters."

For a while the room was silent, the afternoon shadows growing longer. The A-G leaned over and poured the rest of the whiskey into his cup.

"We have to let him go," he said to no one in particular.

"Okay," said the Commissioner after a period of

thought. He rinsed his cup and motioned to Parkwood. "I'll let them know."

They left the office and rode the lift to the basement car park. After they exited, Arnold laid a heavy hand on Parkwood's shoulder.

"Could this be a fake?"

Parkwood held his stare, then nodded sadly. "Yes," he said. "Yes, it could be. But the truth is, there is no way to tell with computers."

***

Darius waited for Fraser in the prison car park. He watched the sallow-skinned man edge his way into the light and make his way towards him, shielding his face from the sun.

Darius saw that Fraser noticed him and sat in the car motionless, the engine idling in anticipation. A throng of cameramen and furry microphones had formed a solid barricade around the prison reception, watched by guards with silent contempt.

They both acted at the same time. Fraser dodged one cameraman and tipped him off balance, then leaped over the tangle of protesting newsmen and threw himself onto the bonnet of a nearby car in a paratrooper's roll. As he landed on his feet on the other side of the car, the Mercedes was already moving in the aisle just ahead of him; he covered the remaining distance with a single leap, wrenched open the door and landed heavily on the back seat. Darius rammed the accelerator and bolted out of the car park, tyres squealing as he turned out of sight.

Once they were on the street and approaching cruising speed, Fraser opened the door he held until now and shut it tight. He stretched the seat belt across his long frame and exhaled in relief.

"Free at last," said Darius with irony.

"Not bloody likely," replied Fraser, staring at Darius through the rear view mirror. "What is that you want from me?"

"All in good time," replied Darius in a measured tone.

Fraser sat back and looked at the rear view mirror. They both noticed the tail right away, a turbo-charged version of a cheap Japanese sedan skilfully camouflaged as its poorer cousin but given away by perfection with which it bolted around slow-moving cars.

Darius swung the wheel without any warning whatsoever and rammed the car over the curb. Fraser tensed, expecting the leading tyre to blow out, but the vehicle bounced heavily onto the footpath and just fitted between sagging barriers of treated pine, accelerating across a football field of a suburban park.

The tailing vehicle stopped abruptly, but there was scarce sense in following them over exposed space.

Darius hurtled along the alleys of the park, thankfully free of pedestrians. He returned to the bitumen by ramming a wooden turnpike, slowing down just enough to prevent damage to the heavy rubber bumper.

"And that's why authorities hate four-wheel-drivers," said Fraser lightly. Darius acknowledged his frivolity with a courteous nod without looking away from the road.

They entered the freeway and drove in silence for an hour, watching the city give way to suburban blocks, then to green paddocks. Darius had the car on cruise control just below the legal limit and chuckled as they passed a police cruiser, its tail backed into roadside bushes. The camera's dead eye stared at them as they drove by, but the cop inside hadn't even glanced in their direction.

They pulled off the highway onto a dirt track, the car gliding smoothly over corrugations. The track ended at an abandoned quarry, its centre filled with malodorous pool of rainwater. Darius drove past a few abandoned cars and scanned them carefully.

Only when satisfied that they were alone did he switch off the engine and let the car glide to a stop. Without waiting for it to become stationary, he slipped off his seat belt and turned to look at Fraser.

"I need you to do something for me," he said in the same unhurried tone.

Fraser drew himself to attention in his seat and snapped off a perfect salute.

"I hope it's not sex. Sir," he said in a mock military tone, his hand remaining rigid at his temple. "Otherwise I'd rather go back to jail."

Darius stared at him in disbelief, then burst into thunderous laughter. He roared, shaking his black curls, huge yellow teeth bared in mirth. It took a while to stop, his black eyes glistening with moisture, head still occasionally shaking in amused disbelief.

He swivelled back towards Fraser.

"Ego te saluto, O simia," said Darius solemnly. "Rex tenebrarum, dominus malorum, terror mundi et princeps mortis spiritum tuum liberum salutat."

[I salute you, monkey. King of shadows, lord of evil, terror of the world and prince of death salutes your free spirit. - Latin]

Fraser continued to look at him, then snapped the salute down smartly.

"I'm sure you'll explain if it's important."

"Of course," said Darius.

***

The hearing was a vicious enough affair, with Farrell and Internal Affairs hurling poisonous sarcasm across a small room permanently embalmed in the odours of fear and hatred.

Turner felt happy enough as nobody managed to land a solid hit on his actions, but it didn't feel like a victory, the disciplinary board casting him looks normally reserved for the terminally ill.

As he walked away to his car, a lifetime of discipline under fire helped him cast aside the whirlwind of angry and frightened thoughts to concentrate on the problem in hand.

It was then that he discovered he didn't have a problem. His personal life was a bare, featureless plain, his friends in no immediate need of his presence, and his job apparently no longer his concern. He was super-fit, still young, highly trained in a variety of marketable skills and not at all about to get upset about office politics.

So he entered his flat and emerged an hour later, freshly showered, shaved and clad in a leather jacket, which showed off his powerful torso to maximum advantage. By way of warming up, he walked half a mile to a nightclub, whence he emerged with a young theatre nurse from the local killing field some minutes before midnight.

Their athleticism made for the best sleep he had in weeks, and he awoke to the hurried dressing of his new friend at dawn. She refused his offer of a certificate by a crooked doctor – there was nobody to fill her rostered position if she declared a sick day – but accepted a limousine service.

He resisted the urge to perform this favour wearing his dress uniform cap but not much else and drove her to the hospital. Phone numbers were exchanged in a traffic jam, then she waved as she ran through the glass doors, and he was alone once more. He stowed her number carefully and memorized it for good measure.

He hoped she wasn't in for a hard day at work.

***

"I want a certain girl," said Darius in a sombre tone, his eyes flashing a dark flame which did not accord with his level tone.

Fraser smiled, but Darius remained silent and grave.

"What, kidnapped?"

"Yes. Then I may need your help to get both of us out of the country. Possibly."

"Let me see," said Fraser. "The prime minister's brat?"

"No."

"Someone royal? With a regiment to guard her?"

"No."

"Quartered, skinned alive, what? Why me?"

"You are very good, that's all. The job should be straightforward, but I am a stranger to these parts, and you seem to know your way around," Darius extracted a picture from his briefcase and passed it over. Fraser looked at a reasonably attractive late teenager with auburn curls, but he was damned if he could recognize her or see anything special about her.

"Where do I locate her?"

"The details are all here, Mr Fraser," Darius handed over the rest of the material. "She is a simple farmer's daughter, neither protected in any particular way nor is she expecting you. I need her completely unharmed, otherwise you can do what you like."

Fraser studied the details briefly, pausing to admire the expertly forged driver's licence.

"I need a few things."

Darius handed over a large wad of cash.

"I need a weapon, too," said Fraser. "I can buy one, but it will take time and I don't want to be seen where I'd need to go."

Darius nodded, then reached under the seat and handed over a cloth bag. Fraser slipped it open and retrieved a snub-nosed .38. He spun the chamber and snapped it open to check the barrel.

"Okay," he said. "Ammo?"

Darius handed over another cloth bag, using all of his great strength to lift it with one hand. Fraser slipped the revolver into his jacket and accepted the bag with both arms.

"We need to talk about the rest," he said.

"I hope you are not expecting more money," said Darius. "I got you out of jail."

"No, not that," replied Fraser. "But I don't think I want to stick around afterwards. I'd like a passport."

"Buy one."

"Certainly, and I know where. But I shouldn't be seen there either, and I won't be able to do it after this job. It's only fair that I have that fixed first."

"Point accepted," said Darius nodding briefly. He pointed his laptop at Fraser and pressed a button on the side, then checked the picture he captured and closed the computer. "I will post it to you at the address specified. The post box key is attached to the papers. Anything else?"

Fraser thought, ticking off points on his fingers.

"A phone," he said. "You need a credit history for a good one. Can you do the honours?"

"First thing tomorrow," agreed Darius. "At the post box, but pick it up in a few days. You will need a lot of sleep right now – I don't want you to start until you are refreshed."

"Fair enough," said Fraser. Darius started up the car and drove to the nearest town, dropping Fraser in the side lane behind a motel.

"Goodbye, Mr Fraser," he said into the rear view mirror as Fraser opened the door. "If all goes well, you get another chance to live."

"Ah, thank you," said Fraser, suddenly feeling his fatigue.

"Quite. But one thing!" shouted Darius, his voice suddenly rasping and hard.

"Yes?" said Fraser, his body going cold with a fear he very seldom experienced.

"Two things," Darius lowered his voice again. "First, no distractions. Until the job is over, no fun at the roadside, no fights and no noisy fornication. Absolutely nothing to attract attention. Drink water and eat cottage cheese. Got it?"

"Okay."

"Second. When you take her, do not hurt her in any manner. Above all, do not molest her. Don't even look at her the wrong way."

"No problem," said Fraser. "Not my style."

"Oh yes," smiled Darius slightly as he put the car into gear. "I do forget – your tastes require a resemblance to certain figures from your childhood, do they not?"

Fraser shut the door gently and watched Darius drive away. However Darius found out, Fraser decided not waste his energy on wondering about it.

He loved his work and had some to do.

Part II:
The Master

Fraser sat in a powerful Toyota utility with customized suspension, which he bought off a bankrupt 4WD enthusiast. He tested the machine off-road and was satisfied with its ability to charge through obstacles that would stop police vehicles.

The enthusiast was too pleased to complete the transaction to check the details and signed the registration transfer sheet without looking at Fraser's ID. Fraser wrote his old neighbour's name on the transfer, knowing that the old coot moved to some beachside caravan park ever since losing his job and had probably even died without anyone knowing about it.

The gun was tucked underneath the dashboard within easy reach of the driver. Fraser unscrewed one of the panels and passed a shoelace around a plastic screw that held the panel in place. A tug on the lace brought the panel down and out of the way, revealing the gun secured to the steering column with a thick rubber band.

He now shaved his blond curls and the stub of the beard, leaving his skull stark and smooth underneath a woollen cap, which he stretched over the hairline. A pair of wrap-around sunglasses completed his disguise. Fraser wore a mechanic's overall with an elastic belt and opted for steel-toed boots rather than runners. His hands were covered by latex gloves.

In his pocket were two industrial wire ties held together by a third, which made excellent handcuffs.

A cotton scarf lay on the seat next to him with a hip flask half-filled with chloroform, courtesy of a vet in a nearby town, who left the key to his surgery under the doormat.

A large plastic syringe filled with Rohypnol-laced vodka was resting upright in the toolbox inside the tray of the ute, its vinyl cover fully retracted and secured with spring clips, revealing a link of loose chain with an open lock at the end. The ute was covered in mud after Fraser's extensive testing, and a large quantity of mud was thrown with a shovel over the front and rear, totally obscuring the number plates.

The ute was parked in a small clearing near the road. Through the trees, Fraser could just see the gates of the Stewart farm. The sun was rapidly rolling towards the horizon, its late rays entirely without warmth. He had the window down, letting the cold breeze cool his sweating forehead.

Every few moments he beat down the anxiety levels by rehearsing the job in his mind. Wait until the bus goes, drive up, grab the girl, knock her out, tie her, feed her Rohypnol and padlock her to the tray. Secure ute cover and drive like hell to where Darius said to tie her to the tree, make the call and look forward to the long trek to Latin America, where the drug lords were always short of security personnel. Fraser even knew a little Spanish.

He heard more than saw the bus, and his anxiety

peaked, ebbed, then left him a cold-eyed machine with a singular purpose. He started the engine and eased down the track to the road, letting the bus pass and emerging to follow it just a fraction after it turned the corner, leaving Maggie to lug her heavy school bag down the long drive to the farmhouse all by herself.

She turned at the sound of the ute approaching her from behind and stopped, frowning against the low sun. Fraser left the engine running and got out, the hip flask open in his pocket and the rag tucked into a sweatband on his wrist.

"Who are you supposed to be?" asked Maggie with a hint of disapproval. Fraser opened his mouth as if about to launch into an odd story and pointed behind her with the left hand.

As she turned to see, he covered the remaining distance with a single boxing leap, his left arm flung like a steel spring around her waist, its hand closed in a tight fist around the rag. His right hand drenched the rag with chloroform from the bottle, then shot up to clamp the rag to her mouth.

The stranglehold around her waist choking her breath, Maggie slammed her elbow backwards into Fraser's stomach. He saw it coming and tensed his muscles with all his strength, but the reverse blow still made him exhale and lose muscle tone. He caught the next blow into the cup of his hand and pushed it back, but Maggie jackknifed her legs high into the air, nearly hard enough to break the stranglehold, then brought both heels down on his shins.

Fraser let out a short scream of pain and dropped her. She hit the ground and rolled over to rise into a fighting stance three feet away, then swung a vicious kick into the side of his bowed head.

He ducked, letting the foot swish over him, then drove his body over hers as she turned to complete the kick. Maggie couldn't compete with his weight and hit the ground hard, which dazed and winded her. The sweet-smelling scarf was clamped to her mouth again, and her consciousness faded.

Fraser picked her up and ran to the back of the ute. He heaved Maggie over the side into the tray and wrenched open the tool kit. With Maggie starting to stir, he forced the syringe into her mouth and held her head against the side of the ute facing upwards.

Maggie gagged a little, but the fluid largely found its target. Letting her drop back on her side, Fraser tied her arms behind her and padlocked the wire ties to the short chain welded to the tray. He tore at the spring clips holding back the cover and pulled it over the length of the tray, then ran around to the open door and leaped inside.

He looked up from the dashboard to see an ageing but powerful man run out of the distant farmhouse. As Fraser pulled the door, the man stopped and put something to his shoulder. There was a distant retort, and Fraser heard a loud crack as the bullet shattered his right headlight.

The ute surged backwards as Fraser stood on the accelerator, not bothering to look at the man firing at him. He heard another loud thud; the bullet had lost its momentum over the distance and cracked the windscreen instead of passing through it.

Finally out of the gates, Fraser swung the ute and gunned it away from town, heading into a maze of forest roads and fire tracks. For some minutes the vinyl cover over the tray danced to Maggie's kicks, then Rohypnol reached her brain, and she passed out.

It got dark an hour later. Fraser turned the dashboard light dimmer to the minimum setting and flicked on parking lights. He edged along the forest road in near-total darkness, but almost invisible from the air. He set himself a monumental task – to cover nearly three hundred kilometres without leaving the mountains, to emerge in another state, where he hoped to steal another car before returning to the main highway.

He made just one stop as soon as darkness fell, to relieve himself and to check his prey. Maggie was still deeply unconscious, but her pulse and colour were fine. Fraser now padded her with a foam mattress and sleeping bag in a position that did not strain her arms against the handcuffs.

Then he got back in the cabin and resumed his relentless progress north.

***

James Stewart sat at the kitchen table, his gnarled bulk bent in silent grief. Old Nick McMillan sat at his side, his hands clamped about his police radio. Nick remembered getting drunk at Maggie's christening.

The description went out, and the roadblocks went up. A large number of serious people were on the way to the town, and a tent was quickly erected on the side of the driveway to preserve a trail of broken glass from Fraser's headlight for the forensics.

But Nick knew that a dark ute made a needle in the haystack of a large swathe of virgin forest to the north, and that once he crossed the mountains, the kidnapper had a wide choice of arterial roads and means of obtaining another vehicle.

What frightened Nick most was the absence of motive. The more he turned it over in his mind, the worse it all looked. He knew Maggie and her father. Their poverty made any kind of property crime senseless in the extreme. Maggie had neither the time nor other means to get herself mixed up in anything serious like drug distribution. Nick knew that – his own son had left school not long ago, and Nick could vouch for the absence of any large-scale drug operations on his patch.

Finally, the doctor came. He took Stewart's blood

pressure and forced him to take two Valiums, and Stewart staggered off to bed. Nick helped him get his boots off and watched him curl up under an old blanket, the look of fear and pain slowly blurring in his eyes.

***

Maggie came to a number of hours later and in great discomfort. Her body was cold and stiff, both shoulders and arms throbbing incessantly from the time spent twisted backwards. She moved her fingers experimentally, finding them numb but responsive. She also wet herself during her drug-induced sleep, which added to the cold and the discomfort.

The ute seemed to be labouring up a steep forest track, the suspension flexing over deep ruts and the engine growling whenever the wheels lost grip on wet clay. She guessed that she was deep inside the state forest, where the rolling hills around her home became steep mountains. It was a totally uninhabited area, where people were seldom encountered. Maggie's friends often used it for various nefarious purposes when they didn't want to be interrupted.

Maggie took a deep breath in and out and lowered her arms to her backside, then pushed them down as far as possible and started to thread her legs through the wrists, bound behind her back.

She had to take a break after the backs of her knees touched her handcuffs and lay there panting until the pain of sudden stretching subsided in her shoulders.

Then she took another deep breath in and out and pulled her ankles through the arms, twisting her body so that her handcuffed wrists were now in front of her.

She saw that she was tied with two plastic ties linked by a third, which was also padlocked to a chain. Maggie tugged on the chain and confirmed that it was secured to the truck somehow. She then looked around and heard the rattle in the toolbox even before she saw it in the dim light under the tray cover.

***

Fraser glanced at the phone when he laboured to the top of the hill, but the signal was too weak to contact Darius.

He swiped his forehead with a sleeve already damp with sweat and threw the ute down the hill. His head buzzed slightly from lack of sleep, but the current section of his route was a nasty, neglected fire track. He tried to pick up speed now that it was light, but the ruts prevented him from getting to the fourth gear, and he drove on grimly, scanning the upturned mirrors for any signs of aircraft.

He started to worry about petrol. Not having anticipated the difficult track, he was now down to half a tank with a third of the journey to go. He decided to slow down slightly – time was the only thing which he budgeted properly.

He was glad of that decision moments later as he cursed and started to brake, fearful of letting the vehicle spin out of control down the steep incline. He managed to bring it to a halt within feet of a large tree fallen across the track.

Fraser got out of the ute and walked around the tree. Either side of the road was lined with tall saplings that he was probably unable to run down. The tree blocking the road had the thickness of a man's torso and probably weighed many tonnes.

***

Maggie reached over and opened the toolbox with her foot. In the top draw she saw a rusty pair of pliers with a wire cutting edge in the jaws. She scraped the bottom of the draw with her foot, the pliers sliding to the end, then rising off the bottom and falling onto her other leg outside.

A moment later, her handcuffs were cut away from the chain.

She heard Fraser walk into the bush to start clearing a path around the log with short, vicious axe blows, taking care to fell saplings without leaving sharp stakes.

Maggie scrambled to the rear corner of the tray and pushed open the cover, rolling over the edge. She hit the ground awkwardly, bruising her side, but the pain only made her move more urgently. She replaced the tray cover and ran into the bush.

As soon as she was invisible from the road, she increased her pace, running with her hands still cuffed in front of her. The sounds of Fraser's axe were no longer audible, but she continued to run, choosing the path which least imposed on the undergrowth. She ran until her strength gave out and stopped to peer in the direction of the truck from the cover of a large tree.

She only faintly heard Fraser's furious shouts and couldn't make out the obvious threat within. As soon as her breath recovered, she turned and started jogging away from the sound of his screams downhill.

When his voice had faded, she stopped to cut the plastic ties with pliers, tossing the lot into a long hollow log as she got on her way with renewed vigour.

***

Fraser pulled up at the designated intersection, noting a small rock wedged in a split tree trunk as he and Darius agreed. He hurtled down the fire track until he saw the black Mercedes next to a large campfire in the middle of a small clearing. Fraser's unease increased, but he now had no choice in the matter. He blew the horn and stood next to the ute.

Darius emerged from the undergrowth wearing a long black robe, which concealed his muscular bulk. His expression darkened as he approached Fraser.

"She escaped," said Fraser simply. "Sorry."

There was a flash at the side of his vision, and he found himself lying on the ground on all fours. As an accomplished student of violence, he was no stranger to being hit with a lot of force, but what really terrified Fraser was the speed – seldom was he attacked in a way that left him so out of control.

Something suggested that he shouldn't get up, and he slowly rolled over onto his side, then sat down on the ground, his cheek numb with distant pain. Darius stood over him, an expression of fury contorting his features.

"I gave her a pretty large dose of Rohypnol," said Fraser. "But she must be used to drugs – it wore off within six hours."

"Is this the best you can do?" asked Darius hoarsely. His torso was still tense and ready to spring.

"Now that I know what I am up against, I'll do better," said Fraser, anger now overcoming his fear. "Oh, and by the way – thanks for telling me she is a karate expert. Anybody else she would have flattened right there and then."

Darius chuckled, his posture now loosening.

"I told you everything I knew," he said, turning away from Fraser and staring into the fire.

"Look," said Fraser. "I'll fix it. I am not giving up. But you need to level with me."

"It's good of you to volunteer," said Darius without turning around. "But I am still wondering whether to kill you and do everything myself."

Fraser made an instant decision not to explore that issue. He got up and stood next to Darius, just far enough to buy some time if things got out of control.

"Okay," said Fraser. "First, why did you get me in the first place?"

Darius slowly swivelled his head and fixed Fraser with a dark stare.

"I mean, you seem pretty capable of doing the work," said Fraser, gesturing to where he was knocked to the ground. Darius nodded slowly in contemplation of the question.

"I am a stranger in this land," he replied. "People remember when I pass by."

"Right," nodded Fraser. "But why her?"

"You don't need to know, monkey."

"I don't want to, either," said Fraser irritably. "But what I don't know may interfere with the operation."

Darius looked up and stared at him for a while.

"That is something you will have to work with," he said at last. "Because I will give you one more chance. Contact me when you have succeeded. If you give up, kill yourself, otherwise I will find you and torture you to death. The bad news, Mr Fraser, is that you are no longer at the top of the food chain."

He walked towards his car and started the engine. Fraser watched him swing the vehicle towards the entrance to the clearing and stop next to him. Darius rolled down his window and tossed a large envelope at Fraser's feet.

"You can't but need this," he said. "But ask for anything else, and you are a dead man."

The Mercedes rolled out of the clearing and disappeared in the bush.

Fraser sat down, fighting an attack of nausea. He retched into the fire, but his stomach was empty apart from a few drops of bile. He spat them into the ashes and sat still for a while, his cheek ignited with stinging pain. He was a little dizzy from the slap that threw him off his feet and got up slowly.

He had never seen a man of his weight and strength flattened like this with a back-hander. He did not quite know who Darius was, but knew that the answer would frighten him further, even if such a thing was unimaginable now.

Fraser reached down and picked up the envelope. Inside was chequebook in his name, and a single sheet of paper fell out of the chequebook as he opened it. He squinted at it and realized it was a copy of the deposit slip for a generously large amount, with his signature reproduced almost perfectly at the bottom. He did not stop to think where this signature could possibly be copied from, given the years he spent on the run under false names.

Fraser knew that he was perfectly free to run further. Darius gave him everything he needed – money, gun and passport. The car had to go – the bullet hole in the headlight was a difficult feature to explain, and he had no doubt of Maggie's ability to recognize every single object related to her abduction.

He slept by the fire and awoke in darkness, its coals long grown cold. He started the car and drove to the highway, where he gunned the engine uphill to blend with passing cars and drove for an hour, being careful as he rounded corners that may conceal police cars.
Where highway bisected the railway track, Fraser slowed down and pulled into the service lane. He drove across the grass and found himself on a dirt track that ran next to the rails, following it for a distance until he reached the foot of a long climb. He concealed the vehicle in the bushes and walked back to the railway, his gear in a small day pack on his back.

It was a very long wait, and he got very cold sitting

still on the shingle. But around midnight he saw the signal lights change in the distance and heard the rumble of the locomotive through the earth.

From his concealed position behind a clump of rebellious undergrowth, he watched a long goods train approach and attack the steep hill. As gravity did the inevitable deed to the struggling diesels, he started running uphill and grasped the ladder of a passing cattle car.

Although the train was already quite slow, Fraser still felt like his arm was being wrenched out of his socket, but he tensed his body and sprung onto the ladder, one boot connecting with the slippery metal and obtaining purchase. He slid open the grimy door, pulled himself up into the truck and settled in for a long trip north.

***

Maggie only allowed herself to stop and take stock of her situation when it was too dark to go on.

She was somewhere in the state forest, which left only one strategy that made sense. She needed to get to the Mitchell river, which was studded with human habitation. That was the only large river in the area, which meant that walking downhill would eventually lead her to safety.

Her resources were a little thin, beginning with no food or water for over twenty-four hours. She wore good boots and socks, for which she was now very grateful. Her clothes were less useful – sturdy jeans but a thin pullover that did little to keep out the wind. If it rained, she would be in a lot of trouble.

There was no way of starting a fire and no knife of any kind. She needed a drink, but her thirst was tolerable for the time being. She broke off a few fern fronds to make a lean-to.

She lay in her improvised lair as the light grew dim and the forest sounds faded with nightfall. She huddled into a ball to keep out the icy mountain breeze and fell asleep as the last vestiges of an appalling day faded into the purple twilight.

***

Fraser stared at the forest through a crack in the boards lining the cattle truck. Cold air forced into the car by the train's motion stirred the smells left by its previous passengers – goats, in Fraser's limited experience with husbandry. Otherwise, he was reasonably comfortable physically, but more afraid than in his entire life.

That was a new experience to Fraser, an angry and violent man who always viewed danger as something he sought and dispensed rather than something he suffered.

What was worse, he couldn't understand that fear. It was true that Darius was a very formidable figure and one whose mercy Fraser obviously couldn't rely on.

But deadly opponents were nothing new to Fraser. He never felt terror in a fight.

The best Fraser could do to define his fear is to note that Darius seemed completely devoid of humanity and at the same time appeared to be omnipotent. This total lack of scruple coupled to a seemingly unlimited power was a rare combination in Fraser's experience, and a very dangerous thing every time.

The train rattled on, slowly chewing up the distance to the north. Fraser thought about it once more, but decided that sleep was more useful than chewing on inadequate information.

He huddled in the straw and let the rolling motion take away his consciousness.

***

Maggie awoke in her shelter, which did a remarkable job of keeping out the cold.

Nevertheless, her body was stiff and sore. She lay curled up in a ball until there was enough light. She was aware of many odours, none of them flattering, but ignored the lot and sprung out of the shelter to do some stretches. When the blood again flowed in her extremities, Maggie started to walk downhill.

It wasn't long before she made it to the river. Taking care not to get her feet wet, she gathered icy water in her palms and drank a lot of it, rubbing her face with wet hands to prevent them from going numb.

Maggie then climbed away from the water to get out of the dense, snake-infested vegetation lining the river. She started to walk downstream, looking for breaks in the vegetation that might signal the edge of cultivated land.

As the cold left her body, her breath started to become heavy, melting in the frosty morning air. She found a wombat trail that followed the river bank.

Her speed now increased to a brisk pace that taxed her attention to the ground in the pale morning sunlight occasionally interrupted by heavy clouds. Maggie eyed the ominous western sky and hurried on.

It was later in the morning that she encountered a brown snake, which stared at her from the rocks, the ugly narrow head rising aggressively. Maggie stepped well back and threw a small rock from what she judged to be beyond the snake's visual range. The creature jerked angrily as the rock bounced over its coils, but decided to do nothing other than dart towards the river.

Maggie waited until the ripple in the undergrowth moved well away from the trail and hurried on.

***

Stewart the elder woke up late, the sun already well above the horizon. The police were gone, having started an early morning search. A number of men from the town had followed them into the state forest, but Stewart's presence was succinctly and incontrovertibly discouraged by a note he found wedged in the front door. It asked him to stay put in case Maggie turned up or called.

The helicopter was up, defying the low cloud cover. One of the local policemen was directing, the other scouring the bush below with binoculars. They didn't know the range they needed to cover and had no real idea what they were looking for; nobody truly believed that the suspect would just continue on in the same vehicle.

***

The train was slowing down, and Fraser stretched awake to the sound of bells at the boom gate. He saw that the train was crawling through a large town, many streets crossing the tracks and slowing down the huge locomotives, which had no real way of stopping at short notice with such load.

He stood up and stared through the crack, trying to discover his current location. He saw the station in the distance and readied himself to look at its signs, peering intently outside.

The horn blew, and the train crossed another railway crossing. Fraser saw the cars stopped at the boom gate and froze.

Darius stood outside his Mercedes, parked next to the boom gate. His eyes were precisely locked onto Fraser's, tracking him as the train passed the crossing. He made a motion towards Fraser with his right hand and pointed in the direction of the rail tracks, then dove into his car and disappeared behind the tinted shield without any further communication, clearly wanting none in return.

Covered in cold sweat and tying to control the light tremor of his hands, Fraser gathered his belongings and put on the backpack, pulling the straps tight. He opened the door and looked into the distance.

Darius was racing alongside the track, the vehicle majestically swaying on its suspension as it barrelled down the rough trail. It overtook the train and started to slow down far in the distance, stopping on a crest of a long hill.

Fraser saw the cloud of exhaust belch from the locomotive, then felt more than saw the speed slow as the large mass started to lose its momentum. He got ready for a paratrooper's manoeuvre, but as his car got close to Darius, the train was moving at no more than running speed of a man. Fraser made it to the ground without losing balance and ran to a stop, approaching Darius with a false smile.

"Where were you going?" asked Darius with no emotion whatsoever.

"To see my contacts up north," replied Fraser with a similar air. "I need to change my appearance and talk to some people about backup."

"What if we go together?" asked Darius in a businesslike fashion.

"We have to now," replied Fraser. "That train was slow, but nobody would look for me on it."

"Don't worry," said Darius. "The cops are concentrating on the local area looking for the girl. We can make the border in three hours by the back way."

* * *

Maggie heard the helicopter instantly, even though it was little more than a faint whisper on the cold breeze. She turned, desperately trying to localize the source of the barely detectable sound, then ran towards the water.

She waded into the river just as the machine appeared over the crest of a nearby hill, approaching her at what seemed like impossible speed. She waved her arms frantically, but the helicopter did not appear to slow down at all. It was only moments before it would fly over her and disappear into the mountains.

Maggie made her decision instantly. Hoping like hell that the crew of the helicopter contained at least one young male, she tore off her top and quickly pulled her bra over her head. She stood ankle-deep in freezing water waving both articles of clothing over her head, her not insignificant breasts dancing to the motion of her arms.

She need not have worried. Both pilot and co-pilot were single men, whose eagle eyes could spot a female breast from a distances at which no other detail was discernible. The sight of Maggie backed by river sparkling in the morning sun was as perfect an end to a mission as they ever had.

Their only regret was that the victim was not at all hysterical. As the helicopter clearly marked her position and started to circle, she calmly ceased her majestic performance and restored her clothing to its rightful place before they could turn around for the next pass.

The reunion at the Stewart house took place less than an hour later. The helicopter set down a hundred paces from the farmhouse, after which Maggie was deposited in her father's quivering arms.

Later that day, after she had a hot shower and managed a little sleep, the detectives from the nearby town found their way to the farm. They didn't turn down an offer from the diminishing stock of Stewart beer and waited until Maggie got up before asking her an interminable amount of questions.

The ute, which Maggie described perfectly, was located by the helicopter the next day, to the considerable relief of those who were manning roadblocks looking for shaven-headed people. An extensive amount of fingerprints was found, and fibres from Maggie's top in the tray confirmed her story to a word.

The enthusiasm quickly faded when the previous owner of the ute was found precisely at his address and in the arms of a very large female, who reacted to the disruption with a stream of expletives. After de-escalating the emotions of the situation, he was able to produce copies of the transfer paperwork, which he duly posted on the day of sale.

After sizing this up, Maggie was barricaded in the back room of the house, which, for reasons most likely related to the sobriety of the builder, ended up with no windows and served as the guest bedroom. She took a variety of sharp instruments to bed, and her father had thrown down a mattress outside her door, sharing his improvised bed with a loaded rifle.

As a final touch, he let the dogs out in the yard and went to sleep listening to the crackling noises emitted by the rapidly cooling roof.

***

Darius dropped Fraser off in the nominated beachside suburb and shot him a menacing stare. Fraser merely nodded and went into a maze of alleys between old terrace houses now densely populated by semi-legal businesses.

He walked into a small Russian restaurant and selected the most distant table from the windows. As he placed an order, he handed the waiter a small note.

His pelmeni arrived, the steam announcing their buttery taste. Fraser started to eat, dipping them into a small bowl of vinegar. He didn't bother looking up.

His confidence was entirely justified. As he was washing down the last of his meal with mineral water, a lean dark-haired man abruptly sat down at his table, pocketing the keys with a BMW tag. He stared at Fraser and shook his head slowly.

"Very impressive," he said with a slight accent. "You know, Fraser, I deal with pretty mad people. Hey, I am pretty mad myself. But you – real maniac. How did you get out?"

Fraser calmly tipped the last of the mineral water down his throat and threw a few notes on the table.

"Let's go some place quiet, Grigoriy," he said with a short smile. "I am not here for fun."

Darius had considerable trouble tailing the BMW in heavy traffic, as its driver expertly took advantage of his car's acceleration. He lost it but picked it up again where Fraser suggested, as the Russian was stuck in a queue to enter the multi-storey car park. Fraser noticed the black 4WD and nodded imperceptibly. If Grigoriy did see the tail, he chose not to mention it.

An hour or so later Fraser emerged from the car park on foot and alone. He was dressed in a business suit and wore an expertly fitted dark wig. He strolled up to Darius' car and walked straight past it. Darius started the engine and followed him around the corner, where Fraser dove into the back seat and motioned to Darius to drive away quickly whilst crouching out of view.

There were no signs of them being followed, and Darius drove south. Fraser straightened up in his seat but remained silent for some minutes.

"Enlighten me," said Darius heavily as they were crossing the Harbour Bridge.

"They'll do it," said Fraser simply. "My contact just needs a few days to get his equipment and people together. I am meeting them at the border."

"They will do what?" asked Darius.

"Provide covering fire," replied Fraser. "I told them that this whole thing is about getting the girl out unharmed. They will just attend to anyone who tries to make it inconvenient."

"Good, are they?" asked Darius doubtfully.

"Not bad," said Fraser. "All former KGB thugs. Mainly escort drug shipments and provide enforcement, but keep themselves in shape with the occasional bank robbery. Totally merciless – shoot people between restaurant dates. Being targeted by them is like tripping over in the path of a bus."

"They sound okay," nodded Darius grudgingly. "Do you require anything else?"

"No, said Fraser. "Drop me off just here and expect the call in three days."

Darius pulled up outside a large used car yard and watched Fraser march inside. He drove off before witnessing Fraser's selection to pursue arrangements of his own.

***

There was no rendezvous as such – just a couple of very brief mobile phone calls, a series of three-ring dials that went unanswered but were immediately returned. Not being connected, none of these signals were logged by the telephone company.

Then the cars started to converge on Maggie's town, some occupants disguised as fishermen, others as campers and a few as surveyors of the local timber company.

Maggie's safe return did not at all make the locals less irate about the kidnapping, the like of which had never taken place in their town. It was eventually decided that Maggie was not a specific target, but all young women – and, who knows, young men – were probably in danger, especially as the kidnapper came away empty-handed.

To the dislike of the constabulary, guns were very much in evidence, many more than known to be registered to local inhabitants.

The grim-looking denizens had the decency not to display the most illegal of assault rifles in public. But from the rush delivery of large-calibre ammunition to the general store, Nick McMillan knew that many stoppered PVC pipes came out of the soil, and many automatic weapons, the possession of which would earn one a lengthy term in prison, had left their subterranean homes for the first time in years.

McMillan made a decision not to pursue this. He wrestled with it for a while, but then decided that this was not the time to preach surrender of illegal guns, especially in a town where guns have never been used in the commission of violent crime, as opposed to beer bottles, knives and axes, not to mention the occasional tractor.

In addition, the experienced cop who grew up in Sydney couldn't convince himself that the business was over. It didn't smell like a random act, and he quietly ensured that all police patrols of the area ended up circling around the Stewart farm. The neighbours left the gates opened, providing a few shortcuts.

With nothing firmer than his intuition, he couldn't do much else for the time being. So McMillan sat back and waited for further developments, fearing them as much as he needed a clue as to what they may be.

**

Maggie was emerging from the supermarket as it happened. A motorcyclist careered from across the street, revving the powerful dirt bike in low gear and skidded straight into her side, pushing her across the pavement, her purchases spraying from burst plastic bags.

His colleagues arrived from the opposite direction. They were in a non-descript sedan of a common make, but with a supercharged engine and a six-speed manual transmission more commonly found on police pursuit vehicles. As it slid to a halt, two doors opened on the same side, with two beefy men hauling Maggie to her feet and dragging her into the car.

An old van driven by the local chainsaw mechanic slammed into the sedan's grille, bursting the radiator and displacing the engine block. The motorcyclist produced an automatic pistol and emptied the clip into the van's fuel tank, but it leaked diesel harmlessly, the bullbar of the van continuing to push the sedan into a supermarket window.

When the sedan was firmly lodged in the window

frame, an island in a sea of nasty-looking glass fragments, the occupants emerged very slowly, keeping their hands well away from their concealed weapons.

They had excellent reasons to look like men of peace, surrounded as they were by a circle of inward-facing gun barrels – many more than they ever saw in this very tranquil land.

The sight wasn't reassuring at all, the barrels belonging almost exclusively to military weapons, outdated and possibly not well cared for, but more than sufficient to shred them to bloody pulp.

Those staring at them along barrels were hardly more reassuring, a bunch of ageing but very strong men, totally at ease with their guns and in a mood turning more lethal by the minute. The fact that they all stank of beer from drinking with their weapons in the neighbouring building made the Russians even less inclined to argue.

The only one to escape was the motorcyclist, who picked up his machine and ducked behind the van to start it. A few shots were loosed in his direction, but he was both fast and lucky, disappearing into the forest in a cloud of dust.

***

The second team was waiting in the bush just outside the Stewart farm. They noted the opposing forces, but were hoping that the large number of armed louts would get tired of the near-freezing weather and go home to their beer.

Towards midnight that appeared to be happening. By one am the Stewart's farm was empty. The dogs were attracted to the team's location by chunks of meat and shot with anaesthetic darts.

The team ran across the paddocks, dodging both cows and their produce, making it to the wall of the house without noise or casualties. The leader, sweating profusely in the black ski mask, waved his men towards the window of Maggie's bedroom.

Inside Nick McMillan responded to the infrared sensor he installed in the yard shrieking into his earpiece. He clicked the button on his police radio three times in quick succession and thumbed the safety catch of the pistol he was holding. Next to him, James Stewart slid back the bolt of the old SLR, its rasp a deliciously illegal sound for which McMillan was most grateful.

Together they watched adhesive plastic film of the type used to coat schoolbooks being applied over the glass, then a butt of a sophisticated assault rifle expertly tapped the window, creating a crack that traversed the pane with a just-audible thud.

The first man through the window died of multiple

wounds. The others responded by tossing a stun grenade through the window. By then Stewart and McMillan, both Vietnam veterans, were back in the hallway. The effect on them was minimal, the smoke being sucked out in the rush of warm air exiting the house through the broken window.

They returned to rain fire into the shattered window, hitting a few more of the assailants as they were coming through. They ran out of ammunition and retreated from return fire, then sprayed the room with bullets from the corridor blindly, their efforts rewarded by a gurgling sound of someone choking on arterial blood.

McMillan sneaked a look in and saw two bodies bleeding on the floor and another draped over the sill of the broken window.

By then there was a sound of wailing sirens coming from across the valley, and the rest of the attackers were running back across the moonlit paddock. They made no sound whatsoever as they dived over the fencing wire into undergrowth abutting the Stewart property and made their way to vehicles waiting in the bush.

***

Darius listened to the story with a darkening expression. Fraser stood by the car door, knowing what that expression meant.

The leader of the Russians, Grigoriy, a man with enormous wiry strength in his black-clad body stood close to Darius. Grigoriy didn't care - he saw the expression too, and he was apologetic, not to mention aggrieved enough professionally – but not at all afraid of a stocky middle-aged man who glared at him with hatred. No spring chicken himself, Grigoriy was nevertheless a very old hand to applying deadly force, often to armed men who did their best to return the favour.

His extensive unarmed combat skills were backed by a Czech machine pistol tucked into his trousers behind his back, within easy reach from either hand hanging loosely by his side. Then there was the small matter of his comrades, standing a few feet away with similar equipment and experience.

None of them even saw Darius whip his hands around Grigoriy's head and twist with enormous speed. Taken completely off-guard, Grigoriy tried to resist, but still ended up with his back to his assailant. Then his neck was broken with a sickening wet snap, and Darius dropped the body, firing Grigoriy's weapon into waiting men in short, disciplined bursts of automatic fire.

Fraser plunged behind the nearest car as its windscreen disintegrated into a spray of fragments. He concentrated as much of his body as he could behind the front wheel, helped in his concealment as the opposite tyre burst, dropping the car closer to the ground. He heard a few rounds strike it from underneath, with ricochet vibrating inside the bonnet.

The Russians did very badly. Only two of them managed to return fire, shooting blindly over the bonnet of the rear car. Darius hit the ground as a few rounds found his direction.

Then one of the men crawled into the car from the front passenger's door and started the engine. Still sprawled over the front seats, he slammed the gear shift in reverse as the other survivor opened the rear door and fell inside. Without anyone to work the accelerator, the vehicle reversed slowly, but enough to soon be out of reach.

Darius dropped the pistol and ran to one of the bodies, lifting an AK-47. He slid back the bolt and sprayed the moving car.

Most rounds went through the windscreen and bounced off the bonnet, yellow-green fireflies in the gathering darkness. The car continued to reverse down the fire track, frantically zigzagging between the undergrowth on either side.

Darius emptied the clip, tore it out and reversed it, briefly pausing to check that the other side was full. He pointed the rifle again, but it blew apart in his hands.

At first he shook his head in consternation, holding aloft the hands bruised by the shattering impact. Fraser fired a few more rounds into the stock, forcing

Darius to drop the remains of the rifle on the ground.

Then Fraser replaced the clip, cocked his pistol and lowered its barrel to the ground. The car with the Russians had disappeared from view, then there was a squeal of tyres as the driver scrambled into the seat and spun the vehicle around, gunning the engine as he had never gunned one in his life. Then all sounds faded.

Darius stood still, looking at Fraser darkly. There was little point in doing anything else – even he couldn't cover the distance between them before Fraser would bring up his weapon to fire.

Fraser stared back calmly and submissively. A slow smile spread over Darius' lips.

"Do you have any idea who I am?" he asked Fraser brightly.

Fraser opened his mouth, swallowed, trying to form the words, then shut it again. Finally, he nodded without breaking eye contact.

"So what was the point of trying to stop me?" asked Darius.

"You were wrong," answered Fraser slowly. His head started to swim, but he stared back at Darius with a neutral expression. "The Russkies were not responsible for what happened."

"Truly," muttered Darius, kicking away the remains of the shattered assault rifle. "A serial killer with principles. Just my luck."

His anger cooling, he walked towards his car, motioning Fraser to follow him. Fraser safed the pistol, tucked it into his belt and followed Darius around the car. He got into the front passenger seat and sat across it, leaving his door wide open. Darius sat down behind the wheel without looking in Fraser's direction and reached for the ignition.

"Wait," said Fraser. Darius slowly swivelled his head and fixed him with a dark stare.

"Is it all true?" asked Fraser.

"Usually not," said Darius curtly. "But please be precise."

The sunset ignited the last patch of sky behind his head, his striking profile black against the fading streak of crimson light.

"So there is a God?" asked Fraser.

"God?!!!" Darius chortled explosively. He stared at Fraser with amazement. "How on earth would I know?"

"But surely..." Fraser trailed off, furiously combing his vague memories of bible classes.

"I have nothing to do with God. We certainly never met. He may or may not exist, but you can be sure that I do."

"But there is a hell?"

"Oh yes." Darius' eyes flashed in the gathering darkness. "You should know that. Your stepfather. Prison. The people you met on those lonely roads – they went to hell alright."

"But that's not what I..."

"Oh, you want the hot place where your soul goes to be tortured after you die? But why? Who needs psychotic mediaeval imagery of sulphur and gnashing of teeth – when people are tortured to death every day, right here. If you want evidence that hell exists, young fellow, you haven't been paying attention in your latter years."

"But is evil..."

"Evil can happen with no effort on my part, you know. Chaps like you do all the work, and creatively so, if I may mention. My kind happens to find evil useful. You are not a part of a master plan. "

"Your kind... So there is more than just one?"

"Oh, indeed."

"So what makes you different?" asked Fraser. "I

mean, from us?"

"We look similar, but there are major differences you may have already guessed."

"Where does your kind come from?"

"I don't know. That's shrouded in speculation. It's not recorded or passed on in any way, but I believe that we separated from humanity a very long time ago."

"Do you meet many others?"

"No, we go our separate ways as we mature. I will probably never see one, unless one of us succeeds – and it will only take one."

"How old are you?" asked Fraser.

"Quite young, would you believe. I appeared as the last of bubonic plague ravaged Europe. I received a lot of training during the world wars, and now I am at about the peak of my powers and experience."
"So you are not forever?"

"Now, that's an area of cultural sensitivity – I don't know if we really want to get distracted with such details. But I do wish for successors, and there are certain requirements. Which neatly brings us back to the girl I asked you to fetch."

"So you need to service her..."

"Do you mind?" asked Darius with annoyance. "I am not a farm animal. Don't anger me, primate – that part of my reputation is richly deserved. "

"Sorry," said Fraser. "I just can't see why someone of your capabilities needs to waste your time with something as silly as a young girl."

"Careful," said Darius gruffly. "Approach matters of the heart with caution. Anyway, it's more complex than you can imagine."

"Does she really have to be a virgin?"

"Yes."

"Why?"

"A sad story. It seems that somewhere along the way our kind wandered into a genetic dead end, and our women began to develop some kind of an ovarian tumour. It usually kills them in early childhood, but if they survive to adulthood, they still get the damn thing when they fall pregnant. They usually die before they can give birth."

"So... how does it work?"

"We need human females. Fortunately, our main characteristics are genetically overpowering - the males are always like their fathers. Well – usually, let us say. It works well apart from one small problem."

Fraser stared at him open-mouthed.

"Your ladies seem to be allergic to our sperm. They say it burns, then there is some kind of an inflammatory reaction. It turns out that women who are exposed to human sperm make antibodies to it, and if these antibodies are present, the reaction to our seed is very severe, so we cannot impregnate them – all sperm cells are killed off by the inflammatory process. Plus the woman suffers for days, which makes for a dull marital life."

"So, virgins."

"Yes. Very tedious, especially in these liberated times, and for one time only. One has to leave with the child before the mother finds out what her child really is."

"That may not be all bad," said Fraser darkly. "Mothers are distinctly over-rated."

"Indeed - but you can see why we don't have large families. Now, the boys have to be instructed in strict isolation and security, otherwise they soon come to harm. In the past priests used to burn them, and today they are snatched by military to see what makes them so special. Or they come to grief trying to flex their muscles before their brains are mature enough."

"At any rate, I am going to try a different system. No snatching - I want to find a mother who knows what she is in for and stays the course."

"What for?"

"Because I wish her to do it repeatedly. I believe that modern technology can bypass the antibody problem, and if I am right, my race can again breed alongside yours."

"Why struggle?" asked Fraser. "If this isn't about God and or hell, what's the big deal? Why not just amble along?"

Darius shook his head gently. "You don't seem to understand, monkey," he said with mild disapproval. "You will become very important. I will need you to run many errands, and you will be supreme among your kind for the rest of a very long life."

"But what for?" repeated Fraser.

"You people are all the same," grumbled Darius. "What for, to what purpose, what meaning? Why, why, why? Why not, for heaven's sake?"

He smiled and waved off an imaginary gnat.

"Just a turn of phrase, he said. "Don't get excited."

Fraser stood still, a look of fear imprinted on his features.

"You humans are so pathetically weak," said Darius expansively. "All this power at your fingertips, and not a single useful action. Look at the mess your UN made of Bosnia – crimes that make Nazis look like boy scouts committed under the noses of Western troopers in their crisply laundered uniforms. Too bad there was no ground action – I'd love to see three sweaty Serbian gentlemen grab some cologne-scented NATO officer for the purpose of ethnically cleansing his quivering anus."

"Your society tears up mountains to run freeways to ski resorts, but children sleep on your streets, prey for some paedophile."

"You make your most productive people suffer, and the resources they produce at such cost to themselves are lavished on scum."

"Your most talented ones are forced to blend in with morons. From cradle you teach them to hide their ability."

"You are countless, and your communities teem with people. Yet most of you live in complete loneliness."

"It's time for a new idea, Fraser. A return to your roots when small tribes lived in harmony with their environment. You must not spread to reproduce this same clusterfuck on a cosmic scale."

"Yours could be a society without prejudice or preconceptions, with no prisons, marriage altars or divorce courts. A society with no barriers, but one where betrayal leads to expulsion, and expulsion leads to a painful death."

"Imagine a world where every parasite is crucified on a roadside post – not for being an incompetent parasite, but for being one at all."

Fraser stared at Darius in fascinated silence.

"Imagine, monkey," continued Darius. "A world without guilt. A world where scores are always settled. A reality where failure has consequences and success always leads to rewards. Can your tiny brain imagine a world like that?"

"No," answered Fraser in a hoarse whisper.

Darius brought his face close to Fraser's.

"I can make it happen," he said, holding his finger and thumb a fraction apart. "I am this close. Help me, monkey."

Fraser slowly sank to his knees and lowered his face to the ground, but Darius stepped back quickly.

"No, no," he said impatiently. "I don't need your worship. I don't want a slave."

Fraser looked up in fear.

"Get up. I need your initiative," said Darius. "I want those sparks your mind is able to strike. I want that man who was laughing at death when I got him out of jail. A free agent, not an automaton."

Fraser clambered to his feet without taking his eyes off Darius.

"What do I need to do?" he asked.

"See, there it is," said Darius irritably. "You can talk about the fate of the world all day, but no attention to the problem at hand. I want the girl, all right?"

"Yes," said Fraser acridly. " I remember that bit."

"Very good," nodded Darius, indicating his pleasure at Fraser's insolence. "Now, here's the slight difficulty: we don't know where they've taken her. Let's not even worry about what resources we need to take her once we know where she is – how do we even find her?"

"Right," said Fraser. "She will be with someone from the witness protection unit. There seem to be fewer of them these days, so they are likely to find a hole and stay put."

He thought for a few minutes.

"So," he said finally. "Here's the best shot: they probably have her in medium-level protection. Just a place in the suburbs somewhere, nothing distinctive from the outside but not very secure. Then we give them a little fright and make them come out of the bushes. They move her to high-level protection, and we follow them. Then we work out what we need to take her."

"Good," said Darius hoarsely. "You know how to do all this?"

"Yes," said Fraser. "Easy. Let's go and see a friend of mine."

He picked up his pack and got into the Mercedes.

"Yes, let's," said Darius. "Any friend of yours is a friend of mine. But my friend first."

***

Bristow recoiled at the sight of Darius and tried to shut the door in his face, but Darius carelessly slapped his forearm into the cheap panelling, and Bristow found himself flying back to slam into the opposite wall. Darius walked in, followed by Fraser who mimicked Darius in reverse, shutting the door with a backward movement of his elbow.

Then Fraser dragged Bristow off the floor by his collar and pulled him into the kitchen, where he allowed him to sit on a chair. As Fraser stood behind his target, Darius circled around the front and sat opposite Bristow. He briefly glanced at a magazine that was spread open on the kitchen table, his eye caught by the startling mound of flesh, then he fastidiously picked up the publication with the tips of his index finger and thumb and tossed it over his shoulder into the grimy sink.

He stared at Bristow, a predator sizing up prey.

"I wonder if you could do me another favour," he said casually.

"Can't wait," replied Bristow sourly.

Fraser sank his knee into the back of the chair, thrusting Bristow forward with enough force to move the entire table. Darius caught the edge of the tabletop to stop it from sliding into his midriff.

"I am in the market for some telephone numbers," said Darius. "This time there will be a fee for service."

"Right," said Bristow, breathing heavily. "Who are you after – the Commissioner's whore or do you want his daughter?"

"Not today," replied Darius. "Just the witness protection unit."

"Anyone in particular?" asked Bristow, sarcasm returning to his voice.

"Oh," said Darius absent-mindedly, as if caught out. "No. Make it all of them. Land lines, extensions in headquarters, mobiles and satellites. That be fine."

"No way," said Bristow. "I am not going to jail. An ex-cop inside… No. Just kill me."

Darius leaned forward towards him, his eyes boring into the space between them. His right hand slowly formed a mallet-like fist in mid-air and hovered above the table.

"Wake up, little man," said Darius vehemently. "I am about to put that into your arse and drag out your insides for you to eat. Understand?"

"Yeah," said Bristow. "Sounds painful. But then I will pass out and die in a few hours. In jail they will do me all day and patch me up so they can do it the next day. Go ahead. I am not going inside."

"All right," said Darius. "Have it your way, then."

He got up and grabbed the edge of the table, upturning it out of his way with enormous force. With a single leap he cleared the space that separated him from Bristow and thrust his hands around Bristow's neck.

"Wait," said Fraser. He grabbed Bristow in a headlock, covering the man's ears. "Have you ever considered something? You may get all we need out of this guy if you just tell him what you are going to do."

Darius froze in mid-movement, staring at Fraser for a moment. His coal-black eyes went wide with contemplation, then he nodded briefly.

"Please go back to the car," he said to Fraser. "I won't be long."

Fraser let go of Bristow and walked outside. As he got into the 4WD, a power failure blacked out the entire suburb.

***

"What is it, boss?" asked Turner into his headset.

"Pull over," was the terse reply. Turner indicated briefly and swerved into a side street. He cut the engine to hear better and picked up the phone.

"Okay."

"Have a job for you," said Garrison. "I'd rather not have you near the shop, but we are a little short-staffed, if you know what I mean."

A tide of bitterness washed over Turner. He didn't go to the funerals of his friends because some people said that he caused their deaths. The thought still rankled.

"It's a weird one," said Garrison. "I'm having you picked up from your place in an hour."

"Great, boss," answered Turner into the dead microphone.

***

The helicopter landed on the roof of the city headquarters, and the Stewarts were escorted inside. They took the elevator down to the basement, where they were ensconced at McKenzie's.

Jim McKenzie, which was not his baptismal name, lost a leg in a violent hostage drama. A man held his girlfriend hostage with a double-barrelled shotgun after mixing a large quantity of various drugs, and the armed protection unit was quickly deployed to talk him into surrender.

The strategy failed miserably, the druggie managing to kill one of the elite police with a head shot, then letting off another round that caught McKenzie just below the left hip.

The blast from a hand-loaded buckshot cartridge simply removed his entire leg, leaving McKenzie to spray his lifeblood all over the pavement.

The gunman died an instant later, killed from three different directions with deadly-accurate shots. His hostage ran aside, and one of the cops tore an amulet on a leather thong off the dead man's neck. He tied the thong around McKenzie's leg stump, exactly as he was taught not to do, and so saved McKenzie's life. Thanks to the wonders of prosthetic science, McKenzie remained employable.

The amulet on the leather thong was meant to join all other evidence in a plastic bag, but the surgeons who untied it later gave it to McKenzie, who never took it off his own chest since.

He now ran the official welcome part of top-level police protection. His empire was a small part of the basement, which was converted into what looked like a comfortable family home but without windows. There was only one way in, through a steel door on heavy hinges, which could be barred from inside with a heavy bolt of steel. It wasn't that McKenzie feared an attack on his charges inside the headquarters – but he wanted them to feel its impossibility.

McKenzie didn't mind relocating to the headquarters permanently. The shotgun blast also shredded his penis, and his wife left the family home as soon as she heard. The last news of her was from a fashionable resort up north, where she was living with a younger man.

Maggie and her father were each allocated tiny bedrooms, where they collapsed into clean-smelling sheets and passed out.

***

"Get your stuff while I talk."

Turner faced his locker in silence for a few moments, then slid in the key. He started to lay all his equipment out on the bench between the rows of lockers.

"Right," said Garrison. "It's a girl and her father."

He spoke at length. Just before he finished, Turner straightened up from adjusting his ankle holster.

"Boss," said he. "What is this shit?"

"Not sure," answered Garrison with an angry shake of his head. "That's what they told me, word for word. Okay?"

"What about the guys arrested by the vigilantes?"

"Not a word," said Garrison. "A couple ended up resisting arrest, too."

"How thoroughly?" asked Turner.

"Oh, apparently one got his hand caught in the car door," replied Garrison with heavy sarcasm. "Didn't mention it to the arresting officer for a while, apparently broke every bone. Moaned a lot, but not a word."

Turner shrugged helplessly.

"Never mind," said Garrison. "Just look after these two. Don't think too much."

"Oh, no chance of that," replied Turner, slotting nine millimetre hollow point rounds into the magazine. He stuck the full magazine into a pouch on his belt and tugged on the collar of his boiler suit to straighten it under the weight of the equipment harness. "Let's go."

"Don't let me down," said Garrison. "You really shouldn't be here."

***

"So how did you turn out the power?" asked Fraser.

"Oh, not again," Darius switched off the ignition and glared at Fraser in irritation.

They were in a street recently wrested from the green paddocks on the edge of the city. Bare earth surrounded tiny new houses, lit by the harsh glare of sodium light in dusk rapidly turning to fog.

"I have to say something," said Fraser. "Look, I am human. My kind has wondered about this for eternity."

"Let it rest," begged Darius. "Not now."

"Well, let me explain," said Fraser. "It's proving a bit of a limitation of mine – I can't get this out of my head."

Darius shook his head in amazement.

"Your bravery is commendable," he said gruffly. "I

would say that you just don't know the consequences of angering me, but you do. Make it quick."

"What is the source of your power?" asked Fraser.
"Ah," said Darius. "Are you hoping for something that breaks the laws of physics? A magic of some sort?"

"Something like that," replied Fraser.

"Well, you will be disappointed," answered Darius. "It's much simpler than that. Consider this ignition switch. Is it magic when I use it to begin internal combustion?"

"No. It's a simple physical law translated into very nice German engineering. Why does it work every time? Because the stalwarts who built it did their homework. No miracle – just unfashionably hard work. But to a savage its action may seem like contradiction of physical laws. To a slob its reliability may be a marvel. But to a disciplined and skilled being, this switch is mundane reality. This was always my kind's advantage over yours."

"All right then," said Fraser tapping his index finger on the dashboard stubbornly. "So does my kind have advantages?"

"Oh yes," said Darius. "More than I care to recount."

"Such as?"

"Wild imagination," said Darius. "Irrational courage. Rampant optimism. But above all, you can act without a plan. My kind usually cannot."

"Surely that's not entirely true," protested Fraser. "Otherwise you'd be helpless."

"No, it's almost a total lack of spontaneity, I am afraid," said Darius sadly. "We do compensate, though – mostly our plans are sophisticated enough to include all likely outcomes, and by the time we live for a few human lifetimes, most challenges can be met with rehearsed responses."

"But you can't spend your entire youth planning!" said Fraser, amazed. "Someone will eat you as you plan!"

"That happens a lot," admitted Darius. "That's why my kind ended up deep inside caves. They only came out when they fully mature. It's a lot easier now – modern society panders to people who live without any kind of foresight."

They alighted from the car and Darius locked the doors. Fraser thought for a while.

"Imagination, courage, optimism – those are not qualities we could be without," he said slowly. "This is what got us to the Moon and back."

"That's right," answered Darius. "Your very finest moment, that Moon act, all very good stuff. But let me tell you something you don't know. Those your kind calls Neanderthals had that and much more."

"Look what happened to them," said Fraser.

"Indeed," said Darius. "But not in the way you believe. Heard of evolutionary dead ends?"

"Oh yes," said Fraser.
"Well, then," Darius dropped the keys in his pocket. "Let me introduce you to a new concept. The Neanderthals did not become extinct."

Fraser stood still, staring at Darius as the cold wind stung his eyes.

"The real dead end is your kind," said Darius. "Neanderthals were a noble race your kind had nearly exterminated. They were better than you in every way. They could outrun you, outthink you and even outfuck you. But you hunted out their animals, and nearly all Neanderthals were starved out of existence."

"So what happened to the rest?" asked Fraser.

"Why," Darius shook his head in bewilderment. "You don't understand this at all, do you? They evolved, monkey. The survivors developed qualities which made up for their small numbers. Those few seemed to have become a spectacular success, apart from being unable to breed like our ancestors."

He watched Fraser and nodded at the spreading expression of recognition on his startled face.

"That problem will be solved very soon. Let's go."

They crossed the road to mount the naked porch of a modest home entirely immersed in darkness. Fraser knocked on the door.

There was a long period of silence, followed by a burst of muffled curses. After a while the door flew open to reveal a thin man of medium height with a dishevelled shock of blond hair. His large blue eyes rimmed with swollen lids glowed in street lighting with an unfocussed look of bewilderment and pain. He was naked apart from grimy white underpants, the bulges of his lean muscles reflected in the orange light.

"Drago," said Fraser genially. "I called, remember?"

There was a rush of footsteps inside, and a small boy holding a large teddy bear ran into Drago's leg and hugged it tightly, looking up to the strangers. There was nothing childlike about his eyes, which bored into Darius and held his stare before sliding across to his father's face.

"Wait," said Drago to Fraser in a voice cracking with fatigue. He slid to his knees onto cheap carpet and embraced his son's neck. His head bent down to the boy's ear in a gesture of defeated endurance.

"Please, bratko," said Drago without lowering his voice. "Help dad. Go on, Alex, go back to bed."

"Daddy," said the boy, his voice as terse as his father's. He stared at Darius again. "Are they bad people?"

His father's hand around the small shoulders quivered visibly.

"They are okay, bratko," said Drago, turning away from the boy. Darius saw two glistening tracks sprout on the tall cheekbones. "Dad just needs to talk to them. Go back to bed."

The boy turned around and trotted down the passage into the darkness.

"Don't cry, daddy," he said tonelessly as he disappeared around the corner.

Drago clutched his face with large palms. The wiry shoulders shook in muffled agony, his blond head dropping onto the chest.

"I'm sorry," whispered Drago as his hands slowly fell from his face. He rose unsteadily, clutching the door jamb for balance as his lean body swayed alarmingly. Darius shot out his hand and steadied him by the shoulder. Drago simply stared past him, unseeing in his hell.

"Let's go inside," said Darius gently.

Drago nodded mechanically and turned, brushing a switch. The light burst into a neat lounge, its floor bright with strewn toys. Drago sat on the vinyl couch, watching Fraser lock the door and sit opposite.

"Sorry," repeated Drago, his voice now stronger and more melodious. "My wife ran off with her boss last month. Her lawyer is having the place auctioned next week."

"Ah," said Darius. "I've heard about this kind of madness. I understand."

"No you don't," said Drago with an involuntary sob. "Her boyfriend's a paedo. He tried to touch Alexander. That's what he's really after, and my wife's too dumb to see it."

Darius stared at him with a rare look of sympathy, as they sat in silence for a few minutes.

"Forgive me," said Darius at last. "But isn't that enough to land him in jail?"

"Apparently not," spat Drago with profound bitterness. "Cops said I was making it up and told Alexander what to say."

Fraser's features tightened into a look of pure hatred.

"Tried the courts?" he asked.

Drago nodded glumly.

"They told me that the child will be supervised," he replied. "By the mummy, okay?" He shivered at some unsavoury memory as he stared past them. "Three glasses of champagne, and she stays unconscious all night. Besides, she's completely in love with that bastard. Must have used his tongue on her – that means he really cares, right?"

"Drago," said Fraser. "We are here about a job. Cash."

Drago simply nodded.

"We have a list of mobile numbers," said Fraser. "We want to access their cell locations for a few weeks."

Drago swallowed.

"I am on leave," he said. "I can't arrange real-time feed."
"Not a problem," weighed in Darius. "A few hours' delay is fine."

"That should be okay," began Drago uncertainly. "There is a server which does log dumps on demand. I can write a daemon to access it regularly. All I need is a laptop and a modem."

"Can it be traced back to you?"

"Nah," said Drago. "Any techie knows the password.

Cash, you said?"

"Oh yes," said Darius. "Dollars. Make it real dollars – American. You need to visit the old country for a while."

"Can't," said Drago. "She got an order that stops my boy from leaving this fucking city. I take him skiing, they can put me in jail."

"Is that so?" said Fraser and Darius at once. They looked at each other, Darius curving his lips quizzically.

Fraser took out a pad and wrote something down. He tore the sheet from the pad and handed it to Drago, who read it slowly, his eyes slowly widening in the sockets.

"She docks in a few weeks," said Fraser. "Make sure you give the skipper this paper."

He scribbled on the next sheet and handed it to Drago.

"Now, memorize this and destroy it," he said. "If I don't get this message by her return voyage, the captain is going to die a very unhappy man. I'll see to it myself."

"Don't mock me, man," Drago's eyes welled up with fresh tears. "Fuck, it hurts. Don't make fun, okay? Fucking kill me if you like, just don't laugh, all right?"

"I am not laughing," rasped Fraser through clenched jaws, making Drago look up in fear. "Why don't you take charge for once in your miserable life? Think of your son."

"I believe he means that as a favour," said Darius. "We are still offering cash. You can do as you like, but think it over."

"Okay then," said Drago uncertainly. He swiped his eyes with the back of his hand and sized Darius up for the first time.

"Okay…"

***

The lift stopped at the basement, then Garrison used his security pass to operate the door. They stepped into a small lobby, devoid of furniture apart from a single fisheye camera lens mounted above a large steel door.

"Please show your passes," rasped McKenzie's voice through the metal grill. Garrison and Turner removed their security passes and displayed them to the camera. There was a loud buzz, and the door slid open, revealing completed darkness spilling from a long corridor. It shut as they stepped in.

The lights blinked on, then after a brief delay they saw McKenzie emerged from behind them, his gun gleaming blue-black in his hand.

"Fuck," said Garrison. "This is a little cops-and-robbers, eh?"

"Not with these ones, sir," replied McKenzie. "It's all a little strange. Hi, Jack."

"Good to see, McKenzie," said Turner. "Can't be too cautious."

"Not when you don't know what's happening. Guns please."

They handed over their pistols, Turner adding a heavy flick knife, which he produced from his sleeve. McKenzie and Garrison both rolled their eyes at the sight of the illegal weapon.

McKenzie went into a small room near the steel door and returned empty-handed. They followed him to the corridor.

Maggie and her father stood up as the protection officers entered the room. Garrison put his hand on Turner's shoulder.

"This is Jack," he said gruffly. "An ugly bugger, but he'll be the best in this business when I die. Do exactly what he tells you from now on."

"Hi," said Turner. "Look, can we talk for while?"

"Got all day," said McKenzie.

"I haven't," said Garrison. "See you all later."

He nodded to McKenzie and left.

"I'll make some coffee," said McKenzie. "Sugar?"

"Two," said Turner without taking his eyes off Maggie. She stared back pointedly, but then softened her expression and smiled.

***

Darius and Fraser watched Drago pull up next to the Mercedes, parked in a scrub off a lonely road. Fraser waited until Drago emerged from his small car, clearly alone, then put away his pistol and followed Darius into the clearing.

Drago nodded at them bleakly and pulled a disk from his shirt pocket. Darius went to the rear of his car and emerged with a laptop, which he opened on the bonnet of the Mercedes, brushing a large raindrop from the screen. He glared at the heavens angrily.

Drago installed his program on the laptop and opened the back cover. Darius handed him the modem cable, which he connected to his phone.

Whilst the connection was being established, Drago looked up at them.

"I am going like you said," he said heavily. "But I need another favour."

"Go on," said Darius courteously.

"A gun," said Drago darkly.

"Are you planning on making someone sorry?" asked Darius.

"Nah," replied Drago with a short shake of his blond head. "Not enough bullets for them. Not in the entire world. I just want a little protection on that ship."

"You don't need to worry..." started Fraser.

"Oh, I think the man has a point," said Darius with a waving motion of the palm. "Those rust buckets are not exactly crewed by model citizens. But make sure you toss it overboard before you get to port. Soon as the vessel berths, all right? We don't want you arrested."

"Right," said Drago with something resembling enthusiasm. "Now watch this."

He pulled out his mobile phone and entered its number into the laptop. The screen turned black as if the machine crashed, but then Drago turned on his phone. The laptop blinked a few seconds later, showing its cell location on the screen.

"They've upgraded the software," said Drago. "Look, it's almost real-time feed. And a full log dump. Gives you everything."

Fraser nodded, then added his phone number. The location was also returned correctly. He looked up at Darius, who nodded.

As Darius finished counting out the cash, Fraser entered the numbers of the entire surviving witness protection squad into the daemon, a program that woke up periodically to interrogate the distant server. He initiated the first session, receiving a display of all cell locations, which he studied with curiosity.

Darius handed Drago the Czech machine pistol he used on the Russians and a few clips of ammunition.

"It's marked," he said. Drago stared at him without understanding.

"It's been used in action," explained Darius. "The police will be looking for it. Don't get caught with it."

"Oh, I won't," said Drago. He ran to his car and drove off quickly.

Darius stared after him, then shook his head in wonder and glanced at Fraser who held out the pistol questioningly. Darius shook his head emphatically and signalled Fraser to get into the car.

"Wait," said Fraser suddenly. Darius rounded on him

in frustration.

"What now?"

"Just one thing," Fraser swallowed. "Is your name really Darius?"

"Really," Darius chuckled, shaking his head in disbelief. "Of all things."

"Is it?"

"No!" howled Darius with annoyance. "I don't have a name! I don't need one, all right? It's to make it easier for the likes of you."

"Why Darius, then?"

"Darius was the last great king of ancient Persia. Your history is a little unkind to him, but in truth he had a lot of style. Besides, the word has a nice ring to it."

***

The protection squad settled on a vehicle after a lot of wrangling - a bulletproof van with courier markings. Its mercilessly hard suspension made it highly manoeuvrable, but even that was no substitute for the slits that could be used to fire in every direction from inside without opening doors or windows.

Turner sat inside with the Stewarts, a military

shotgun resting on its pistol grip between his knees. He watched the traffic incessantly. Maggie chose the seat next to him, he noticed with an inward smile. As the van swayed around corners, her elbow occasionally came into contact with his. He did not react visibly, but found this quite a distraction.

They drove a circuitous path through the older suburbs, where any powerful vehicles stood out in the stream of ageing sedans filled with tired people crawling back to their suburban illusions. Soon Turner was pretty certain there was nobody following, since there were no cars at all for quite a few miles. He let his body relax slightly, his biceps now making light contact with Maggie's shoulder.

The van rumbled into a tongue of undeveloped land, whose market gardens awaited despoliation by town planners yet unborn. They bounced along a dirt road, then turned into a long driveway of a house standing alone on an acre of cabbage rows, planted to make sprinting across open ground a difficult and dangerous activity.

The door to the garage was opened by the guard as the van approached, and shut just as quickly as it rolled in. Turner waited for its milled steel to clang onto concrete before he unlocked the van.

"Here we are," he said with a hollow cheer as the lights came on.

Two men watched from behind bulletproof glass as

Maggie and her father alighted from the van and walked to the reinforced door, with Turner displaying his ID to the camera above.

They walked into a small lounge room that had one strange addition to the 1960's décor. Large sheets of steel covered all windows behind drawn curtains, preventing any possibility of shot penetrating the glass. The UV levels being what they are, the accountants determined this to be far more cost-effective than bulletproof glass, which deteriorates in the sun. The security experts did not disagree with this recommendation, demanding only latches that could be undone in case of fire from inside.

The Stewarts were shown to different bedrooms. Sleep overtook them, as well as it can overtake someone whose every night on this earth could be the last.

***

"Watch this, simian," said Darius jovially. He parked at small row of shops living out the last of their long grimy lives.

They sat in the car for a short time, gusts of cold wind coming off the sea and shaking the tall sides of the car. The engine clicked noisily as it cooled, as Fraser sat without a word, staring ahead.

Then two teenage girls came across the road and went into the grocery store. They emerged a short time later, their faces aglow with a guilty secret. Darius nodded to Fraser knowingly and started the engine.

As the girls started on a path towards the beach, Darius drove into the beach car park and reversed the car to point its bonnet at the exit.

"Won't be a moment," he said lightly. He left the engine running and left the car, strolling briskly towards the walking path.

Sally and Melinda were startled by his figure springing from the bushes and snatching the brown paper bag from Melinda's hands.

"Now then," said Darius with a predatory smile. "What's this? Dear me – that looks like marijuana, does it not? And look here – the ribbed Xtras with a large reservoir! Great! Planning ahead, are we?"

"Give it back, you big fuckwit!" yelled Melinda. "That's mine!"

"You're right," said Darius placatingly. He tossed the bag on the ground. "Not certain who'd poke either of you – unless blind drunk? Oh yes, that must be how. But that's not what I need to know right now."

He grabbed Melinda by the arm and spun her around, his elbow locking like a steel tube around her slim throat.

She yelped as his gloved hand snaked to the side pocket of her jeans, thrust inside and removed a small mobile phone. Then Darius pushed the girl aside and started walking towards the bushes.

"Give it back!!!" screamed both girls at the top of their voices.

Darius stared at them for a moment. "This is when you get to run away, unless you want to me to try the condoms."

"Bet you couldn't get it up with a girl!" screamed Melinda, retrieving the paper bag.

"What?" asked Darius turning to her ominously. "You filthy piece of garbage, how dare you?"

He took a step back towards them, and fear spread over their faces. They backed away, then turned and ran into the park.

Darius shook his head and dialled a number he memorized just before. It was answered by a middle-aged woman.
"Wait," said Mrs Garrison sourly. "I'll get him."

She dropped the receiver on the table and crossed the lounge back to the table.

"It's for you," she said to her husband, who dropped his napkin and stood with his facial expression mimicking hers.

"Yeah," he said into the phone. "Garrison here."

"Listen carefully," said Darius. "The little Stewart bitch and her father. Hope they have their funerals prepaid."

"What do you want with them?" asked Garrison evenly.

"I'll kill them," said Darius. "Slowly. You got that?"

"I think so," said Garrison. "But why?"

"Have a good night," said Darius. "Your lady sounds eager."

He thumbed the switch on the phone, and threw it into the bushes.

***

Turner listened intently, nodding into the phone.

"Moving out now, boss," he said curtly and cut the line.

"Hey, listen," he said to the waiting colleagues. "I say it once only. Get the subjects, get your weapons and start the cars. We have to be out of here in thirty seconds."

It happened only a little slower, but they were soon racing towards the freeway. Nobody was left in the house – risks were no longer taken in the protection squad.

"Hmm," said Darius, staring at the laptop intently. "We have lift-off."

He thrust a long finger with a manicured nail into a row of numbers, which Fraser leaned in closer to track.

"I'd say this is the one," he said pointing to a row in the table. "Whose is it?"

Darius minimized the current screen and consulted a spreadsheet from Bristow.

"His name is Jack Turner," he said thoughtfully. "Sounds familiar."

"Yeah," said Fraser. "Heard it on the telly in jail. He lost a canary, and they blamed him for it. Big job – five cops dead."

"Ah," said Darius lightly. "Difficult stuff, losing colleagues, what?"

"Yes," agreed Fraser. "Very distracting, such business. Must be a weight on the poor boy's mind."

"Know him?" asked Darius.

"Yes," nodded Fraser. "Lost a shooting match to him a few years ago."

"Good, is he?" asked Darius. "Must have been."

"Good," confirmed Fraser. "Another ex-Army. A real hard case."

"Ah well," said Darius with a slight sigh. "Catch as catch can, kind of thing."

"They'll be headed back to HQ," said Fraser, looking at the laptop. "So what do we do next?"

"You know," said Darius. "I was going to ask you the same thing."

***

McKenzie took the return of recent guests in his stride. The steel door was locked and bolted, the cameras were turned on, the guests were served a weak tea, and Jack stole a few hours of sleep in the spare room.

Then Maggie awoke from what little sleep she managed to steal and went to the toilet. She washed her face and went to the lounge room for a drink of water.

Turner was there at the desk, polishing the slide of his automatic with a rag. He looked up and smiled. Convention required him to put the gun away out of sight of a civilian, but he never obeyed that rule anyway, and something about Maggie's eyes told him that he especially didn't need to now.

He went on polishing. Maggie got a glass of water and sat opposite him, watching his practised hands on the metal. He became aware of her stare and looked up.

"They are coming, aren't they?" said Maggie.

"Nah," said Turner immediately, but looked away from her stare with moderate discomfort.

"Please," said Maggie. "Tell me the truth."

"They might be," said Turner. "I don't know."

"Will you stop them?" asked Maggie.

"You mean, can I stop them?" asked Turner.

"No," said Maggie. "That's not what I meant."

Turner looked up and studied her eyes carefully.

"Yes, I will stop them," said Turner slowly. "Unless they kill me first. Okay?"

 Maggie held his stare.

"Okay," she said.

He gratefully dropped his eyes and reassembled his pistol. Maggie continued to watch him, cupping her glass of water with both hands. Turner reloaded the clip and replace the pistol in the holster.

"Just stay calm," he said at long last. "It's got to work out."

***

Sandy Woodward scratched his stubbled chin and threw the papers on his desk.

The new tax system was killing him. He ran a small building firm for most of his adult life, somehow blundering through the economic downturns, a divorce and assorted building disasters imposed by the force of gravity and various insurance companies. He could cope with all that.

But the new tax forms defeated him. His brain, so adept at juggling his schedule and estimating required quantities of building materials, baulked at alien terminology introduced by the latest generation of bureaucrats catching a career ride on the latest wave of reform.

He was startled by the ringing phone, a rare enough event in the aftermath of the tax reform, which saw most people cease all non-essential economic activity rather than think.

"Woodward Constructions," he said cheerfully into

the receiver.

"I have a proposition," said Darius. "Is there a place we can meet?"

***

"Want you to wear this," said Turner, handing the Stewarts two Kevlar jackets. He opened his shirt to show them how it looks.

"All the time?" said Maggie.

"Yup," confirmed McKenzie. "Never take it off when you have people shooting at you."

"What do we do then?" asked James Stewart.

"This is the hard bit," said Turner. "We sit right here and wait. Nothing outside is safe."

"You think we are safe in here?" asked Stewart senior with contempt.

"Not from his breath," said Turner, pointing at his colleague. "Other than that, yeah. I don't think anything can get us in here."

"Do you play cards?" asked McKenzie.

"Sure," replied Stewart.

"Let's get set up then," said McKenzie. They left the

armoury for the lounge room, leaving Maggie and Jack together. As soon as they were out of sight, Maggie quickly undid the buttons of her heavy chequered shirt and took it off, standing before Turner in a tight-fitting singlet. She saw his discomfiture and took utter delight in it.

"Help me with this, would you?" she said in a businesslike tone. Turner sighed and picked up the bullet-proof jacket.

***

Drago sat on a torn sofa hugging his son as he waited for the first mate to emerge from his cabin.

The first mate was a large Norwegian and not a pretty sight with unkempt red beard and red, swollen eyelids. Reeking of stale liquor, he stepped forward unsteadily and hurried to take a seat.

"The captain iss on shore leave," he said with a heavy accent. "But iss'okay. I can help. I unnerstant."

"Indonesia?" said Drago eagerly.

"No," said Norwegian. "Nos' so goot. Too much trouble. Not goot place for young boy, okay?"

"Where then?" asked Drago.

"We go next to Phillippines," said the Norwegian. "You stay below, keep real quiet, yeah? In Manila you disappear. No one cares. No police."

"Right," said Drago. "The price all right?"

"Yeah," said the Norwegian. "Fraser goot friend. No problem. You go below now. Your boy keep quiet?"

"I'll be very quiet," said Drago's son indignantly. "I want to come with Daddy, all right?"

The big Norwegian's bandit face creased into a big lopsided smile. "Oll rightt."

***

"Yes, you heard that correctly," said Darius.

"You want to buy me out?"

"Yes, yes," said Darius impatiently. "What's the problem – isn't this a legitimate business?"

"Course it is," said Woodward, wiping sweat off his face. "It's just that..."

"You have no customers at the moment?"

"None."

"Well, that's not a crime in the current economy, is it?"

"No. Suppose not."

"No problem. We have an urgent job to do, and we need a lot of equipment. We don't actually want to take over existing contacts."

"Were you thinking of a particular offer?"

Darius removed the chequebook and wrote out a deposit. Woodward only shook his head in wonder.

"Who is your solicitor, please?" asked Darius. Woodward dug in the filing cabinet.

"This is the guy I use," he said hoarsely. Darius pocketed the card.

"Time is of the essence," he said with a dry smile. "Please call him and ask that he cooperates."

***

From his hiding place Fraser watched the men sweep the car park in the gathering darkness, then stepped into the open, his hands well away from his sides.

He was immediately surrounded by men dressed in black, hornet-angry at having their perimeter penetrated. He gave them a bright smile. After removing his gun they escorted him to the small van with darkened windows. The side door slid and Fraser got inside.

Fortunately, Russian gangs don't interact other than swapping bullets. The man he spoke to had not heard of a wave of recent funerals in his ethnic group, and he would not have cared even if someone told him.

Fraser emerged from the vehicle some minutes later and walked away through a seemingly empty car park.

The van drove away followed by decrepit-looking but powerful cars full of very experienced men.

***

"We are putting up some structures for a large cultural event," explained Darius to Bienvenutto, who was still out of breath. "It's urgent."

Luigi Bienvenutto, the lawyer on whom Woodward constructions had been bestowing its custom, was a busy man. He did a lot of petty crime work and meddled in the ugly little divorces that abundantly took place in the wastelands of the local housing commission plot.

It was thirsty work, a lot of petty nastiness from people not schooled in hiding their frustration from a society that parked generations of their families in a dead-end siding.

His office, perched above a corner pet shop, was neat enough, but one of the window panes was missing and replaced with a sheet of plywood, over which some homely soul – Darius guessed the same large-breasted Italian matriarch who greeted him in the waiting room – had placed a cheap but leafy pot plant.

Life went on, reflected Darius, with the overall effect being probably nicer than the view out of the unbroken window.

The second-hand smells of stale clothes and various smoked substances clung to the neat furniture that probably once adorned the Bienvenutto family lounge. Curtains were dispensed with, giving the room a much lighter air than its size and contents deserved.

Mr Bienvenutto was very eager to cut his session at the local Family Court when he heard the particulars of the Woodward transaction. He adjourned not one but three separate cases, warning clients that Her Honour appears to be in a delicate part of her menstrual cycle and should not be approached by anyone who does not wish to lose custody, access and the shirt off their back to their ex-spouse.

The clients eagerly accepted this display of legal perspicacity and adjourned their cases to various drinking establishments.

The reason for Bienvenutto's haste was the bonus – Darius offered to pay Woodward's legal fees, and generously at that, as compensation for the speed with which the transaction had to be conducted.

Woodward Constructions was not normally a prompt

payer, and ridding himself of a troublesome client whilst being handsomely and promptly paid for the final transaction suited Mr Bienvenutto very much.

What Darius was proposing was simple enough. All of the company's assets, its good name, the existing client list and the list of subcontractors was to be transferred to the ownership of Darius Holdings, a bona fide company registered with all the appropriate seals and approvals in the same jurisdiction.

The conveyancing was very straightforward, as the said assets were mainly well-used tools, a couple of battered trailers, a bulldozer and a brick hoist.

There were some consumables for which Woodward accepted a modest lump sum: left-over bricks stored at the respective building sites, a couple of sets of cheap bathroom fittings, an account in credit with a local timber supplier and a quantity of miscellaneous items.

An asset mentioned separately was a shed Woodward housed on a block of industrial land owned by the local cement supplier, who received various housekeeping favours from Woodward Constructions in lieu of rent. The two small businessmen managed to finish school together and both were let loose onto the unsuspecting world at the same time, both of them now having plenty of regrets about being born.

This property was surrounded with a proper cyclone fence and had a resident Doberman. This was where

Woodward kept a couple of lines of stock that may attract unwanted attention. There were a dozen boxes of ammo for the nail guns, expensive brass door handles from a bankrupt job which left Woodward unpaid and a quarter of a tonne of industrial dynamite.

The latter proved a little more difficult. Whilst the bulldozer and the vehicles didn't have to be operated whilst in the possession of an unlicensed owner, something Bienvenutto simply noted in the contract, the mere possession of explosives and nail gun ammunition was an offence without the proper paperwork.

So Bienvenutto was much relieved when Darius produced a commercial license for handling and using industrial explosives as well as a comprehensive firearm permit, complete with a rare centre-fire endorsement.

A smile of victory creased Bienvenutto's broad face as he retrieved the contracts from the laser printer and witnessed Darius' signature.

Sandy Woodward came in a few hours later and signed too, leaving a very large bundle of keys and a wine box full of assorted papers, the mere sight of which gave Bienvenutto's heart a jump. Fortunately, none of these needed his attention, Woodward explained, as they were mainly receipts for various items in stock, a bedraggled book containing the client list and a very thin ledger of recent transactions.

The contracts and bank cheque were exchanged, everybody smiled widely, and Bienvenutto popped a bottle of cheap but surprisingly good champagne, of which Mr Woodward seemed to have drunk the most amount.

He was a very happy man when he extracted his Land Cruiser from a tight parking spot, making a mental note to have the Woodward Constructions logo removed from the doors.

After remaining in town just long enough to see the bank cheque go through, he hightailed to his favourite place, a fishing village on the ocean beach where he had not been for nearly a decade.

***

After nearly a week without action Maggie and her father started to acquire a look Turner had seen in the field – a calm vigilance that never quite settled, becoming superimposed onto the personality of the combatant. Smiles, jokes and banter started to break through a curtain of constant tension and sense of danger.

Turner was right at home in this situation – it was what he did best, and his system knew it. He never felt more alive than during such operations, especially if his conscience was not in the constant niggle mode about whether the people he was protecting deserved it.

This was no such problem now. Whilst nobody even claimed to understand why the Stewarts were targeted in this venal and determined manner, it was put down to some event in the realm of mental illness.

An early theory that their farm was somehow involved in the drug industry was thoroughly discredited. The well-known captains of that industry denied any knowledge of the Stewart family. They solemnly swore, on the blood and various solid organs of their venerated ancestors, that they had no designs on the Stewarts.

They all undertook to notify the authorities at once should they become aware of the miscreants who caused the police to disrupt their trade with inquiries. That promise was quite credible. Whoever was attacking the Stewarts did not appear to respect the rules of sustainable criminal behaviour.

***

Ivan Karpov, a former history lecturer at Moscow University, was now living much better than the stunted imagination of a Soviet citizen would ever allow him to dream.

He drove a latest model Mercedes, smoked Cuban cigars and ate food of the finest quality. His wife, who largely disapproved of his career change, was separated from him for some time.

Fortunately, she did not produce any children, which was why her departure was tolerated. She was also wise enough to choose religion as her next love, residing at a small Russian monastery near Sydney, where she helped the good brothers keep their library and avoided any mention of her husband.

Karpov occasionally slept with a selection of his business associates. He found young Russian women superb in his line of work. Coming from a society where equality of the sexes was enforced regardless of the consequences to women, Russian girls were a stunning combination of ruthlessness, lateral thinking and loyalty.

Not that loyalty was a problem in his organization – Karpov never cheated his employees, the result being a re-enactment of a mediaeval enclave in which the warlord and his cut-throats interacted according to a strict set of rules whilst raping and demolishing the surrounding countryside.

In many cases, loyalty was reinforced by the simplest possible means – money was reliably dispatched to miserably poor families in Russia, along with some commodities which even money cannot buy in Russia, such as physical safety and quality medical assistance.

Karpov was a balding, non-descript man of medium height and slack facial appearance, which belied the speed and the nastiness of his attack.

He had to do a lot of attacking earlier on, when his chain of nightclubs started selling fashionable recreational drugs, forcing out itinerant dealers who chose not to work for him. Changing their minds was wet work, as the KGB once called it, with electrocutions, beheadings as well as the occasional dismemberment using the towbars of two Range Rovers.

Karpov prided himself on drawing from his expertise in history to revive this Viking custom, which quickly gained popularity amongst his ancestors. The ancient Russians tore people apart used galloping horses or treetops bent to spring apart with unstoppable force, whereas Karpov enjoyed the low-ratio gearing of powerful luxury vehicles, capable of doing the job without anyone touching the throttle.

Vikings understood an important issue, he would tell his few confidants, usually over a bottle of excellent red wine. Tearing someone apart got everyone's attention, even in an era when violent death was a welcome release from the crushing hardship of daily survival.

Now Karpov was confronted with the strangest proposal in his entire life. In general, he did not kill those who did not interfere with his business, for money or otherwise, and didn't like those who did. But ecstasy and other stimulants poor young kids had to take before they could interact with one another were hard to come by and even harder to use.

They seemed to Karpov an imperfect class of chemicals, full of impurities and dangerous side effects. The latest batch was particularly inconvenient. It appeared to cause some salt imbalance, which made the brain swell up inside the skull and kill the poor young twit who took it. The only warning signs were a very high body temperature and confusion.

Karpov was grimly bemused at that warning – confusion in a drunken teenager was not a simple thing to detect, although the temperature bit was more promising. Alas, one of the bouncers had to be permanently deployed near the toilets to listen for anyone with more than a healthy interest in cold water. The victims were immediately dragged outside and forcibly injected with a diuretic, which countered the salt imbalance - usually in time.

Dollar-wise it was all worth it, a single tablet selling briskly for more than a bottle of good whiskey. But the side effects annoyed Karpov, who felt a certain loyalty towards his customers, even as young and as stupid as they were. Karpov was willing to go to a lot of trouble to clean up that act for another simple reason. The prospect of sudden death in embarrassing circumstances deterred punters from trying the drug.

Darius was the first man who made sense, which is why Karpov consented to meet with his agent. Fraser was known to Karpov, who once employed the former cop for some delicate advice.

There was a time when one of Karpov's subordinates broke some traffic laws and ended up in jail for wrestling with the police who stopped him. Fortunately, they never looked beneath the back seat of his non-descript Korean model, where they would have found enough material to put the driver away for the rest of his conceivable lifespan.

Instead, after they finished roughing him up and locked him inside the police van, one of their number parked the man's vehicle securely on the side of the street, from where it was nonchalantly removed by one of Karpov's girls as soon as Karpov found out the next morning.

Fraser called in some contacts in the prison underworld – the one of prison staff rather than inmates – to see that the delicate-featured prisoner with soft blue eyes was unmolested until he was sprung on bail and decided to try his hand at ocean sailing. To this end, he was hired as a personal assistant by a Peruvian gentleman who sailed the South Seas in search of pleasure and good drop-off points for drug distribution. Neither was seen in this part of the world again.

What Darius proposed and Fraser conveyed to Karpov made very much sense. A laboratory with a Harvard-trained biochemist sounded a much better bet than the chemical pigsties run by half-crazed motorcycle brothers, who kept the best stuff for themselves anyway.

Even at a higher price, Karpov was certain it was worth the extra trouble, if the dark man was right about a dirty metabolite being the cause of the salt imbalance.

Samples provided by Fraser in a poorly lit car park turned out to be everything promised. For a whole week there were no casualties, and the bouncers were removed from toilets, much to the delight of those who used them for a variety of alternative interactions. Business was again running itself.

Karpov was troubled only with the nature of the proposed transaction. He would be glad to accept the entire sale for more dollars, but Darius asked him to provide labour. This worried Karpov, even though they were free agents and he merely served as a talking address book.

His orderly academic mind knew this feeling of vacillation. It normally signified that he was not adequately informed, most likely deliberately.

He selected a prepaid mobile phone card and pressed the chip into his phone, then keyed in its access code. He dialled Darius.

"Professor!" said Darius pleasantly. "Are you ready to work with us?"

"I am not sure," replied Karpov with disarming honesty. Darius reached over to the stereo and toggled the switch that channelled the conversation to the speakers. Fraser looked up intently from a map he was studying and began to listen.

"What do you need to be convinced?" asked Darius earnestly.

"This operation you mount," said Karpov. "It's a problem. Can I just pay cash? I will pay more. You can use the money to set everything up without my help."

"Afraid not," said Darius. "You see, I need to eliminate a certain... obstacle before the operation is able to proceed. It's not a separate transaction, I regret, and you are the only man with the right resources."

"I understand," said Karpov. "Your target?"

"Police headquarters," said Fraser into Darius' microphone. Darius nodded his approval at the brevity of that statement.

"Oh," Karpov was now certain. "Unfortunately, I cannot do this."

"Why is that, Ivan?" asked Fraser.

"Times have changed," explained Karpov. "I am criminal, yes, but now organized criminal. We sell, do business. War is not good for business."

"What war?" said Darius smoothly. "Just a short

sharp operation."

"Oh yes, like Afghanistan," said Karpov. "Please, I am old enough to remember. Police and I work together now. They look away, I keep nasty people in line. No disorder. Good for business. You want commandos to attack police. That is war. Very much disorder."

Fraser silently mouthed a curse and moved to cut the connection. Darius grasped his wrist and stared at him, shaking his other index finger.

"One moment, please," said Darius and put the call on hold.

"He'll be just fine," said Darius. "After his electricity fails."

"Ah," nodded Fraser. He went back to reading his map. Darius took the call off hold.

"Just a few moments of your time face to face, professor," he said. "I believe that you will be impressed. Say, tomorrow?"

***

At noon of the next day Darius was shown into the inner sanctum of the sprawling house, most of which was immersed in twilight. This did not affect the infrared camera through which he was being watched. Its bright red LED was the only object clearly visible in the near-darkness.

Karpov came in, accompanied by a very trim young man in an impeccably cut business suit, who stayed in the shadows near the door. Karpov himself was attired very informally, in a plush dressing gown and slippers.

"I don't wish to take much of your precious time," said Darius with a flash of his large teeth, as he got up, shaking Karpov's limp hand. Karpov nodded perfunctorily.

"Are you a man of religion, professor?" asked Darius.

Karpov reeled from him in amazement and turned to his associate. Both erupted into sardonic laughter.

"Please," guffawed Karpov. "I was brought up in the Soviet Union. I don't believe in God."

"Then how about Satan?" asked Darius.

Karpov chuckled.

"Satan has more credibility, yes," he said with amusement. "Plenty of evidence that he is active."

"Very well, then," said Darius, the look in his eyes darkening and focussing on the blurred facial features of the man opposite. "Do you have an open mind?"

"Oh, I assure you there is no mind more open," said Karpov. "I come from a three-bedroom flat which was shared by three families to this," He circled his hand around the tall ceiling of his mansion. "So yes, my mind can accept anything. If my life was possible, anything can and does happen."

"Yes," said Darius. "I do like you, Russians. You find the notion of devilry so acceptable."

"Excuse me," said Karpov. "But we have some business to attend to, yes? I hope you haven't come here to entertain me with stories of mythology."

"Mythology," said Darius in contemplation. "Well, so be it. But you know, all mythology is based on some fact. Is it not so?"

"Frequently," said Karpov's companion crisply.

"Oh, Valeriy," Karpov turned to face him. "Come into the light and I will introduce you. Mr Darius, this man is an expert on ancient myth. I rescued him from a career of digging in Scythian garbage dumps on the Volga and put him in charge of my distribution network. I was very impressed with how his digs never ran out of any essentials when nothing in Russia was where it should have been."

"Very pleased to meet you," said Darius, shaking the man's hand. This time he met a rock-hard grip, which he only just countered, avoiding a contest of strength. "You will also find the following of considerable interest."

He removed some folded papers from his pocket and passed them to Karpov, who glanced at them half-heartedly. Then his facial expression tightened to absolute concentration, and he held the document up to dim light, staring at the figures intently. Finally, he passed it to Valeriy.

Valeriy's reaction paralleled Karpov. He glanced at his boss with horror.

"Do be a good boy and check these numbers," said Karpov, his voice now a steel rasp. Valeriy ran off.

Darius stepped out of his way and stared at Karpov, who met his eyes with horror. They stared at each other with silence for minutes, Karpov realizing with icy fear that he more than met his match.

Valeriy returned. He said nothing, merely nodding twice. Karpov's face now betrayed a severe fright.

"Here we are," said Darius. "A lifetime of cynicism – and look at you now. Weak as newborn puppies. Humans, you are naught."

He stopped to hear a reply, but neither man managed to speak.

"Yes, here it is," continued Darius, looking into the distance in contemplation. "So much for scientific atheism. All the mad old women, all those drunken peasants and all those lecherous priests were right. And believe me, they could only guess at the power I have."

"What do you want from me?" asked Karpov in a shaky voice.

"Ah, professor," said Darius, turning to Karpov as if suddenly reminded of his presence. "Not your soul, that's a fact. That commodity would be hard to peddle indeed."

"Now, pay attention. I asked for a small favour, and I want it transacted. Then we can go ahead with the other business. If you want a better deal, I am willing to negotiate – but please let's get it out of the way now."

"No, the money is not a problem," said Karpov. "But the soldiers... It'll take time..."

"Hmm," said Darius irritably. "Time is the one commodity neither you nor I like to lose. Please snap out of your present state and fix it. By the way, you will find these an interesting addition to your scrap book."

He took out a small bundle of photographs from his jacket pocket and passed them to Karpov. The Russian merely shook his head with an expression of horror as he leafed through them, lingering on one shot which he passed to Valeriy, his hand shaking lightly.

Valeriy took one look at the picture, rushed over to a pot plant and vomited into its soil.

"I'll leave you to it," said Darius, gesturing at the vomit. "Don't bother, I'll show myself out."

He strode out of the darkened house and got into the Mercedes, where Fraser napped in the back seat. He awoke and stretched like a cat as Darius started the engine.

"Any trouble?" he asked lazily.

Darius smiled widely into the rear view mirror as he put the car in gear.

"Oh yes," he replied. "Lots."

***

There was nothing terribly original about the plan of attack – its scenario could describe any action recently fought by the Russian army. The enemy is softened up by an overwhelming artillery barrage, then the infantry pours in behind tanks.

Instead of artillery a large bomb was placed next to the outer wall of police headquarters, disguised as a street cleaning machine whose garbage receptacle was packed with explosives. The driver left the yellow light rotating, then walked across the street to the public toilets and casually strolled down the stairs. Then there was a roar of explosion, which tore a ragged hole in the steel-reinforced wall.

One block away Sandy Woodward's bulldozer growled awake and was driven at top speed towards the hole, smashing through its jagged sides and dropping a few feet onto the floor of the basement car park. Its treads hung limply for a few seconds, then the driver found the right lever. This raised the shovel, causing the front of the treads to drop onto the concrete of the basement car park.

Feeling the treads bite, the driver pumped the accelerator. The machine's rear clanged onto the floor of the car park and it rumbled towards the large steel door near the lift well.

A number of figures in black poured into the hole left by the explosion and advanced behind the bulldozer. Sirens started to wail outside, but more dark figures emerged from the shadows in the street, firing at emergency workers as they jumped out of their vehicles. Most targets went down immediately. Ambulances spun around to accelerate out of the reach of bullets.

More distantly, police wagons cordoned off both sides of the street, officers hiding behind the bonnets of their vehicles from the hail of gunfire.

Turner was thrown awake by the blast impact and had his gun out before he was fully conscious. He ran to where the Stewarts slept in adjoining bedrooms.

Maggie met him in the corridor, her father just a second behind her. Turner grabbed Maggie with his free hand and pulled her towards the back room. Then he suddenly changed his mind and ran to the lounge, gesturing for them to come along.

They met McKenzie near the monitor, which showed a bulldozer crawling towards the steel door separating them from the outside. Then one of the figures stepped out behind the bulldozer and fired a single shot into the camera's lens. The screen went dark.

"It was good to work with you, Turner," said McKenzie calmly.

"You too, arsehole," replied Turner affectionately. "Got any spare guns?"

McKenzie tore open a draw and palmed the keys, with which he opened a wall safe concealed behind a wall hanging. Turner helped himself to an assault rifle and a few magazines, then started tossing weapons at McKenzie, Maggie and her father. As he turned to grab the last weapon, an ugly sawn-off double-barrel shotgun, he watched Maggie snap a magazine into a sniper rifle with cool competence.

There was a shattering thump as the bulldozer slammed into steel. Puffs of brick dust burst from around the door frame, metal shuddering and shifting visibly.

Turner found cover by upturning a reception desk as the bulldozer was reversed with a loud scraping noise, then the rumble of the diesel became louder and culminated in another crash into the door. This time the steel buckled.

The third impact saw a section of the wall give, bricks tumbling across the vestibule as the door was detached from one wall to hang from the last, mangled hinge.

A man dove into the opening, dead from Turner's bullet before he hit the floor. Answering small arms fire exploded around Turner, forcing him to crouch behind the desk, but he raised the assault rifle over the edge and sprayed the jagged opening with lead.
As he changed magazines there was a moment of relative silence, with the rumble of the bulldozer punctuated by the chatter of automatic weapons outside.

Turner focussed on a fragment of glass panelling left in the window behind him, which reflected the breach. He could just make out the yellow of the bulldozer, but there was no movement.

When that changed, it was a blur of two lean bodies diving head over heels into the lethal space and flattening themselves on the floor. Turner dropped onto carpet and emptied the magazine through the bottom edge of the desk. Its side disintegrated from the first few bullets, then two screams told him what he needed to know. He reversed magazines and focused on the glass again.

The bulldozer rumbled away and returned with its engine screaming, smashing into steel again. This time the entire door frame nearly parted from the wall, still hanging by one corner.

The bulldozer driver gunned the engine, forcing the scraper further into wounded steel. The door groaned, lifting away from the brickwork slowly as the bulldozer's treads spun over concrete.

Turner acted. He emptied the rest of the magazine into the gap around the torn door, then dropped his assault rifle, vaulting over the desk. As he rolled over his head, he extracted the sawn-off shotgun from its hiding place behind his belt. His ended the roll crouching on his feet beneath the door hanging from the bulldozer's blade. With not a second to waste, he fired both barrels point-blank into the machine's radiator from the ground.

They were loaded with illegal solid slugs instead of buckshot. Both slugs cannoned into soft metal of the radiator and penetrated as if passing through hot butter. Barely slowed, they pierced the engine block, shattering its alloy wall and destroying the first piston in their way. The rod was immediately driven into the cylinder wall by the engine's last thrust.

The bulldozer came to a shuddering, clanging halt, its driver scrambling from the cab and running away.

Hot oil pooled on the concrete like blood collecting beneath a fresh corpse.

Turner only just had time to dive for cover as bullets sprayed all around him. As he lay still, he heard the Stewarts and McKenzie return fire furiously. He scrambled out of the way and crouched in the rubble with just his pistol at the ready. Bullets whistled around him furiously.

He didn't get to fire another shot. The attackers retreated and concentrated their fire on one of the street cordons, through which they broke despite a number of casualties from the hail of return fire.

The helicopter was now in action, snipers shooting from skids into the circle cast by its giant spotlight. The attackers scattered into dark side alleys and blended in with crowds in the nearby shopping mall.

There was no more action in the basement, but Turner sat still, his gun at the ready, until he heard a familiar voice outside.

Part III:
The Absolution

The police minister slowly alighted from his limousine into a lightning storm of reporters' cameras, which he ignored with contempt. Two cops in flak jackets and helmets were assigned to escort him. He curtly nodded as they fell in behind him and started walking towards the scene.

He was outwardly calm and grimly composed, but his face was pale. He never felt so out of control in his life as he did in what was an instant war zone amid a dull capital of his middle class society. War was something young men went to wage overseas, sometimes for better, sometimes for worse. Now he walked amid war in his own city.

He saw a wide street sealed with crime scene tape and strewn with smoking car wrecks. Stately colonial building façades were pocked with marks from automatic fire. It was clear that something quite alien had invaded on his watch, and there wasn't a thing he could do to stop it.

He bent under the crime scene tape, which was stretched by his escorts to near his height, but not quite so. As he walked towards the headquarters, he stared at the yellow chalk outlines on the bitumen marking the bodies that were taken away at dawn.

There were a lot of these marks, he saw, especially behind a police wagon that appeared to have been blasted with a rocket-propelled grenade, causing it to explode and overturn on his side. One of the shredded tyres was still on fire.

He walked into police headquarters through a wide breach left by the blast. The force of the explosion bent the structural beams inwards, and they circled the entrance with twisted and blackened limbs. Masonry rubble was scattered throughout the car park, also dotted with many chalk marks.

All people at the scene appeared to be still. No pictures were being taken, no videos shot, no notes written. Most people stood around, their glazed eyes slowly swivelling towards him as he strode inside without acknowledging any of them or altering his pace.

He marched to the destroyed bulldozer, taking in the size of the machine, its oily lifeblood pooled on the ground and cordoned off with tape. He inspected a head-sized hole in its radiator, through which the shattered engine block could be seen inside.

He rounded the steel door hanging precariously off its frame and found himself in the vestibule of the witness protection unit.

"Halt please," said McKenzie unpleasantly, blocking their way. The minister stopped sharply, glancing up at his obstacle with sudden hatred.

"Robert Parsons, arsehole," he said vehemently. "Out of my way."

"Whether or not you are an arsehole, you have no

business here," replied McKenzie in an equally acrimonious tone. "I have protected persons inside that I prohibit you from approaching."

"I am the police minister," said Parsons ominously. "I'll have you arrested, you dumb mutt. Get out of the way."

McKenzie stood impassively.

Parsons turned to the policemen accompanying him.

"Arrest this idiot," he said curtly.

"On what charge, sir?" asked the older of the two.

"Insubordination. I have invoked emergency powers this morning, which makes me the commander-in-chief of the entire force. None of you are allowed to disobey my direct orders."

The cops stared at each other, uncertainty soaking their postures. Then they turned to McKenzie.

"All right," he said harshly. "Arrest me. That's the only way your boss is coming in."

"Forget all that," crackled a voice on the intercom. "I am locking you out."

Turner saw the entire scene through closed circuit TV and operated three sturdy electric bolts which locked the bedroom door, another contraption of solid steel.

The switch was hidden in the door jamb to prevent clients from using it, but its location was known to all protection officers. It was the ultimate backup, installed in case a long chain of adverse events allowed a hostile party to come this far.

"I have to speak to your clients," said Parsons in a clear voice into the camera above the door. "In private."

"Absolutely no chance," answered Turner. "I am not leaving them again."

"I'll have you arrested too," said Parsons.

"You can even convict me," replied Turner. "But in absentia. I'm staying here."

There was a commotion at the door, and the lights were turned on in the corridor. Parsons turned to see the Commissioner enter, with Garrison walking just behind him.

"Welcome to the Wild West, sirs" said Turner through the speaker. He turned up the volume to ensure both heard.

"Turner, what the fuck is this?" said Commissioner Arnold irritably. "We have a war zone outside. Automatic fire and grenades in the city centre, for fuck's sake! Eighteen of your colleagues are in the morgue along with at least fifteen assailants with military training!"

"Yes, sir," answered Turner with a wild cheer that overtook him in desperate situations.

"All that," continued the Commissioner. "And the only people who know why this happened are with you in that room, got it? Now get them the fuck out because I want them to tell me why all these men died."

"No, sir," answered Turner. "They don't know a thing, and I am not letting anyone near them. Not even you."

"Are you suggesting some form of impropriety on my part?"

"No sir," said Turner. "I am just saying that I am not opening this door until I feel safe."

"Turner," rasped the Commissioner. "You are disobeying a direct order."

"Oh, that's one for the lawyers," replied Turner. "I am not exactly an ordinary copper. Protection officers have wide discretionary powers, remember?"

Arnold stopped in his tracks, snapping his fingers with annoyance. He turned to the others.

"He is right," he said to Parsons. "After the Boleros incident, remember?"

Raul Boleros was a most unpleasant man who landed in these green shores to establish a local chapter of one Colombian cartel. He had himself arrested for drunk driving, as he was not a fan of the product he peddled.

He attempted to buy off the policemen who pulled him over with a bundle of US dollars, but that effort did not pan out. Out of sheer lack of experience both of them were so startled by the sight of foreign money that they detained Boleros, in the process of which he accidentally tripped and broke his jaw.

Despite handicap imposed by jaw wires, Boleros talked. A lot. He said a lot of things that attracted frenzied interest from the FBI. In due course, a deal was struck to relocate him to America in exchange for a box of DVD's containing FBI's observations of Hong Kong triads selling guns, drugs and women to distributors from Sydney.

When it came to transferring the prisoner, a Lear jet was hired especially for the purpose. History is a little vague about subsequent events, but available facts suggest that one protection officer objected when he met the pilot. The officer made a loud phone call to headquarters questioning the pilot's identity. Naturally, he was asked to shut his trap and get back to work.

They never found the plane after it dropped below radar cover. The assumptions which had to be made after an extensive search suggested that it either made a clandestine landing to take on enough fuel for a transoceanic flight or that it was ditched in the ocean. For once, nobody suggested an accident.

Of those on board none were ever seen again. After that regulations were amended to give protection officers a unique privilege – they were allowed to go above the chain of command if they suspected foul play.

"Are you going to cuff me or what?" asked McKenzie with a note of impatience in his voice. The officers on both sides looked at Parsons uncomfortably. He shook his head and turned away, his face a mask of rage.

"Well, I'll be in my office if anyone wants to arrest me," said McKenzie. He limped away without another word.

"Fuck it," said the minister quite audibly. He pulled up a chair from the corner desk and sat down, still staring at the ceiling-mounted camera. Turner remained silent.

"Sir," said Garrison. "Let's ease the pressure off him. The man had just had to fight for his life."

The minister opened his mouth to say something, then thought for a while and closed it.

"Sir," said Garrison. "This can wait a while until he calms down. He earned it."

"No," Parsons stood up and leaned into Garrison's

face. "It fucking well can't wait. If we don't get them out, what next – an air strike? You want more dead people in your uniform?"

"Sir," Garrison ignored the outburst. "We do have a determined enemy, but they are not going to try a failed tactic twice. If we move Turner and the Stewarts out now, we risk another attack. I can't think of any place more secure."

"I can," said Parsons. "Listen closely – this needs to be done fast."

***

The man in a khaki uniform was examining his passport, bearing stamps of various European countries that Drago had visited in the last happy years of his life. The official clearly had an infinite amount of time and was not at all pressured by a queue of loud Americans, whose cruise ship has just graced the local harbour.

Finally he reached for the stamp, carefully applied it to a fresh page in the passport and put the document aside. He then picked up Alexander's passport and stared at it intently.

The picture Drago obtained with Fraser's help showed a blond toddler. Stamps made in that passport for the previous year matched the entries in the father's passport for the good and simple reason that they were stamped by the same individual in a seedy shop in Melbourne. Drago had the forger reproduce the stamps of countries he still remembered from his travels.

The customs officer stared at Alexander, clearly trying to imagine him a year younger. Well-briefed in advance, Alexander was busy undoing his father's shoelaces.

A smile creased the man's weathered face as he gestured to Drago's feet. Drago looked down, then raised his hands in a gesture of frustration and began to retie the laces just in time to conceal a drop of sweat, which fell from his forehead to the floor.

He wiped his face before straightening up.

"Vellcome to Phillippines," said the customs officer, handing him both passports.

"Thank you," said Drago calmly. "We'll have a good time."

The customs officer turned away and reached for the passports of an elderly American couple, who were eager to be parted from their omnipotent dollars.

Drago wheeled out the trolley with their luggage, Alexander sitting on his shoulders. They made their way past the press of the arrival lounge to the taxi rank.

He asked for the nearest hotel to the city's markets.

***

"I told you this won't to be easy," said Fraser stubbornly.

"So you did," echoed Darius, his tone sombre.

They sat in Karpov's dining room, doing justice to the professor's Shiraz supplies. Fraser was fascinated – he never actually saw Darius eat or drink anything before tonight. He seemed to enjoy the wine but did not appear to be a prolific drinker.

"'A very costly operation," said Karpov unhappily. "So many men killed."

"You were paid," replied Darius. "As for the dead, they were soldiers. They knew the risks."

"It's a question of supply," said Karpov. "They were all veterans. There is no one like them in Russia."

"Oh," said Darius. "Is that what you are worried about?"

Karpov merely stared at him.

"Well, relax," said Darius. "War is around the corner in Russia. Soon you will have all the veterans you need."

"How do you know this?" asked Karpov caustically. "Satan himself doesn't know what happens in Russia!"

"Not so," replied Darius with a cryptic smile.

"Forgive me," muttered Karpov. "I didn't mean it this way."

"Care of it no further," said Darius expansively. "I have a more important problem for your rare brain, professor. "Was anyone taken alive?"

"Apparently not," replied Karpov. "Informants say that all of our people in police custody are quite dead."

"Excellent," said Darius. "That leads me to the next point. Can this operation be traced back to you?"

"Not at all," replied Karpov. "I am not crazy. All men I give you will die under torture rather than speak. We feed their families in Russia."

"Good show," said Darius. He sipped his wine appreciatively. "But it's not over, of course. I want the girl."

"Right now, mister, you can't have her," said Karpov vehemently. "They will have the entire force with her tonight."

"That's right," said Fraser. "Anything we do will only

make them more wary."

"Yes," said Darius, putting an empty glass down on the coffee table. "You are right, gentlemen. It is time to sit back and wait for a while. We will be in touch if we consider you of further use."

He bowed politely and turned to leave, Fraser following him. Valeriy opened the door, his face seemingly frozen in an expression of shock, Darius staring at him as he walked past. Valeriy shrank from his glare.

They got into the car and closed the doors, at which point Darius sniggered with mischief.

"How did you like that, monkey?" he asked, driving away from the house, where Valeriy still stood in the doorway, staring after them.

"Most impressive," said Fraser. "So what was it that shocked them so much? Is this a trick of some sorts?"

"Of the cheapest variety," answered Darius, glancing at Fraser briefly.

"So what did you show them?" asked Fraser.

"Only some family reliquiae," said Darius. "Nothing supernatural, but these gentlemen didn't know that certain facts were remembered and certain photographs still existed. Then I got on a powerful computer and made some images of what their minds simply never allowed for. One forgets, I suppose, that he who lives by the sword can die by one."

"Hmm," said Fraser. "I thought Karpov was a tougher nut than that."

"Oh, he is as tough as they make them," replied Darius. "But there are things that I can visualize much better. My kind lived in the dark. They spent much time dreaming dreams of when they could live in the light."

"So what did you show Valeriy?" asked Fraser.

"You don't want to know," replied Darius firmly. "It will have an effect I can do without."

Fraser nodded slowly and stared into the window for a while.

"So why didn't your kind do better on the surface?" he asked suddenly.

"Very tough competition," said Darius. "There was a constant problem with food. Then they decided that it was a good idea to cull the numbers to concentrate on quality."

"Eugenics!" said Fraser.

"Yes, eugenics," answered Darius. "Thirty five thousand years before the Greeks spoke the very language your term comes from. A very visionary move, but poorly coordinated. It thinned us out a little too much because one of the seemingly perfect survivors carried a fatal flaw, and she ended up being the mother of all survivors after another run of bad luck."

"So what did they do?" asked Fraser with rekindled interest.

"Oh, just the same as the Greek eugenicists," replied Darius. "Retrospective abortion. Over a few generations we killed all those who failed to show sufficient promise – in youth, before they were able to resist."

"Pretty harsh," said Fraser with awe. "No sentiment whatsoever."

"As harsh as can be," answered Darius gravely.

"How did they do it?" asked Fraser with professional fascination.

"Clubbed on the head, then boiled and eaten," replied Darius. "Their parents needed all available resources to continue reproduction. We have a little problem with that at the best of times, and malnutrition shuts it off very quickly. No room for tender feelings."

He passed an intersection where a homeless man stood limply in the middle of the road with a bucket and a windscreen brush. Darius stared at him, and the man first leaned towards his window, then backed away, following their departure with the same expression of frozen horror as Valeriy.

"Do they still do that?" asked Fraser.

"Kill the weak young?" said Darius. "Of course."

"Why?" asked Fraser.

"Oh, for the same reason the tradition began," replied Darius. "There is no point letting weaklings loose in the world to compete with humans – it's kinder to kill them with a single blow. That's a much better end than the weak can expect from your kind."

"Are we that nasty?" asked Fraser.

"Yes," said Darius. "Yes. Yes, you are. Those who came before humans were more impressive athletically, but nothing compares with your kind when it comes to a deadly fight."

"And Neanderthals?" asked Fraser.

"They were much stronger and tougher. But they had this… sense of harmony," Darius glanced at Fraser, and his eyes briefly glowed with involuntary expression of emotion.

"Neanderthals were at one with their surroundings and other species – they took no delight in violence. Then you appeared. Nothing was sacred to your ancestors. If they couldn't eat it or rape it, they would destroy it anyway."

"Well," said Fraser dreamily. "Maybe that's what we are supposed to do on this planet."

Darius nodded thoughtfully and mulled it over for a while.
"Interesting, monkey," he said at last. "I never thought of it that way. Perhaps you are even right. But I will not allow it for much longer."

"Can you ever stop us?" asked Fraser.

"When I succeed," confirmed Darius. "I, the successor of the truly worthy. I am this world's sole remaining defence against its defective offspring. Yes, I will stop your outrage or I will destroy every one of you. Whichever is more expedient."

"Every one of us?" asked Fraser incredulously.

"Look in the glove box," suggested Darius.

Fraser sprung open the glove box and extracted a fat wallet, which he hadn't seen Darius use before. He hefted it in his hand.

"Open it," said Darius gravely.

Fraser unfolded it in his lap and saw a stack of identification cards, neatly held together with a rubber band.

"Yes," said Darius after a quick glance in his direction. "Have a look through those."

Fraser took off the rubber band and wound it for security around his fingers. He began to rifle through the cards, icy cold spreading from the pit of his stomach.

The first card was in Arabic, showing Darius with a deep tan and very short hair. It contained no Latin characters, but Fraser recognized the corner logo as the flag of Iraq.

The next was in English, belonging to Dr Arthur Darres. According to it, Dr Darres worked in the research section of a facility run by the US military at an unspecified location.

The third card was in French, showing Darius with a shock of silver hair and a rather pasty complexion. It was from the Pasteur Institute in Paris.

Fraser stopped at the fourth card, which was in a totally unfamiliar language, although Fraser recognized some of its characters as Cyrillic. Darius stared in the photograph in a peaked officer's cap with a large red star.

"What are all these?" he asked breathlessly.

"Just what they say," shrugged Darius. "These are security passes from all the wonderful places where I had the pleasure to work."

"You on a payroll?" whispered Fraser with a hysterical note creeping into his voice.

"Excellent value for money, too," suggested Darius. "I was an exemplary worker at each of these locations until driven out by corridor politics."

"What are they?" asked Fraser holding up the cards he couldn't read.

"Oh," Darius chuckled. "The first is the Al-Mirah milk processing plant where Iraqis developed a particularly vile nerve gas. The French card is from a place where they did a lot of work on the AIDS virus. The other is from a Serbian nuclear plant in Vojvodina, where they produce weapons-grade plutonium for North Korea underneath an oil refinery. That way, if it accidentally reached critical mass, they'd have a cover story for the explosion."

Fraser replaced all cards into the wallet, his hands numb and shaky as if the rubber band he put around a few fingers was suddenly wound tight around his body.

"As you can see, I get around," said Darius.

***

Drago presented the official with both passports and grabbed Alexander across his mid-riff just as the boy took off into restricted space. Alexander laughed and kicked his legs in the air, both sandals coming off. The loud local shirt had ridden up his small body, showing a deep golden tan.

"Did you have a good holiday?" asked the customs man.

"Yes," said Drago. "The best. We will only come here from now on. Right?"

Alexander nodded his assent, still hanging upside down from his father's arms.

"Where is missus?" asked the official lightly. Drago made a frustrated face.

"Work," he said. "She is in America now."
The customs official shook his head at this Western craziness sympathetically and stamped both passports. Drago retrieved them and walked through, nodding his thanks.

Four humid hours later a heavily laden Air France Airbus rumbled down the runway of Manila airport and grudgingly took off. It rose above the city's pollution and set course for north west, where Europe was beginning to awaken from the depths of its winter.

***

Turner watched the others leave the vestibule, unlatched the door and came out.

"Jesus Christ, boss," he said shakily.

Garrison put a heavy hand on his shoulder and guided him to a chair.

"Yeah," he replied when Turner was seated. "It's the original, Biblical clusterfuck, son. Don't ask me how this one could be put to bed. Ever."

"Any ideas why?" asked Turner.

"No. Not about that. It's all pretty psycho, except this psycho has hired a private army, and psychos are not normally in a position to do that. No, we don't know and we are not even guessing."

"Any idea what to do next?" asked Turner.

"Yeah," said Garrison glumly. "Write to the Guinness Book of Records. What a show."
"We need everyone here," said Turner unsteadily. "Call in the SAS. Get them to surround the place."

"No, son," said Garrison gently. "We have to think of the public now."

Turner recoiled in horror.

"But your idea has merit," said Garrison quickly. "And that turkey in a suit agrees. He wants you flown to an army base. He declared an emergency, so this is no longer a civilian matter."

Turner looked up.

"In that case," he said carefully. "Can we go right now?"

"Ah," said Garrison, making the mental calculations. "Yeah, you probably should."

"Where, boss?" asked Turner, his brain now in gear and ready for the next assault.

Garrison got up and made a gesture to still his impatience.

"That will have to be seen," he said pointing with his gaze upstairs. "But we'll arrange it properly. This time they will need a real army to get to you."

"I want us all in the same copter," said Turner. Garrison nodded his assent.

Then he walked out, and Turner locked the door behind him.

Maggie and her father looked up expectantly when he came back in. He told them the guts of the story. Maggie sat opposite Turner, her eyes grave and wide.

"I am frightened," was all she said. Her father put his arm around her thin shoulders.

"You are one tough lady," he said affectionately. "You're only afraid now? I've been frightened out of my brain since it started."

"Dad," Maggie gestured towards Turner. "These guys are not in control. Thanks for saving our lives and all that, but I think we better go hide some place."

Turner stood motionlessly and looked at her with sadness across the table. As a professional, he acknowledged the truth of her assessment completely, much as it rankled. But her action plan was patently flawed, and he waited for her to come to that realization herself.

Maggie stared at him angrily, then the corners of her mouth softened, and she lowered her head.

"I'm sorry," she said staring at the steel door. "I don't know what to do."

"It's okay," answered Turner. "You are right about the control bit. No, we don't know what we're doing or what we are up against. I don't know who is after you, I don't know why they have a small army and how they knew where we were. But we know that we have to try something else. In this game staying still means losing."

***

Darius extracted a bottle of Shiraz he liberated from

Karpov from the boot and applied a Swiss Army knife to its cork. He found two plastic glasses and filled them to the brim without spilling a drop. He offered one to Fraser, who had to grasp it with both hands to prevent spillage, and sat down on the rear bumper.

They were at a mountain lookout perched on the side of a steep cliff. It overlooked a long valley framed by steep mountains. The wind had a hint of winter to it, but the mid-morning sun shone strongly over the long panorama.

Darius raised a toast to the bleak sun and tasted the blood-red liquid. Fraser dropped his anorak on damp ground and sat a few feet from the car, facing Darius.

"I still have a problem," he said. "Can I ask you now?"

"Oh, why not," replied Darius. "You are in luck – this wonderful invention of humanity always makes me more accommodating."

He sipped the Shiraz, letting it roll around his mouth.

"When were you born?" asked Fraser.

"Born," Darius chuckled at the term. "Yes. Around five centuries ago."

"Right," continued Fraser. "Now, what you are doing is clearly very important to you."

"Where is this going?" asked Darius with a little edge in his voice.

"Well, it's just that you must have tried it before," said Fraser. "Or did you?"

"Of course," said Darius expansively, signalling with his wine glass. "Frequently. So?"

"Don't take this the wrong way," said Fraser. "But why didn't you succeed? Or did you?"

"No, I did not," replied Darius gloomily. "Succeed, that is. I did try, and things went wrong. If I did succeed, I wouldn't have needed to try again."

"But surely," said Fraser. "Five centuries is a very long time."

Darius swivelled his head and stared at him briefly, then chuckled.

"What a brave man you are," he said approvingly. "I will even give you an explanation."

Fraser nodded eagerly.

"I cannot just announce myself when I feel like it. The time has to be right."

"How?" asked Fraser.

"Oh," Darius waved his hand airily to indicate

protracted complexity. "Many factors. Mainly, to put it in one sentence, humanity must be at a cross-roads."

"Ah," said Fraser. "I think I am beginning to see."

"No prizes for that," replied Darius. "It's a simple concept."

"Do you mean the lack of religion?" asked Fraser.

"In a narrow sense, yes," said Darius. "Religion can get in the way. But it's not religion per se. It's a matter of picking when society loses its moral compass. Lack a frame of reference, if you like."

"Well – we've really lost it now, haven't we?" asked Fraser.

"Oh yes," answered Darius vehemently. "What a mess. I am more comfortable with a serial killer than with police minister."

Fraser chuckled, but his eyes turned icy.

"At least I could understand what you did," said Darius. "It isn't awfully fair, but I can understand what happened to you. That son of a bitch has no such excuse."
Fraser nodded without turning around.

"Yes," said Darius. "No doubt, that's what's wrong with modern society – it selects the very worst people to run it. People are born no different nowadays, only better nourished and less diseased – but what they are taught cripples them from birth."

"No," said Fraser. "Some are still born bad."

"Of course," said Darius. "As they must - standing still means extermination. A species needs to experiment constantly, and experiments will go wrong. But what you do with these aberrant people is what makes the difference."

"So what would you do with my step-father?" asked Fraser, turning to pierce Darius with a searing stare.

"Same as with you," answered Darius. "I would send you both off to war to live brief but glorious lives. People would adore you until you got your head blown off, and ballads would be composed about your heroic death."

"Didn't work out that way," said Fraser with a bitter smile.

"Of course not," said Darius. "How could it – they don't like natural killers in modern armed forces. Nowadays they go for sensitive types and smother them with sunblock and deodorant. You were just born at the wrong time. Both you and the man who made you as you are."

"Good to know it's that simple," said Fraser bitterly.

"Yes it is," nodded Darius dreamily. "Armies used to know what to do with people like you. They would service all your needs, just make sure you never went near normal society. Everyone was happy back then."

"But wasn't the place constantly at war?" asked Fraser.

"Certainly," said Darius. "A good thing, too. Lots of self-important people got out of everyone's way to live in army camps. They sent the killers and the madmen into front lines and had them butchered in the name of glory. Everybody else just thumped their chests and twirled their moustaches, then returned to society, impregnated maidens and bored their offspring with war stories for the rest of their lives."

"An all-out military carnage is a relatively modern idea. Traditionally, most soldiers died of infectious disease, often horizontally acquired. That moved the economy too."

"Interesting perspective," said Fraser.

"No, not all," answered Darius. "It's as plain as dirt for all to see. It's just that all your textbooks are written by people who repeat each other's lies. They have to do that if they want to be published. Then everyone reads them, and the next generation rewrites the same lies in a language it can relate to."

"I don't agree," said Fraser. "It sounds like a strange thing for me to say, but I am glad I didn't live back then."

"Fool," Darius flashed his eyes angrily. "Humans are made for conflict. You cannot put more than a few of you in one place without starting a war. You stagnate when you have to make nice."

"That's a dim view of humanity," said Fraser.

"Well," Darius shrugged his shoulders. "Like I said, a superseded model. Just an experiment that had its uses, but there is someone better now."

"We can't be that inferior," said Fraser. "There's an awful lot of us."

"Oh, I grant you," said Darius. "Evolution is a tortuous process. You are not bad given your flaws, and I even need most of you – but there is still a better design. You'll see."

He drained his glass and tossed it to the ground, springing to his feet. He walked to the cliff's edge and stretched his powerful frame above the horizon, blocking the sun.

"Damn it all!" he thundered towards the distant valley. "All I need is one clear shot!"

***

"Lord," said Stewart senior. "That's the youngest copter pilot I've seen."

They rushed through whirlwind under its blades, climbing into the camouflage-painted machine surrounded by armed men. Turner helped them strap in and sat next to the pilot, who indeed looked barely old enough to drive a car. The pilot nodded to him and looked away to starboard.

"Hey, Airedale," shouted Turner above the turbine angrily. "Are you paid by the hour? Let's go!"

"Hold it," shouted back the pilot, his grey eyes flashing contempt. "I need these orders confirmed. This is a civilian mission, for Christ's sake. I thought that was completely illegal."

"We are in danger sitting like this, jackass," shouted Turner. "Take off or we disembark right fucking now!"

The pilot put out his hand placatingly, pointing to his earphones with the other. He nodded without enthusiasm and said something into his helmet, then signalled thumbs-up to Turner.

As Turner strapped in, the pilot reached for the instrument panel and keyed in a row of numbers into an onboard GPS.

"LZ," he shouted to Turner, pointing at the coordinates.

Turner stared at them in consternation, but decided to wait until they took off to pursue the matter.

He watched the men around the helicopter sprint away as the rotor picked up speed. His gaze followed them to the entrance into the elevator shaft, and Turner saw Garrison standing next to the door, sturdy frame buffeted by the rush of air from the helicopter.

Garrison locked eyes with Turner, his expression grim. Turner gave him thumbs-up, which Garrison did not reciprocate. But as the helicopter skids cleared the pad, Garrison's hands formed tight fists, and he held them in the air in front of his chest, a gesture willing Turner strength. He waited until Turner nodded, then turned and left the roof.

***

"What is your business in Bulgaria?" asked the official in comically accented English.

"I am a telephone engineer," replied Drago in clear, slow tone. He extracted a card from his wallet and handed it to the official, who studied it, taking in the logo of a mobile telephone.

The card belonged to Drago's former colleague who retired a month before Drago's life detonated. The man's farewell piss-up was Drago's last memory of a normal life event.

Drago used the name because the former colleague bought a sturdy Land Cruiser and disappeared into the desert to do some opal mining. Given that little of this activity was subject to taxation, his whereabouts were likely to remain uncertain for some time.

Drago then produced a letter from a suitably dubious start-up company in Boston, which invited him to study in person the prospects of selling mobile telephone services to the burgeoning democracies of the Balkans as well as advising of a hefty deposit for travel expenses.

The official understood enough of the letter to be impressed by the Australian's evident value but not enough to wonder why Americans should resort to his services in particular. He nodded and handed it back to Drago, then noisily stamped his passport, reaching for the next document.

He opened Alexander's passport, and his ill-shaven face creased in a smile as he looked down to compare the photo with its subject.

"My boy," said Drago, grasping Alexander's shoulders.

"Good boy," concurred the Bulgarian warmly. "Where is wife?"

"Job," said Drago. He made an exaggerated rubbing gesture with his free hand indicating a large amount of money. "Couldn't come."

"Oh-key," said the official. He stamped Alexander's passport and handed it to them. "Good boy."

Drago pocketed the documents.

"I have four," the man held up four fingers. "Three boy, one girl."

"You are a strong man," answered Drago. With Alexander looking elsewhere, Drago pumped his pelvis lustily. The customs official's smile turned into a brief leer, then he jerked his head, indicating that the queue was becoming impatient.

Just before leaving the terminal building, Drago stopped at a post office and handed over a few US dollars. He was shown to an ill-smelling telephone cubicle, where he picked up the receiver when signalled by the clerk.

His call threaded its way through twelve thousand kilometres of fibreoptic cable, bounced off a satellite and ended up being broadcast through a tower on a hill overlooking a long valley.

There were numerous rings, then Fraser answered cautiously.

"The Balkan," said Drago. "Please acknowledge."

"Acknowledged," answered Fraser. "Fuck every one of them."

"You bet," said Drago and terminated the call. He nodded to the clerk and returned to Alexander, who sat on top of their luggage trolley outside.

They emerged from the last airport Drago was hoping to see in his life and walked into the car park, where dented Trabants and Russian Volgas mixed it with shiny Mercedes and Citroen offerings.

They kept walking away from the terminal building until a large elderly man dressed in baggy trousers and a soiled white shirt stepped away from his old Fiat.

Only then did Drago's composure fail, and he was streaming large tears as he reached the man's powerful, sweat-scented embrace.

"Uncle," he rasped in half-forgotten Serbian. "It's good to see you."

"And you, Dragomir," answered the tall man, slapping his large hands around Drago's back.

"Welcome home."
He released Drago and looked at the boy. He reached to pick up Alexander – but stopped halfway into the action and squatted next to him instead.

He said nothing, knowing that the boy only spoke English. Instead, he extended a calloused hand to Alexander, who clasped it with his, the boy's delicate fingers disappearing inside the sunburnt fist.

Alexander's face did not change. His large grey eyes shone with a solemn, grave stare, which bored into the scarred and wrinkled face searchingly. At last he let go of the large hand and looked up at father, who was pulling a sleeve across his eyes.

"Daddy," said Alexander. "I think this is a good man."

Drago mutely nodded his assent, tears streaming down his tortured face.

"Like you, daddy," said Alexander pointedly. "Just like you."

***

They gained altitude above the city centre and headed north west, clearing a layer of pollution and rising above the hills. Turner glanced at Stewarts a few times and turned back to stare at the instrument panel, his mind racing.

The flight path took them over virgin bush, gleaming bright in the morning sun. The helicopter pilot largely ignored Turner, speaking into the radio at frequent intervals. He clearly had orders to stay in touch.

Suddenly Turner knew what was bothering him. He turned to the pilot and tapped his shoulder. The pilot glanced at him reluctantly.

"Got a map of the LZ?" shouted Turner.

The pilot reached across to the console and touched a few buttons on the GPS. Its screen lit up, indicating the landing zone location on a topographic map.

Turner stared at it intently, his face congealing to an expression of hatred.

"No," he said mouthed silently.

The next time the helicopter pilot glanced sideways, he found himself staring at the barrel of an automatic pistol. Turner was now wearing the intercom headset.

"Listen, fuckface," said Turner. "We are not landing there."
He gestured to the Stewarts. James unstrapped his harness and made his way forward.

"We have a problem!" shouted Turner, gesturing at the GPS screen. "Look where they put the landing zone. I think it's a set-up!"

Stewart examined the topographical symbols on the glowing screen, recalling things from a long-ended war.

"This is where the barracks are!" shouted Turner, jabbing the finger into a corner of the screen.

A look of recognition flashed over Stewart's face. He nodded furiously.

"You dumb little fuck," hissed Turner to the pilot. "Can't you see you are flying into an ambush?"

"That's what they ordered me to do," said the pilot into the intercom.

"Don't you fucking know anything?" shouted Turner furiously. "Look, moron – there's only one way out! Can't you see where it is, for fuck's sake? You can detonate a nuclear bomb at that site, and nobody will hear it at the base!"

"Sorry," said pilot. "Orders."

"Wake up!" replied Turner. "They will kill you too – can't you see that? We've been sold out!"

The helicopter pilot shrugged. Turner clicked off the safety and brought the gun to the side of his helmet.

"We are not going there," said Turner distinctly and calmly.

"Look, bud," said the pilot coldly. "If I was afraid of anything I wouldn't fly these things. We get killed all the time, you know."

"But you'd be a damn fool to die for nothing," shouted Stewart angrily.

The pilot shrugged dispassionately.

"At least I'll leave a beautiful corpse," he said without interest.

"All right then," said Turner, his voice tight with rage. "All right."

He clicked the safety back on and reversed the pistol in his grip. The pilot's contemptuous expression turned to horror as Turner slammed the pistol butt into the GPS screen. The glass buckled under assault and cracked loudly, releasing an evil-smelling plume of smoke as it faded.

Turner reached across and sank the pistol into the radio console, with a satisfyingly similar effect.

"Shit!" shouted the pilot. "Do you know how much paperwork you just caused me?"

"Oh yeah," answered Turner gleefully. "I'm ex-army."

"Well, fuck you dead, ex-army!" shouted the pilot. "What do you want from me?"

"Ah," said Turner with satisfaction. "That's more like it. I want you to take a new bearing. Zero-ninety, to be exact."

"I've only got fuel for thirty-five!" shouted the pilot.

"Great," said Turner. "I don't want you back in the air after you drop us off. Now turn, you little creep."

The pilot altered the course, and they flew east for another half-hour.

"That fuel is getting real low," said the pilot ominously.

"Find us a highway and land one click away," answered Turner.

The pilot cleared a wooded ridge and pointed his machine into a valley, where he crossed what appeared to be a significant highway, flew over a short stretch of forest and landed in a paddock. He reached out to power down the engines.

"Uh-uh," Turner knocked his hand out of the way. "Let her run."

Ten minutes later the fuel gauge was reading critical, and Turner let the pilot cut the turbine. The Stewarts were waiting by the door as Turner grabbed his backpack.

"Next time use your brains, dickhead," said Turner as he slid the door open and jumped out. "And stay in that helicopter until I can't see you. I meet you, I shoot you – understand?"

The pilot glared at him hatefully.

"Do you understand or do I cuff you to the seat and leave you to piss in your pants until they find you?"

repeated Turner, stepping towards him.

"I got it," replied the pilot tersely, looking away from him.

They walked to the edge of the forest and entered the undergrowth. As soon as they were out of sight, Maggie grabbed Turner by the arm.

"What's this all about?" she asked furiously.

"Keep walking," said Turner, pulling her along. "We don't have much time."

"What happened?" insisted Maggie.

"We were set up," said Turner grimly. "The landing zone was in an army base, all right – its most secluded part. Whatever they were planning up there, not many people were meant to see it. That give you an idea?"

"Shit," said Maggie with a hint of tears in her voice. "Shit."

"Well, it didn't work," said Turner. "Let's keep that in mind."

"Yeah," said Stewart senior to Turner. "You did good, kid. Thanks - again. It just bothers me that we are down to our last defence. Again."

"Yeah, well," replied Turner. "The last defence is still

working. Let's just keep moving, folks."

They ran onto the side of the highway, where Turner stepped into the path of a truck, holding his badge and his gun in plain view above his head. He spoke to the truckie briefly, and the man gave them a lift to the nearest town in gathering darkness.

They disembarked just outside the police station, but Turner moved them out of sight as soon as the truck left and marched them to the parking lot of the nearest shopping centre.

They waited in the overgrown bushes until Turner spotted a young farmer and his wife pull into a parking spot in an old van. The pair extracted three young children from the van's cavernous interior and ambled into the supermarket without locking any doors.

Turner shot across the open space and climbed inside the van, pocket knife in hand. He spent some minutes bent over the steering column, then the van's engine started noisily. He drove out of the parking lot quickly, pausing just long enough to allow both Stewarts to climb inside.

They sped into gathering darkness, eager to put distance between themselves and the marooned helicopter. Halfway towards the next town they turned off the highway using faded roadside signs to navigate parallel to it. Maggie went to sleep, but her father sat up with Turner, looking out for signs of trouble. He nodded off an hour later.

At eleven o'clock Turner stopped to relieve himself. When he got back to the van, he found James Stewart at the wheel, gesturing for him to get into the back. Turner nodded and climbed over the front passenger seat to stretch out on the hard floor with relief.

The van started off with the grinding of ageing gears and gathered speed. As Turner closed his eyes, he felt a hand take his and squeeze it lightly. He reached over and placed his other palm over Maggie's hand, rubbing it reassuringly. He felt nothing but the warm touch of her hand as he passed out.

***

They found the helicopter at first light. Its pilot thought better of trying to follow Turner to the highway and spent an uncomfortable night on the floor of his cabin.

His colleague located him next to the machine, passing the night's urine a thankful distance away from the helicopter. The grounded pilot let go of his vital organ to give his rescuers a clasp-handed salute.

Nobody failed to link the only local vehicle theft in living memory to Turner's tactical prowess. The van itself was found in the car park of railway station six hundred kilometres away.

The trains were hastily searched, but it was a little

late, the first express for the city having left the railhead at dawn.

Turner and his charges were just ten hours ahead – but they were ahead for the first time since the chase began.

***

"Is that so?" asked Darius. "Now, was it too much trouble to call me earlier?"

"No," replied Parson's scrambled voice. "You knew as soon as I knew."

"I see, minister," replied Darius thoughtfully. "Well, thank you. I'll take it from there."
"And the...er... arrangements?" asked Parsons.

"No need to worry," answered Darius. "I'll destroy the evidence as planned."

Parsons threw down the mobile phone and started his engine in an empty car park next to a deserted boat ramp. The moon was fading over the bay.

"Stupid prick," he said spitefully as he put the car in gear.

He was, of course, referring to his eldest stepson, a heavily-built lad who took very much after his daddy, a drifter with a taste for violence. When Darius sent Parsons computer-enhanced stills from a surveillance camera showing the stepson kicking a still body outside a football stadium, Parsons knew instantly, as only a long-suffering stepfather can know, that the pictures were not faked.

As police minister, he also knew that the stills incontrovertibly associated his stepson with a brutal murder of a drunken spectator, which took place one year before. He remembered that unsolved case well. Parson's Jaguar surged forward and blended into the traffic, headed towards the cemetery for the first of many police services he would attend in the next few days.

***

"Hmm," Darius motioned for Fraser to return to the car. "They aren't coming here after all. Back to work and drudgery, I'm afraid."

Fraser opened the laptop as they drove nearer to town, where the phone worked better. Darius stopped at the local football ground, in clear sight of the mobile telephone tower.

"Here he goes," said Fraser, pointing at an entry on the screen. "Fuck, that's miles from here."

"Hardly unexpected," answered Darius. "Not a stupid man, that Turner. I should have hired him instead."

He started the engine and changed gears violently. The tyres spun as he accelerated in the direction from which they've come the day before.

"What was that phone call?" asked Darius sullenly.

"Drago," replied Fraser. "He managed to get to Bulgaria."

"Oh, good," said Darius with genuine approval. "I hoped he might make it – I hate paedophiles. I plan to execute every last one."

"Amen," replied Fraser. "But let me do it, would you?"

"Deal," said Darius. "You can do the ones who knew what they were doing. Slowly."

***

As they emerged from the train, Turner pulled them into an alcove neatly covered up by the luggage trolley. He extracted his phone and dialled a number.

"Yeah," rasped Smoko into the receiver indifferently. "It's me, Jack," said Turner quickly. "Need help."

"Yeah," said Smoko curtly, his voice now hard as steel.

"I'm in the CBD and need a quiet place for a few nights. Three people," said Turner.

"Call you back," said Smoko.

The line went dead.

Turner stood still for a few minutes staring at the telephone in his hand and thinking. Then the set rang.

"All fixed," said Smoko. "Got a pen?"

"Yup," Turner flipped open his notepad and put it in Maggie's hand. He wrote down an address. "Got it."

"Keys under the door mat," said Smoko. "Got a gun?"

"Yes," said Turner. "No problem there."

"Great," said Smoko. "Now, there's no food there. But the local pizza shop is pretty good. Its pamphlet is on the fridge door. Don't eat out, will you?"

"We won't," said Turner with a sallow smile.

"Need muscle?" asked Smoko.

"Maybe," said Turner. "See how it cracks."

"No hurry," said Smoko. "Thank me later."
The line went dead.

They caught a cab to the address Smoko gave, and Turner let it go at the corner. They walked to the house, which was a narrow-fronted timber home in a small one-way street jammed with cars. Turner liked that – it made sudden arrival of a large number of people impossible, and they could only arrive from one direction.

He was also appreciative of the way the walls came too close to adjacent houses to admit a large number of assailants around the side. There was a ready escape route through a rotten back fence, which lead from the neglected and overgrown backyard to a similar triumph of landscape design on the other side, which had a narrow passage to the street.

The house was surprisingly pleasant inside, old carpets stripped to reveal a beautiful floor laid in hardwood long since reserved for more exclusive purposes. The furniture was sparse, but new and attractive. There was a minimum of electrical appliances and a bathroom splendidly appointed in marble.

Turner got a distinct impression that Smoko used it as a pad for illicit sex and hoped the man could go without for a while. Hell, thought Turner, Smoko could even try it with his own wife.

He arranged sleeping quarters for Maggie and her father, the latter allotted an industrial-sized double bed to allay any concerns an old man may have. Maggie went to sleep on the couch, and Turner stretched out on a thick Persian rug in the hallway with one of the armchair cushions for a pillow.

He chose a position where he was not quite in plain sight of anyone kicking through the door. It would buy a few seconds, he reasoned as he slowly drifted off, the fatigue getting the better of anxiety. Turner was first and foremost a soldier.

When he was finished doing all he could do, he embraced sleep and banked it greedily lest it be impossible in the days to come.

***

The drive back to the city took Darius all day, mainly due to a huge traffic jam created by road works. Fraser napped in the back seat, episodically firing up the laptop to study the readings.

It soon became clear that the fugitives found a place to hole up. Turner's phone was connected to the same cell for nearly twenty-four hours.

That was the good news, said Fraser as they approached the city limits, making modest speed in a column of irate traffic. The bad news was that the cell was in a densely populated inner suburb not far from the waterfront, and the place was packed with every kind of obstacle to orderly acquisition of targets known to humanity.

"Hmm," said Darius. "You'll have to do better than that, primate."

"Give me time," replied Fraser and went back to his nap. They were not too far, but were yet to spend hours crawling through smog-stained streets past city centre before they were anywhere near Turner's hideout.

Darius drove on, his brain pacing furiously. An hour later Fraser awoke again and took another reading.

"Still there," he said cheerlessly. "Must be nice, wherever he is."

"Let's be productive," said Darius. "Can't be a business – today is a working day, and he wouldn't let anyone see him. Unlikely to be a hotel – he wouldn't risk it. What else?"

"I bet it's on the ground floor," replied Fraser. "It would have to have a good escape route, like a house with an exit through a front and a back door. But fuck – that leaves most of the suburb, surely."

"Keep thinking," said Darius. "He is not moving, all right? All we have to do is find him."

Fraser sat up and thought furiously. Then he pulled out the laptop and tapped for a while.

"What are you doing there, my friend?" asked Darius with a note of concern. "I like that instrument precisely as I have it set up, thank you."

"Yeah, right," replied Fraser impatiently, staring at the screen. He typed a few more keystrokes, then his face lit up triumphantly. "Pull over, would you?"

They went to a small park sandwiched between two factories. Fraser placed the laptop on a freshly painted metal bench and knelt in front of it reverently, the closest his obscene being came to worship.

"I recall Drago saying something about full log dump," he said, stabbing his finger at the black screen.

"I do too," said Darius. "So?"

"So it shows this," replied Fraser, pointing at a column of numbers half-visible on the right side of the screen.

"And these are what?"

"Signal strength," said Fraser.

"For each set locked onto the cell?" asked Darius incredulously.

"Yup."

"Wonderful," said Darius, rubbing his hands. "All we need to do now is travel the grid."

"Exactly. Pipe the log dumps into a text file, open it with a word processor and do the grid. All we do is travel the same radius."

"That's superb, monkey," said Darius as they walked

back to the car. "That's exactly what I tried to tell you earlier. You see, I can't make mental jumps like that."

"You did when you got me out of prison," said Fraser critically.
Darius stopped in his tracks and thought for a while.

"No," he said at last. "It wasn't like that. I heard about you on the highway. I heard that the cop who found you was badly injured, and the rest occurred to me when I was driving to the city and saw someone suspicious being flashed by a speed camera."

"Suddenly I thought – that man now has an alibi. If someone accused him of murdering someone at that time, he can wave his speeding ticket. Then I thought of you."

"Oh," replied Fraser with a little disappointment in his voice as he swung into the front seat, holding the laptop carefully. "I thought it was your superior mind."

"Still superior," replied Darius, unlocking the car. "But spontaneous..."

He stared at his car's gleaming instrument panel wistfully, shaking his head. Finally he started the engine and merged into heavy traffic.

***

Turner slept nearly sixteen hours, with Maggie and James simply stepping around him; he awoke when they started to eat, then went into a lighter sleep.

At midday he awoke feeling much better and got up, chasing away a slight headache with some stretching exercises.

He was glad that nobody wanted to go for a walk or cause him any other form of trouble. In fact, he was highly impressed with both of his charges and had no qualms about asking them to share in the duties of their protection, such as taking over the watch as he slept. He enjoyed risking his life to protect genuinely decent people instead of clever scum, who traded some information for the right to shed his blood with his own superiors.

The protection squad didn't normally get involved in looking after ordinary dumb crims, with whom Turner shared much of his world view and for whom he had a lot of sympathy. He usually protected people he would rather shoot for resisting arrest.

Like many front-line policemen, Turner felt that the only good crime boss is a dead crime boss, and he resented having to protect such people at a considerable risk to his life.

He shared a meagre lunch cobbled out of the remains found in the kitchen and began to wonder if he could ever go back to risking his neck for people who did not deserve to live.

***

Darius and Fraser were busy curving a tight circle through the crowded inner suburb. The idea was excellent. Cellular telephones are essentially radio sets, which select the closest tower in range and lock onto it to transmit and receive. Fraser's signal strength was going to be the same as Turner's when they were exactly the same distance away from the same tower.

As a template, they were using the signal from Fraser's phone, which Drago's program identified as the same model as Turner's. Cruising at exactly the same distance form the receiver tower as Turner's phone, they watched for signs of anything unusual.

They determined that the same signal strength was attained by being exactly 2.5 kilometres away, which put Turner's location somewhere on a circle with a five-kilometre diameter, the tower at its centre. Fraser drew that circle on the directory page, and they started to comb the streets, keeping to the pencil line Fraser left on the map.

They circled the area twice, looking for any suspicious places, cars or people, but everything looked entirely ordinary.

Most elderly houses were spruced up commensurate with their newly acquired status as real estate unaffordable by ordinary folk. Most cars parked along the narrow streets were either falling apart or worthy of upwardly mobile citizens who were not yet privy to true discernment of fine motoring or even value for money.

The only persons seen on their circular journey were elderly women living out the remainder of their lives in their newly-moneyed estate, drunks clinging to the region's former reputation and the occasional gentleman in a camel hair coat who stopped to value a property, strictly by invitation.

Apart from the drunks, Fraser would gladly shoot the lot just for the false hope they raised. He grated his teeth every time a sighting turned out to be a clear waste of their attention.

"That was a marvellous idea, monkey," growled Darius as they embarked on their third circle.

"Damn right," snarled back Fraser, who was less afraid of Darius than he was stung by his unfairness. "And still the best idea on the table, at that."

He pulled the laptop open and tapped a few keys thoughtfully.

"Fuck," he said wistfully. "He hasn't moved."

He lurched as the car pulled over to the curb abruptly. Darius pulled the handbrake with a wrenching crunch, then snatched Fraser's mobile phone from the seat.

"What's his number?" he asked curtly.

"Oh, now – wait," said Fraser, holding his hand up urgently. "This may not be a good idea."

"No?" asked Darius irately. "Do you have any other?"

Fraser held up his hand, thinking furiously. Suddenly his face creased into a sly smile.

"I thought you didn't make spontaneous moves," he said.

Darius stared at him for a while, thinking.

"I am not usually supposed to," he acknowledged uncertainly. "Maybe it's the bad company I keep."

"Well, I can't think of a better way," said Fraser. "Do it."

He turned the laptop around to show Darius the number on the screen. Darius dialled it and turned away from Fraser.

***

Turner was in the shower when the phone rang. He furiously turned off the water and ran out of the shower, trickling puddles on the marble floor. He grabbed the phone off the basin stand and thumbed it, just a second after it ceased ringing.

He frantically pressed the keys to check the caller's number, but this was blocked. He cursed and put the phone down, reaching for his clothes.

"So much for my good idea," said Darius vehemently. "Now he won't answer it."

"Wait," said Fraser with a sinking feeling. "Can I have it for a moment?"

Darius tossed the phone over the shoulder, the set landing precisely in Fraser's outstretched hand. Fraser checked the settings, exhaling in loud relief as he confirmed that the phone identity was blocked to those called from it.

"Try again," he said, handing the set to Darius.

***

The phone rang again as Turner finished dressing. This time he was ready and answered on the first ring.

"Mr Turner," said a very deep voice, speaking slowly and precisely with what Turner classed as a South African accent.

"Yeah," said Turner in a business-like manner. "Who's this?"

"Oh," said the voice with a slightly amused tone. "I think you know who I am."

"Sorry to be slow," replied Turner. "But I don't have a fucking clue."

"Never mind who I am," said Darius. "You do know what I'm after."

Turner didn't reply. For the first time in his life he felt completely on his own.

"Mr Turner," said Darius. "I am not interested in you in the slightest, other than to commend your bravery and speed."

"Thanks," replied Turner, checking his gun. "If you're into men, I am not available."

He heard Darius chuckle.

"You heroes are all the same," said Darius. "From Spartans onwards. You fight like a real man yet quiver over your masculinity like a demure virgin. But don't let's get distracted."
"I'm all ears," replied Turner without the slightest trace of interest in his voice.

"Miss Margaret Stewart," said Darius, the lightness evaporating from his voice. "May I speak with her?"

"Not a fucking chance," replied Turner. "Anything else?"

"I will get her, you know," said Darius. "Soon."

"Listen friend," said Turner. "What you will soon get is a bullet. You come along, and I'll give it to you between the eyes at a hundred yards, got it?"

"Mr Turner," said Darius. "You are a man way out of his depth."

"This is not a regular operation," said Turner. "And I am no longer a regular operator. Anyone who gets near us will get his brains spattered over the pavement. Understand?"

"I heard you the first time, little braggart," said Darius, tensing with cold anger. "Now hear this. When the time comes, save one bullet for yourself, because you don't want to be alive when I reach you."

He cut the connection with a jab of his thumb and turned to Fraser, pointing at the laptop, his fingers still white with bubbling rage.

Turner stood for a few moments, staring at the telephone in his hand. Then he threw it on the floor and drew his gun. He thumbed off the safety as he brought it up and fired a single round into the unit.

Pieces of black plastic sprayed all over the wounded

timber floor, as he turned to the Stewarts rushing in from the lounge.

"Okay," he said calmly and carefully. "Get your stuff. We have to do a runner."

Three minutes later they ran into the back yard after Turner dove out the back door and rolled in the tall grass, coming onto his feet as he scanned around him with his gun pointing the way.

He ran into the back fence and simply let it collapse under his weight, continuing into the property on the other side. They followed him around a long, narrow house, ending up in a front yard facing another one-way street. Turner abruptly halted behind the cover of a tall camellia bush, briefly checking the surroundings. He then ran out, vaulted over the low front fence, keeping his gun just behind the fold of his coat, and started walking along the pavement quickly.

They marched along the street, reaching its corner with a main suburban artery, and turned abruptly, marching towards a tram stop, speeding up as the tram approached.

They joined a small crowd of people at the stop, waiting interminably for the vehicle to scrape to a halt to allow a few elderly women with shopping trolleys to negotiate its stairs. Panic rising, they shuffled in the slow-moving queue to the steps and were at last inside, the concertina doors sliding shut behind them.

Turner put a few coins into the ticket machine, and the vehicle set off to the next stop.

***

"Shit," said Fraser, watching the display.

"What now?" shouted Darius.

"He just… disappeared," said Fraser limply.

Darius snatched the laptop from him and put it over the empty front seat. He closed Drago's program and restarted it. After staring at the screen for a few moments, he swore and slammed the machine shut.

"He disabled his phone," said Darius. "Just as I would. Let me tell you, this boy is good."

He started the ignition and moved the vehicle into the centre of the street.

"Get your pistol," he said abruptly.

Fraser yanked his automatic from his belt and pulled back the slide noisily.

"Now listen," said Darius. "We have to circle this place in increasing circles until we see him. If we lose him now, it's going to be a lot of work to find them again. Got that?"

"Yes," said Fraser in a bland tone he used during dangerous situations.

"Now, you know what he looks like," said Darius. "If you see him, don't fuck around. One bullet, and make it right. If, that is, he doesn't see you first. I don't think he will need more than one shot if he does."

"Right," said Fraser. "Let's go."

***

Turner moved into the body of the tram, his eyes sliding over other occupants in search of a threat.

His efforts were rewarded only with sullen and silent retorts, as people stared back numbly. Being past the rush hour, most people in the tram were those sidelined and disenfranchised by society at large – students, pensioners, the odd drug addict and an ageing lady of the night returning from what looked like a difficult shift, her provocative black miniskirt now chastely covered by a long and rather stylish raincoat.

Many pairs of eyes slid over Maggie, then turned away as her father put a protective hand over her shoulder.

Turner signalled for them to sit down at the back and out of sight. He stood just aft of the rear exit of the tram, his hands casually in his pockets, the right ready to bring up the gun and fire through his jacket pocket.

The tram rattled on, disgorging most of the occupants opposite a shopping centre. A few more people lugging shopping trolleys got on, setting their goods along the floor to wheel them to their seat.

Drizzle started outside, the road immediately turning to an oily mirror. It reflected the lights of expensive vehicles, which overtook the tram at furious speed. Turner scanned them carefully, studying the occupants of each vehicle, his hand hovering near the pistol butt.

***

"I think we've lost them," stated Fraser sombrely.

He glanced sideways and saw the familiarly dangerous expression spread over Darius' face.

"Wait," he said hurriedly. "I have an idea. Go right here."

Darius obeyed that directive instantly, his face unchanged. He drove down a wider street quickly.

"Okay," said Fraser. "Don't speed here."

Darius slowed down and drove at the speed limit towards a distant intersection. Fraser leaned between the two front seats from the back and pointed to the side of the road a few hundred yards ahead.

Darius squinted and saw a policeman standing next to a speed camera by the side of the road. He was next to an unmarked car, and Darius saw the wire, stretched from the window of the powerful sedan to the speed camera.

"Turn left just past him and pull over," said Fraser, his voice tight. He pulled out his pistol and checked that there was a round in the chamber.

Darius dropped Fraser off just around the corner from the policeman and sat in the small street without switching off the engine. He watched in the rear mirror as Fraser sprinted to the street corner and dropped back to normal stride.

Fraser walked up to the policeman's car and opened the passenger door.

"Hey," shouted the cop turning around abruptly. "What the hell is this?"

Fraser emerged from the car, pointing into its interior with wide eyes and backed away slightly.

His mouth narrowing, the cop rounded towards him, hand dropping towards his gun as he turned around to the open door and leaned inside to take a look.

Fraser rammed his gun into his stomach and pushed him inside the vehicle with his free hand. The cop didn't resist and sat in the passenger seat of his cruiser stiffly.

Fraser leaned inside the vehicle. Angling the barrel up, he squeezed the trigger gently. The drilled torso shuddered just once and slumped back into the seat. A little blood flowed into the groin.

Fraser looked around carefully, but could see no immediate witnesses. He zipped up the man's leather jacket over the bloody stain and clipped on the seat belt to hold the body upright, then tore a pair of sunglasses from the dashboard pocket and placed them over the eyes already turning opaque.

He ripped out the cord of the speed camera, gathered it up roughly and threw it into the back seat, then ran around and got into the driver's seat.

Darius saw the cruiser with Fraser at the wheel round the corner and pulled out to follow it. Fraser drove very quickly, returning to their hunting ground through small streets. When they were near their circle on the map, he leaned over to spring the passenger door, undid the seat belt of his dead passenger and pushed the body overboard. He accelerated from it abruptly, the door shutting against the slipstream.

Then Fraser picked up radio microphone and touched its button.

"Emergency, emergency," he said in the robotic tone used by trained people pushed beyond the limit of their endurance. "Officer shot, I repeat, officer shot.

Dead, I think. Corner of High and Ramsgate."

The radio cracked to life immediately.

"Copy that," said a female voice with a shade of shock. "What is your car number?"

"You are breaking up, Central," he said, holding the microphone at an outstretched arm from his face.

He ignored requests for his identity for a few more minutes, then brought the microphone back to his mouth.

"Central, I have some information on the suspects," he said. "Three persons, two men, one female seen running from the scene."

He gave a vague description of Turner and Maggie. He remembered her father only from a distance, but gave his approximate age.

"Copy that," said the female voice. "Your number, please."

"Four-nine-nine," read Fraser off the car bonnet, knowing that by now things were too hot for this detail to be looked into. "In pursuit of the suspects westwards down High."

"Thank you, four-nine-nine," said Central. "Stand by."

Fraser hung up the microphone and continued to cruise down the street. As the airwaves exploded, he punched in the code to block all non-emergency transmissions.

"All points," crackled the radio some minutes later. "All points, attention. Attention."

Fraser slowed down for the red light and listened.

"Three suspects in the inner east wanted for questioning over a shooting of an officer. Officer pronounced dead on arrival at the East Medical Centre. Fatal gunshot wound confirmed."

Fraser pulled over, Darius following behind him. He knew that all over the city police dropped what they were doing to listen to the same message.

The police network broadcast Fraser's description of Turner and the Stewarts.

***

The tram slowed down and crawled into the terminus where both tracks converged onto one stretch opposite a perfunctory shelter. Here the line petered out, losing its war against suburban sprawl. All people in the tram stood up and left, the driver staring at Turner pointedly.

"Let's go," whispered Turner urgently, leaving the bench.

They followed the other passengers into the street, marching towards a distant strip of shops, where Turner was hoping to catch a taxi unobtrusively.

They heard the sirens from far away and suddenly Turner swung into the driveway of a house they were passing. He motioned them to crouch behind an ageing Ford parked in the front yard and from behind it they watched a police car drive down the street slowly, its lights and siren belying the slow speed. Both occupants were scanning the street, and Turner put his hand on Maggie's shoulder, urging her to sink below the car's silhouette.

Turner saw that one of the policemen was holding his pistol at just above the level of the door.

"Think they are looking for us?" asked James Stewart.

"Don't know," answered Turner. "See the gun?"

"Yeah," said Stewart grimly. "That's why I'm asking."
"All right," said Turner. "Stay here."

He walked up to the front door and rang the bell. After waiting for the reply, he extracted his knife and fiddled with the lock, the door springing open within seconds. He motioned the Stewarts inside and leaned on the front door, shutting it with his weight. His expression reflected his sudden fatigue.

He picked up the phone in the hallway and dialled a long number from memory, keeping an eye on his watch.

"Yeah," said Garrison on the second ring.

"Boss," said Turner urgently. "What the hell is going on?"

"Turner," said Garrison quietly, as an expression of recognition. "I should ask you the same fucking thing. Did you just shoot somebody?"

"No, damn it," shouted Turner. "They did this! They are using an alert to hunt us down!"

"Christ," said Garrison. "What a mess."

"Boss," said Turner. "I need help."

"Yeah, don't worry," said Garrison after a short delay. "I'll come and get you."

"No, boss," said Turner. "We are on our own. I don't want to come in."

"Actually, that wasn't a request," said Garrison coldly. "We need to talk."

"No boss," said Turner finally. "I'm cutting loose."

"Not the best idea you've ever had," replied Garrison in the same tone.

There were many things Turner wanted to say, but his time was running out.

"Thanks for everything, boss," said Turner, not referring to the last transaction, and hung up. He looked up to see Maggie and her father staring at them.

"That's it," he said. "Now it's just us."

***

Fraser ran out of the cruiser and leaned into the window Darius opened.

"It's just been on the radio," he said, pointing at the aerial of his car. "They were identified catching a tram to the local terminus."

"A tram," Darius smiled in wonder. "You mean that whilst we were stuffing around, those three sat on a tram like sheep waiting at an abattoir?"

"Looks like it," said Fraser with a note of contrition. "What can you do?"

"Hmm," said Darius, his eyes flashing anger. "I hope you are thinking hard, primate."

"Yes, sir," said Fraser, now without any mockery at all.

"Well, I am dying to see the fruits of your labour," said Darius. "Get back to your car until you are ready to share your thoughts."

"Actually, I have one right now," said Fraser. "We should move nearer to the terminus. It's not far from here, but every second will count once they are seen."

"Good point," said Darius with approval. "I'll follow you."

They decamped and Darius indeed followed Fraser to the tram terminus, where they drove in a few concentric circles, gradually increasing the diameter.

Fraser started to sweat. It was only a matter of time before the number of cruiser was checked against the log and discovered to belong to the dead policeman. Yet he dared not contradict Darius.

 He thought of removing the transmitter and ditching the car, but there were too many wires to pull, and the likelihood of Darius allowing him near his car's electrics appeared to be slimmer than his chances of not going to hell – in case Darius was wrong on that score.

If it went right, thought Fraser, I wouldn't need the cruiser. The only problem with that theory was that Turner was well and truly warned by now. He was unlikely to do something simple and silly, like try a taxi, and any resource may prove pivotal.

Fraser thought what he would do in Turner's situation and arrived at the same conclusion every time. He would wait till it got dark, which made each and every search much more difficult, steal a car and drive to a random destination, where they were unlikely to be intercepted or even known, such as a deserted holiday cabin in the nearby mountains.

The possibilities were endless, and Fraser felt the rising tide of panic in his chest. Every time he glanced in the mirror, he saw Darius stare straight at him with absolute concentration.

There was no chance whatsoever that he could take off and outrun Darius in the cruiser, even if the car with a supercharged V8 could run rings around any 4WD. He knew that somehow this plan would go wrong and chose not to test Darius in this manner ever again.

The waiting game continued as the sun rolled towards the purple horizon and backlit the city with a blood-red hue for a few brief minutes. Then it sank below the hills that made up the skyline and left the earth to its devices in the gathering darkness.

Fraser shuddered involuntarily, wondering if he would see the sun again.

***

The search of the house yielded no sign of the keys for the old Ford outside, and Turner was thinking of leaving the house in search of another form of transport when a battered van pulled into the driveway, cutting off their escape.

Turner swore softly and positioned them in a child's bedroom next to the front entrance, leaving the door ajar, as he found it. He waited until the front door was heard to open, footsteps sounded in the hallway, then the front door shut.

He motioned the Stewarts to stay quiet and still and walked out into the hallway. A woman with faded blond hair turned towards him, her mouth opening in fright. She instinctively stepped between Turner and a boy of around ten, who looked at him with wonder.

"Police," said Turner quickly, before the situation got out of control. He held out his identification, deliberately allowing his coat to open, revealing the holster with a heavy weapon at his side.

The woman took the proffered wallet and studied the identity card. It looked right enough, although she knew enough to question what a single policeman was doing in her house if he were up to nothing bad. Nevertheless she decided, with a part of her brain not permitted to submerge into panic, that if the identification wasn't real, the gun certainly was.

"What's going on?" she asked breathlessly.

"I'm a protection officer," said Turner. "I have two persons who are in danger. We were pursued, and I used your house to seek refuge. I am sorry if this inconveniences you. I did no damage to gain entry and we were not seen coming here, otherwise we wouldn't be alive by now."

"My God," said the woman, her neat, oval face paling even further. "What do you need?"

Turner signalled to the Stewarts, who emerged from the bedroom.

"Thank you," said James Stewart to the woman.

"Look," said Turner after a few seconds of frantic thought. "It's better if you stay out of this. We need transport, but none of your cars are good enough, anyway."

"Why don't you just call in?" asked the woman.

"A small matter of police corruption, madam," replied Turner. "It seems that someone keeps selling our position. I took it on myself to hide from my colleagues, and this is when we began to be genuinely concealed for the first time. I think I'll keep it that way."

"Lord," said the woman. "Have you eaten?"

"Not for some time," said Turner, suddenly feeling it.

"Right," said the woman, colour returning to her face. "My name is Rita. This is my son, Mitchell. We will prepare a quick meal, then you can go wherever you are going. You spin a strange tale, Officer Turner, but something makes me believe you."

"Thank you, Rita," said Maggie.
"Okay," said Rita, now totally at ease. "Mitchell, go and start the salad. Do the sausages in the oven. Make tea for everybody. You three come with me. You can take a shower whilst we are cooking."

"Thanks," said Turner. "I appreciate it."

Rita appeared to be a woman worth her weight in gold. Three towels materialized from the linen cupboard, two showers were run at the opposite ends of the house, and by the time they reassembled in the kitchen, dinner was on the table, the son lacking little of his mother's ability to think on her feet.

Turner did take one extra precaution. He and James Stewart eavesdropped on Rita and her son in turns, but to no avail – neither made any attempt to ring out.

They finished a simple and delicious meal quickly, then Turner tried to offer Rita some money. She refused.

"My first husband was a cop," she said sadly. "Blew his brains out."

"I'm sorry," said Turner grimly.

"His sergeant wanted him to go on the take," she said. "To ignore some heroin dealers settling scores. He wouldn't do it. I know all about corrupt police."

"Yeah," said Maggie. "Sounds like a real crash-course on the subject."

"I'm remarried now," said Rita. "Jim's an Anglican priest. He's meeting with some street kids tonight. They run a group for them at the parish."

"Thank you again, Rita," said Turner as they were ready to leave. "Don't say anything to anyone, will you?"

"No, I think I know better," said Rita. "I think Mitchell will understand too. He is my first husband's boy."

They left by the back door, coming around the house through the long driveway on the side, with Turner scanning the street for any sign of threat.

He then emerged into the orange streetlight feeling more naked than at any time in his life.

They walked for a quarter of an hour towards the nearby shops, three pairs of eyes scanning every passing car for any sign of threat.

The shops they reached were a few forlorn businesses struggling to make a living amid increasing isolation and pollution. Still able to cling to survival because of the busy road, they sold a small range of food, wine and newspapers, items which did not justify a trip to the jammed car parks of multinationally owned shopping malls.

The last shop in the street was a take-away kitchen, specializing in pizzas.

"We're in business," said Turner reassuringly. He herded them into the relative darkness next to a vandalized telephone booth.

They waited.

It took another half-hour of rising tension, then they were rewarded by the sight of two large teenagers covered with tattoos and dressed in tight jeans and sleeveless T-shirts, which accentuated their bulging muscles. The young thugs arrived in an old sedan whose engine was evidently replaced by something which throbbed deliciously as the driver remained in the seat. The passenger emerged from the car and lumbered into the take-away after casting a contemptuous glance at no one in particular.

"Stay here," said Turner.

He waited until the man turned to the menu blackboard with what appeared to be a mental effort. Turner walked casually and quickly to the throbbing car, then the Stewarts watched him open the front passenger door and get in quickly.

What followed was only partly visible through the tinted rear window, but the car appeared to rock slightly. They watched as Turner emerged between the bucket seats and slid into the rear, concealing himself in the darkness.

The second thug emerged from the shop and swaggered back to the car. He opened the door and leaned to swing inside, then hesitated for a brief second. The Stewarts saw Turner's arm flash in the dim light, dragging the thug inside, and the car rocked again. The youth's legs protruding from the car went limp, then rapidly disappeared inside.

Turner opened the rear door and ran around to the driver's seat. The car took off into darkness, leaving the Stewarts completely alone. Maggie gripped her father's arm in panic, but James merely stood precisely as Turner positioned him.

A few minutes later the car returned. Without leaving the other side of the road, Turner motioned them to get in. They ran across the vacant traffic lanes and joined him inside the tobacco-scented interior.

Turner took off and drove down the street slowly. Maggie noticed that his left eye began to puff up, and a large clump of hair appeared to be missing from the side of his head.

"You all right?" she asked.

"Oh," Turner gestured reassuringly. "It's nothing. The second was a dumb bastard. Took time to realize that he was knocked out."

Maggie chuckled, relieved.

"What now?" she asked.

"Oh, I thought you had a plan!" exclaimed Turner with mock surprise.

"Yeah, right," said Maggie. "How about we go to McDonald's? How's that for a plan?"

"I'll have fries with that," said Turner happily. "Now listen."

They leaned forward to make sure they didn't miss a word.

"We could go to the mountains," said Turner. "Find a holiday cabin and stay there for a few days. Then get another vehicle and go some place pretty far."

"How about home?" asked Maggie. Turner frowned at the windscreen.

"I'm sorry, Maggie," he said sadly. "Nobody is going home until it's all over and we know that for a fact."

"He's right," said James Stewart hoarsely. "Maggie, we are stuffed. The only way we can get back to our life is if we find out who is after us and have them dealt with."

"Shit," said Maggie. "Shit. How the hell do we do that without help?"

"There may be a way," said Turner. They stared at him as he drove in silence for a while.

"We can just run," said Turner. "But they will find us. Maybe not now. Maybe not next year. Whoever wants you, Maggie, he will find you. You can see that, can't you?"

Maggie hesitated, then swallowed air and nodded just once.

"We need one of them alive," said Turner. "We have no idea who they are, but if we did, that would at least tell you where you can get some rest from them and what they were after. We have to let them come to us and get one of them."

"Yeah," said James Stewart. "That's right."
"Okay," said Maggie. "Let's do it."

Turner snatched the telephone from the dashboard and called the number.

"Yeah," said Smoko gruffly.

"It's me, Yannis," answered Turner.

"Ah," said Smoko with delight. "And here I was, thinking you was dead. Thanks for telling me."

"Yannis," said Turner urgently.

"What do you need?" asked Smoko.

"Guns," said Turner.

"Yeah," replied Smoko. "If I were you, I'd want all the guns I could carry. Call us back."

Turner hung up and pulled over to the side of the road, switching off the lights. He glanced at his watch.

"They will be coming around soon," he said to no one in particular.

The Stewarts didn't reply. Ten minutes he redialled Smoko's number.

"Got a pen?" asked Smoko without a preamble.

"Go," said Turner, positioning a ballpoint pen over his palm.

"Here's the address," said Smoko, naming a street in one of the seedier outer suburbs. "Go there now. Pay me back in the next life."

"I will," promised Turner. "And… Smoko?"

"Yeah?"

"You are a better man than the cunts who put you in

jail," said Turner. "Thank you."

"Yeah," said Smoko. "I'll miss you. Make sure you get to hell in one piece, all right?"

The line went dead.

Turner pulled away from the curb, the powerful engine surging easily. He drove to the designated location through the side streets, found the right cul-de-sac and flicked off his lights, letting his eyes adjust to darkness. He pulled over a few doors away from the right house, reversed to point the car to the exit and got out without switching off the engine.

"Maggie," he called through the open door. "Come here."

Maggie got out of the car and came around to the driver's door.

"You get in and get ready to drive off," he said. "If I am not out within half an hour, go. Any threat, go."

She got behind the wheel silently. Turner shut the door on her.

"James," he said, handing him the pistol. "You'll need this. Maybe."

He turned and walked towards the house, brightly lit by a few cornice spotlights. The Stewarts watched in terror as he rang the doorbell and stood aside in case someone fired through the door.

Instead there was something else. As soon as the door opened, the spotlights abruptly died, plunging the front yard into total darkness. As their eyes adjusted, they could see a tall man standing next to Turner outside the open door. Then they shook hands, and Turner came back clutching two cheap suitcases. His arms were fully outstretched, and his head tilted up at the weight of the load.

Maggie found the boot release catch and sprang it open, watching the lid slide up behind her. Then there were two jolts as Turner dumped his load into the boot and closed the lid, sprinting to the rear door and diving in.

"Go, go," he said quickly. She put the car into gear and drove out a little too fast, spinning the tyres slightly.

They were back onto the freeway for a brief ten minutes, then Turner directed her into one of the quieter roads that lead into the mountains. They drove through the outer suburbs where houses becoming scarce and picket fences intermingled with paddocks. Then they drove into the hills, as the road became dark and windy.

"Pull over here," said Turner.

She stopped at a small scenic lookout, where Turner ran out and opened the boot. He worked for a few minutes, then came back to the front with his catch.

"Oh my," said James Stewart.

He was rewarded with an M1, an old but reliable military carbine, with two magazines as well as a heavy long-barrelled revolver. Maggie got a small Beretta pistol and a few stun grenades.

Turner finally shut the boot and returned to the car with an SKS, a bad-tempered semi-automatic rifle. It did not have a good reputation amongst firearm enthusiasts because of its propensity to jam. It was good for little more than spraying a particular direction with lead, but standing in that direction would be a sad enough occasion for any recipient.

"Merry Christmas," said James Stewart sarcastically. Turner nodded an acknowledgement.

"Go," he said to Maggie.

They drove on until she saw the sign. Turner saw it too, and he told her to turn left.

They started climbing a steep track towards the Observatory, a gastronomic excuse for a steep climb. It was once able to overlook the entire bay area, before that view was permanently drowned in a brown sea of pollution, trapped by ringed mountains encircling the city.

"Right here," said Turner.

They were passing a cutting in a steep hill strewn with mossy rocks and sparse bushes. Turner gestured to Maggie to slow down.

"You see it?" he asked.

"Yup," said James Stewart. "Great place for an ambush."

They drove to a small property owned by the telephone company enclosed by a perimeter of barbed wire fencing which surrounded a few tall sheds. Amid the perimeter stood the mobile telephone tower, a proud steel phallus topped with a ruby aircraft beacon, its proud erection reigning over the hill. Turner got out and shot the lock off the gate.

He got Maggie to park the car between the sheds, facing towards the exit for a quick getaway. They left it and emerged from the gate burdened by their weapons. Turner stopped to hook up the chain to the destroyed lock to hide any appearance of a break-in.

It took a while to pick a spot on the hill from which they could cover the cutting and the nearby road as far as its curves would allow. Turner positioned himself in the middle, with Maggie and James covering the sides.

After they checked their weapons and went over the plan, Turner pulled out the phone and called emergency.

"Police, please," he said calmly. "This is an urgent report."

After a short delay he spoke again.

"I understand you are looking for three suspects," he said calmly. "They were just seen driving into the Observatory car park. I was walking my dog and saw them."
There was another question.

"Oh, bugger what my name is," said Turner. "I am not getting involved more than I am already. Three people who matched your description, okay?"

He listened briefly.

"It looked like an old hotted up... oh, you know," he said vaguely. It was dark green with a spoiler, anyway."

There was another pause.

"No, I am sure about that," he said. "And don't bother tracing this phone. You will find it near the car, where they left it, okay?"

He killed the connection and turned the phone off.

"Here we go," he said simply.

***

"All units, all units," said the radio urgently. Fraser turned up the volume, glancing up at Darius. In the rear view mirror he saw that at that very moment Darius picked up his phone to answer a call.

"Suspects wanted for questioning over Constable Tambling's murder seen entering the car park of the Observatory," said the radio. "All available units required for cordon. Proceed to the foot of the Observatory without music or lights immediately."

Fraser and Darius took off at the same time, Fraser now turning on his flashing lights to get past the traffic to the freeway. As Fraser expected, Darius followed with only a slight delay, able to keep less than two car lengths between his car and Fraser's pursuit vehicle.

At the freeway Fraser dropped to just over legal speed and killed the flashing lights. The traffic was thin, and they made it to the base of the mountain before a proper chain of command was established over the site.

"We are going around the other side to the top!" he shouted at the young officer who waved them to a stop.

The young policeman nodded automatically, even though geographically this statement didn't make the slightest bit of sense.

Fraser roared up the mountain, Darius close behind him. He realized his error a fraction of a second too late, his windscreen already a hail of flying fragments. Fraser leaned behind the dashboard without altering speed, the bullets from both rifles missing him by a few millimetres and grazing the side of his neck.

Darius showed absolute discipline under fire. He killed his lights and zigzagged alarmingly across the road, tyres screaming and smoking. Bullets struck angry orange sparks as they hit the bitumen around him.

He did this so well that not a single round connected with his car, not even as he briefly touched the brakes as he screamed around the final corner, his brake lights presenting his assailants with an inviting target.

Then all went silent.

Darius and Fraser regrouped out of sight of the lethal hilltop and started running to the source of the fire in the undergrowth.

* * *

Turner reloaded the SKS at the top of the hill and froze, listening.

Maggie heard it first and alerted Turner, who listened harder and nodded.

"Is it good or bad?" whispered Maggie.

Turner shrugged his shoulders.

A few minutes hence, there was no further question. There was probably more than one helicopter, and soon the entire mountain would be lit like a Christmas tree. For better or for worse.

***

Darius and Fraser kept climbing. Darius held aloft a small pistol, climbing the hill with large strides, his breath heavy but not at all ragged. His face was entirely serene.

"Slow down here," rasped Fraser, who was slightly in front. "They must be very close."

At Fraser's signal they dropped onto their elbows in the tall grass, crawling towards the hilltop as the thump of helicopter blades grew louder in the distance.

"There," whispered Fraser sensually, pointing just left of their direction. Darius looked over just in time to catch a glimpse of metal flashing in the moonlight.

They moved very slowly and a few meters apart, almost invisible in the grass. The helicopter was now a loud drone in the near horizon, its spotlight slicing the dark chasm at the side of the mountain, as the machine rocked in the rising wind.

They were within striking distance.

"On the count of three," whispered Fraser. "You take the midline to left."

Darius gave thumbs-up. One helicopter was now circling the hill, its spotlight throwing out a brilliant lemon-yellow cone, which danced across the ground.

Fraser waited until the circle took the attention away from their direction – or so he certainly hoped as he started the count.

"One," he signalled with his index finger, rising up on his haunches. Darius did the same and thumbed the safety catch of his pistol.

"Two," commanded Fraser with the middle finger joining in. The helicopter searched the far side of the hilltop and started swinging back towards them.

"Three," his ring finger extended, Fraser jerked his hand forward and sprang from the grass, Darius mirroring his movement.

They were met by a hail of lead - Turner anticipated this manoeuvre completely. He too would have used the helicopter as a distraction, and he now sprayed the assailants with bullets, hitting both.

Darius was thrown backwards, his left shoulder torn by a round that did what all military rounds are designed to.

The bullet's parabolic trajectory turned into a corkscrew, maximizing the damage. Additionally, the slug tumbled over itself as it continued lethal progress through soft tissue, tearing into the deltoid muscle in a spray of shredded flesh. Finally, it spread out into a ragged flat disk that fell more than flew out of a large exit wound in the back of the shoulder, blood spraying from mangled muscles.

Darius immediately took hold of his left sleeve and pulled the injured arm next to his side, backing away behind a small rock.

Fraser stopped three rounds with his torso, yet he did one last thing as he died. Clinically, he was already dead when he did it, but the evil he was taking to his grave would not die as fast as his flesh, driving it past the very end - even as his blood flow ebbed and merciful darkness spread over his conscience.

His arm raised, he emptied the magazine into the centre of the ambush. Then he sank down onto his knees, his body falling to rest on his elbows. He came to rest in this position of worship, his head immersed into what used to be most of his blood, now soaking into the ground beneath him.

Turner replaced the magazine and fired more volleys into the same direction, but Darius already scrambled further downhill and disappeared, leaving behind a trail of dark blood.

The helicopter darted well away from gunfire. Turner looked back and stiffened in horror.

Maggie lay with her head on her father's chest, her body totally still. Turner grabbed her hand, exhaling in relief as she turned towards him with an expression of total bewilderment.

Then he saw that James Stewart remained still on his back. Gnarled hands wrapped around the carbine, a wisp of smoke still drifting from the barrel. There was a gaping hole in the centre of his forehead.

They sat still for a long time until the sirens at the bottom of the hill came closer. Turner put his hand on Maggie's shoulder.

"Maggie," he said quietly, pulling her towards him. She didn't react, and he applied more force. She turned stiffly, the tears starting to roll down her face.

He dropped the SKS onto grass and threw his hands around her. Her resistance suddenly failed, and she slumped towards him. He held her very tight.

"I am sorry, Maggie," he said wearily. "I am really, really sorry."

Her tears were burning into his shirt, as he felt the powerful torso shudder in his tired arms. He became aware of a tingling on his head and took away his hand to run it over his scalp. It came away with a dark stain. He felt a superficial graze and decided to ignore it.

"Maggie," he said, leaning away from her. "Maggie..."

She raised her head to stare at him mutely, tears streaming down her cheeks. Turner felt his own eyes sting and water. His scalp wound started to throb.

"Maggie, listen," he said tenderly. "I am truly sorry about your father. But we have to go."

"No," shouted Maggie, shaking her head frantically. "We can't! What, leave him? No!"

"Maggie," said Turner again. "Your dad was a wonderful man, but he is dead now. There is nothing more you can do for him."

"No," shuddered Maggie, flinching away from him. "No. I can't just leave him here."

"Listen," said Turner forcefully. He grasped her cheekbones between his hands and turned her face towards him. "Your father is dead. You have to live. Say goodbye to him now because if you stay here you will be dead too, you understand?"

She merely shook her head, crying.

"Maggie," said Turner leaning his forehead onto her hair. "He wouldn't have wanted you to die so stupidly."

Maggie turned to face him, her eyes two hollow whorls of pain. She stared through Turner blindly, then slowly nodded. Turner backed away.

Maggie fell onto her father's chest and held his shattered head in her arms, then planted a long, slow kiss below the gaping bullet hole in the forehead. She then straightened and stood up, turning away after one last glance.

She walked over to Fraser's body and stared at it for a few seconds. Then she swung a vicious kick to the head which would have killed Fraser in life. The body flopped backwards, knees slowly rising from the ground as Fraser came to rest on his back, arms outstretched, legs parted and bent at the knees.

Maggie levelled her pistol and shot the corpse through the groin, watching it twitch. Then she turned around, her mouth tight and determined.

"Let's go," she said hoarsely, tucking the pistol into her waste band. "As you say, dad would want me to survive. Make it happen, Jack Turner."
They ran down the side of the hill away from the road and disappeared in the forest where none would wisely follow them at least until the dawn's first light.

***

Darius retained his calm in the presence of hideous pain, but his physiology kept betraying him. He had a lot of trouble standing up because of dizziness, and pain made him dry-retch. He lost his balance and had to brace himself every time his stomach went into spasm.

It took him a while to stagger to the car, where he was at last able to sit down.

It took longer still, the wounded arm feeling paralysed and his conscious state wavering, to dump all the documents into the culvert, leaving a prepared set in the glove box. He threw his pistol over the side of the mountain, the ruined shoulder flaming with agony at this movement.

Darius started the engine and drove down the hill slowly, blood ebbing over the plush seat, until he confronted the police cordon. Only then did he pull the parking brake with his right hand and sank back into the seat, losing consciousness for the first time in his very long life.

***

They crashed through the scrub, sirens yelping on the hill above them. Every now and again the helicopter passed by, and Turner made Maggie hide behind a thick tree. He didn't know if they had time to get the infrared cameras working, but he didn't want to risk it.

His fears were allayed reasonably soon – the pilot's behaviour appeared to be geared to the spotlight rather than anything else. Turner knew the crewmen were wasting their time – there was no chance of being spotted beneath the canopy of that tall forest, one of the few to escape the ravages of bush fires and man.

When they reached the bottom of the hill, all noises ceased. They crashed through the bush past a few tracks, which Turner ignored. He sketched an escape plan in his mind as soon as he settled on his location and now knew exactly where he was going.

He hoped like hell that the accountants hadn't euthanased the narrow-gauge rail line, which ran past the Observatory according to the map. If they had, that would leave them with no choice but to risk exposure to other people.

That was a serious hole in his plan – he didn't want to steal any more cars, knowing that any local theft would be immediately related to the gun battle.

He saw the gap in the moonlight tree line and moaned. The railway was quite a way up the next hillside. He explained the plan to Maggie, who stopped to catch her breath, wiping her forehead with the back of her hand.

"Let's go," was her only reply.

They made it to the gully separating the two hills, and Turner risked using a small burglar torch to check for bog and snakes. There were no snakes, but plenty of mud in the bed of the small creek running between the two hills, and they took much trouble to avoid getting dirty and conspicuous. Turner stopped to wash the dry blood from his face.

During the climb to the rail line behind Maggie, Turner got to reflect on his age for the first time. He was a very fit man by anyone's standards, but climbing a steep hill after a teenager left him gasping.

He managed not to look too exhausted as he made it after Maggie up the railway embankment, and for the first time that night he had good news. The narrow gauge tracks glistened in the moonlight, indicating recent use – and plenty of it.

As soon as their sweat was dry, they followed the tracks to the top of the hill, where a cutting smoothed the upward gradient. Turner selected a suitable location just past the cutting, and they settled to wait.

At nine pm, just as Turner was about to gently break the news about having to spend the night in the open, they heard the putter of the antique locomotive struggling up the hill. His heart thumping, Turner put his hand on Maggie's shoulder and pushed her below the level of the grass.

The locomotive reached the top of the clearing, losing all speed in the ascent. It was coupled to two vintage carriages, both nearly empty. At either end of each carriage was a platform fenced with waist-high railing, a refuge of smokers, vagabonds and joy riders.

Turner spotted a conductor armed with a radio in the first carriage and waited until the train crawled past. Then he and Maggie were up and sprinting downhill to catch the train before it accelerated.

Maggie reached the back platform first and vaulted over the barrier, then reached down to help Turner consolidate his grasp on the railing. He did this with only relative ease and used what felt like the last of the strength in his arms to pull his aching body upwards until his knee got hold of the platform.

"You okay?" asked Maggie with concern, watching the agony on his face as he dragged his legs over the railing.

"Yeah," wheezed Turner. "Just stuffed, that's all."

"Don't peg out on me," warned Maggie. "You have to get me to safety first."

"You bet," replied Turner huffily. "And we have a long way to go."

***

Charles Carson was a lean middle-aged man with a permanently sour expression. Acid bubbled up from his soul, his every movement and expression a statement of resentment.

A superbly promising cellist in youth, he was railroaded in taking advantage of his excellent marks at school to enter medical training.

To this day he couldn't understand how he became an orthopaedic surgeon, a speciality known for its least intellectual rigour. "An orthopod is as strong as an ox and twice as smart" was the comment of his psychiatrist father when Carson passed his surgical exams. These days, dad insisted that he maligned the oxen and apologized whole-heartedly.

None of this was a good foundation for establishing a private life unsullied by his profession, and Carson never bothered. Living in an expensive, barely furnished unit a few doors away from the hospital, he never once took advantage of the exuberant sexuality that overtakes normal people working amid death and tragedy. His aloofness left straight and gay singles of this closely knit environment equally peeved, but he revelled in the resentment he aroused, much as it mirrored the resentment of his own existence.

Nevertheless, Darius was fortunate that CC was on call the night ambulance officers pulled him from a blood-spattered car and dispatched the helicopter to the town's largest trauma centre with Darius under heavy guard.

Carson was amazed by many things he saw during the operation he immediately scheduled after inspecting the damage. He found it amazing that the shoulder looked like it was infected for some days, although the police report was absolutely clear on this point.

Then there was the size of the patient. Not very tall and definitely not young, once stripped of his bloody clothes he looked a champion weightlifter. His gracefully thin stomach tapered to an enormous barrel chest, limbs bulging with muscle even when he was totally paralysed by the anaesthetist.

The nursing staff took advantage of Darius' unconsciousness to appraise his genitals. The consensus in the trauma theatre is that the German had the largest tool in their collective experience, which was extensive both personally and professionally.

They concurred that even in its flaccid state the penis in question would shame most persons who really should remain nameless. To their eternal delight, it responded to the induction of general anaesthesia in a most embarrassing fashion, rising to what seemed an impossible height above its unconscious owner.

But that was the least of the anaesthetist's problems during a relatively short operation, the patient requiring very large doses of muscle relaxant to remain still, and heart throwing off runs of dangerous-looking arrhythmia.

Finally, blood that was taken in casualty revealed a haemoglobin reading of two hundred and twenty, which panicked the anaesthetist. People with so many red cells are likely to clog smaller vessels with clumps of these cells as blood flow becomes sluggish, causing strokes and heart attacks. He opened the drip full-bore and asked Carson not to take his time, as sluggish blood flow is frequently experienced during anaesthesia.

"Fuck off, gas-man," replied Carson biliously. "I don't want to be here any more than you do."

The anaesthetist was a relatively new graduate and therefore did not take it as an insult. How could it be a slight when the surgeon didn't even know his name?

"Look," he said reasonably. "That's a pretty high haemoglobin."

"Wasting your time," said the scrub nurse, who came as close as anybody could to Carson's bed. "CC doesn't remember what haemoglobin is. That takes him back all the way to medical school, you know."

"Hope your panty liner is holding," answered Carson, seizing a bleeding vessel protruding from the bullet wound with forceps. "Diathermy."

His junior assistant grabbed the diathermy and passed it sycophantically. Carson picked up the instrument with his long, slender fingers and applied it to the forceps. He stepped on the pedal, acrid smoke of burnt flesh filling the theatre. The bleeding stopped as the torn artery shrivelled and turned into a black stump. Carson tossed the diathermy back at the assistant.

"I do know something about haemoglobin," he said thoughtfully. "A guy with this build, he must either have a hormone disorder or he is on something."

"A bit old for a body builder, isn't he?" asked the assistant cautiously.

"No, son," said Carson venomously. "No time like middle age to be stupid. Right, let's see if any of you should be working here. What could he be on?"

"EPO," replied the anaesthetist, disgusted at the ease of the question.

"Hey," yelled Carson. "Not bad for a guy who's missed out on his evening pethidine."

He turned to his assistant with a scowl hidden by the mask.
"What's your name again?" he asked with suspicion.

"Richards, Mr Carson," said the resident fearfully.

"Oh, good," said Carson absent-mindedly, his fingers

continuing to weave an intricate ballet across the torn shoulder. "What else could it be?"

"Polycythaemia rubra vera," replied the resident, referring to a rare condition in which red cells are overproduced. "Or erythropoietic leukaemia."

"Hmm," said Carson. "Attention, folks. We have ourselves a frustrated physician. Sees everything except the fucking obvious. Look at his muscles, boy."

"Oh, right," replied Richards with consternation. "Acromegaly?"

"Yeah, I'll pay that," said Carson. "Nursey!"

"What?" asked the circulating sister gruffly.

"You people always think you are clever," replied Carson. "What gives a man with acromegaly a high haemoglobin?"

The sister shrugged and went back to work.

"Even the gas-man must know," goaded Carson. "Why don't you?"

"Okay," said one of the other nurses. "Suppose you reveal it."

"Tell them, gas-man" said Carson as he returned full attention to the wound.

"Hyperplasty of the upper airway," said the anaesthetist importantly. "Sleep apnoea causes secondary polycythaemia."

"Yeah?" said the circulating nurse. "Well, I'm off for a smoke. You boys and girls enjoy your wonderful teamwork."

***

Darius came to, feeling worse than ever.

He appeared to be alone in a windowless room, in a bed that was rock-hard, his head propped by a tiny pillow and held in a neck collar, which appeared to be somehow fixed to the bed. His left arm was encased in a long plaster cast, which was suspended above the bed by a rigid apparatus of clamps and rods.

A drip snaked into his right wrist, and he saw what he recognized as an infusion pump, whose line piggybacked onto the drip. He suspected that the appalling nausea and dizziness he experienced came from the substance in that infusion pump.

The left shoulder still felt as if acid was poured into the ragged track left in his tissues by Turner's bullet. Its fire seared every time he tried to move.

He looked around, and his vision drifted in and out of focus, taking in the head of a uniformed policeman in the glass panel of the door.

***

Their train crawled through the hills, appearing not to pick up any passengers. Turner was relieved that it was moving in the right direction, hoping not to have to spend the night at the terminus. This would have been bad in itself – but the worst part would be to retrace the route to the city past the shootout, where a watch may by then be in place.

They arrived to a suburban train station towards ten pm, simply disembarking as the train stopped. Turner bought two tickets to central station, and they managed an express that got them there before midnight.

Turner found the platform that serviced northbound trains. Avoiding groups of policemen who appeared to be ill at ease, he and Maggie strolled to the end of the platform, where they casually jumped off the end, suddenly sprinting from the light into welcome darkness.

A goods train loaded with new cars destined for the greener pastures of the North crawled past them, and Turner took a chance. They climbed on, hiding between non-descript family sedans manufactured locally by a Japanese company wishing to import its more lucrative products at reduced tax rates. The train rolled on, gradually gathering speed.

After half an hour of observing the surroundings,

Turner was reassured that the train was indeed rolling northwards. He gradually relaxed as the city was left behind.

Maggie was transfixed and numbed as she watched her past recede into the distance. The city acknowledged her escape with a total lack of concern, shrugged and returned to its business, oblivious of the fact that the first part of Maggie's life had just ended.

***

At midday Darius was visited by his saviour. Carson studied the chart at the end of the bed, worried by the temperature. Antibiotics had been poured into the man's system for three days, yet he looked like a freshly admitted vagabond with pneumonia. Soon he would have to cut the cast to examine the wound first-hand.

"Has he regained consciousness?" asked Carson curtly.

"No," replied Richards. "Drifting in and out."

"Get the neurosurgeons to have a look at him again," said Carson. Richards made a notation in his notebook. He did not reply, as he was known to have sound hearing. There was no other reason why Carson's order would fail to be carried out.

"What about the repeat haemoglobin?" asked Carson.

"Oh," said Richards, embarrassed to be prompted. He produced a printout from his pocket. "I had a call from Haematology about this."

Carson glanced at the report, then snatched it out of his assistant's hand and read it again.

"What the ff…" he began.

"It's all right, sir," said Richards. "I don't think he can hear you."

"What is this bullshit?" asked Carson miserably. "Get them up here, for Christ's sake. What do they mean – "not human"? Then whose?"

"It's probably a mistake," said Richards.

"Not knowing my luck it won't be," complained Carson. "Let's go. Who else do I need to see? Delight me, young man."

They carefully washed their hands outside the room, watched by the policeman who was detailed to note everything that happened to this strange patient.

***

Turner woke up from the cold and did a few stretch exercises to warm up.

Maggie stood at the edge of the carriage platform, her hair blown by the crosswind away from her face. She stared at the moonlit woodland that rolled past in a mute farewell, knowing that she would never see that kind of country again.

Turner walked up to her and they stood together in silence, the train eating the miles to destination.

"Who were they?" asked Maggie.

"I am sorry, Maggie," he answered. "I don't think I can even guess."

"Will we ever find out?" asked Maggie.

"I hope not," replied Turner. "My plan is to make sure they never see you again."

"Okay," said Maggie. "Where are we going?"

"Sydney."

"Why?"

"Because from there we can get out of the country," said Turner. "Without leaving a trace."

"Right," said Maggie without a trace of emotion. "A new life."
"Yes, Maggie," said Turner, placing his hand over her shoulder. "I promise."

She nodded slowly and leaned into his direction. Turner led her away from the edge of the platform and hugged her gently.

Her arms rose to embrace him strongly. For a while she just stood still with her face pressed into his chest, then she looked up at him and kissed him hard on the lips.

He returned the kiss for what seemed like eternity, the swaying of the train rocking their bodies and building tension. Then her knees buckled as she pulled him down, rolled over and straddled his hips with hers, all while continuing to kiss him.

He felt her body move over his and began to react. Blood rushed to his face and ran hot across his body. He found himself holding Maggie with all his strength, moving with her and responding to her urgency.

With an effort he pulled away and sat up.

"Wait," he said, catching his breath. "We shouldn't be doing this."

"Why the hell not?" asked Maggie indignantly. "It's good enough to have people shooting at me – and I am not allowed to get laid?"

"You are still at school," protested Turner.

"No, mister," shouted Maggie. She sprang to her feet

and stood over him angrily, her posture edging close to a combat stance. "My school days seem to be over, don't you think?"

Turner leaned towards her, took her arm and tugged on it gently until she sat beside him, still fuming. They sat still for a while. Then he looked in her eyes.

"You are right both times," he replied. "Yes, your school days are over. Yes, you have a right to get laid when people are trying to kill you."

"So?" asked Maggie aggressively.

"We have no protection," sad Turner weakly. Maggie's eyes flashed at him angrily.

They heard a level crossing, and Turner reacted instantly, diving to the floor of the platform. Maggie followed suit.

They passed a lonely road cut by the railway. They needn't have bothered – no cars stood at the boom gate, but they remained still just in case until the crossing was long past.

Maggie draped her leg over him and put her head on his chest. The smell from her hair intoxicated Turner.

"So what if we don't have any protection?" asked Maggie into his chest. "What are our chances of being alive in a week?"

Turner thought it over. Then he put his arm around her and placed his other hand on her breast.

"You are right," he whispered. "I don't know. Let's do what we still can."

* * *

Morphine made Darius nauseous, and it tore his will from its foundation, setting the mind adrift and out of control.

One major drawback of longevity, as Darius understood a long time ago, is the accumulated burden of trauma suffered over centuries. His kind was no more immune against that pain than the humans he so despised. It was merely a matter of refusal to remember, applying the iron will of his species to the task.

But he was never in this much pain, this close to death and this badly frustrated in his task. A combination of failure, pain, fever and drug broke the barrier that held back his memories.

As waves of throbbing pain arose from the wound in the shoulder and spread through his body, Darius found himself powerless against a tornado of his past. He stopped struggling and let it take him.

Darius often reflected on the curse of projectile weapons – it was they which narrowed the seemingly impossible gap between two species. Humans did not invent the bow, he shook his head, alone in miserable darkness, but they proved just as adept at shooting it as those who did.

Yet until cheap and powerful firearms made body armour obsolete, someone of his strength could still wear enough metal to withstand any projectile – and still blend in. His war axe, an old and much derided weapon, once ruled any battlefield. The double blade and the handle were cast as a single piece, far too heavy for any opponent to deflect or block. It was also too heavy for anyone else to pick it up and use, even if they survived having it thrown at them.

That was how Darius subsisted in those days, plying the grisly trade of a mercenary at a time when Europe was one continuous battlefield. Clothes were seldom removed, and his bulk was presumed to be padded with fat. Impossible battlefield feats were observed, but they were always put down to combat fever or simply dismissed as admiration of a drunken comrade afterwards. Life was uncomplicated.

Mercenaries were exempt from normal rules of behaviour and citizenship, and they were largely left alone even if their antics offended the powerful. There were no rules for his ilk – at worst all they needed to do was travel across a few valleys to a different battle, if one cared to make that distinction.

It was during one of these journeys that he was overtaken by a snowstorm at a mountain pass and decided to make for nearest shelter.

The castle he soon spotted was nothing much – a few towers linked by a sagging wall, all built many centuries before to deal with threats of a simpler age. More recent owners let their defences crumble, not even bothering to clear the garbage of centuries out of the moat, and that vital structure was now nearly solid to human weight.

On that day they lived to regret it. A band of marauders, probably his mercenary colleagues let loose in the countryside after being cheated out of their pay, were laying siege to the sagging structure, and their businesslike efforts were bound to yield eventual success. Arquebus fire kept the defenders from dealing with ladders applied to the wall by ragged-looking thugs whose demeanour revealed complete familiarity with combat.

Without overtly knowing why, Darius took an instant dislike to this rabble, although he fought all over Europe with and against such men. He generally accepted their pillage as normal behaviour, observing rapine and slaughter with detached amusement.

The probable reason he chose a different side at the siege, he liked to think afterwards, was realization that the castle was unlikely to provide much shelter if the rabble became its masters. Despite the decrepit battlements its towers looked homely enough, strongly built against the weather. Chimneys belched smoke which bespoke internal warmth he much craved after three days of trudging through snowdrifts.

He dismounted a short distance away from the wall and left his horse untied, knowing that the vicious animal will not fall into enemy hands. Darius walked into the siege line, his axe whistling as he whirled it above his head.

By the time the arquebusiers suffered their awful fate, it was too late for those crashing down from ladders and running back from the wall to stop him. Many were killed by stones and firewood thrown by defenders, who could now safely lean over the wall, and none of the survivors made it past the axe with a giant blade now dull with blood.

At the end of his slaughter the gates swung open, and an older man in dented and rusty armour limped towards Darius at the head of his ragtag army of peasants and house servants.

Neither he nor Darius had a visor which could be raised in salute, so instead they removed gauntlets and shook hands. Darius was led inside like the saviour he for once became, seated before a huge fire in the dining hall, copiously fed and intoxicated with local claret.

Stories changed hands - like all nobles of his generation, the count was no stranger to war. But decades of conflict, failed harvests and appallingly cold winters left his family with nothing but survival rations, and by the time he inherited his castle, it was well beyond his means to rebuild it to a standard mandated by safety of its inhabitants.

There were frequent raids by marauders, but none were able to get near the parapets. Alas, gunpowder now revealed the obsolescence of the count's defences, and the defenders were about to set fire to one of the towers as a desperate ploy to dissuade the invaders from making the final effort. Darius arrived just in time.

An auburn-haired girl the servants addressed as Contessa drank in Darius with his absolutely level demeanour, bulging shoulders so handsomely set out by armour, melodic voice and a humourous twinkle in his eyes, something that disappeared, he stopped to note, after the first instalment of the World War.

Her father noticed her rapture and did not in the least appear put out. He played a cool hand, the old count, knowing the meaning of streaks of blood in his cough and rapid loss of weight from his long frame.

A month later they found his body, fully clad in armour and with ancestral sword in hand, at the bottom of the tallest tower of the castle. Darius told the local priest that the count slipped on some ice whilst inspecting the battlements, keeping one hand on the handle of his dagger as he said it. The funeral went ahead in the traditional manner.

There was no ceremony to mark their union, but

Darius and Contessa simply drifted into behaving as spouses. They continued, as was custom of the day, to reside in different towers of the castle, but ended up spending more and more time together.

Darius found this release from mayhem that comprised his entire life confusing. He was programmed for destruction and predation; peace that invaded his life was a strange thing that he cautiously embraced after a long period of uncertainty and consternation.

The Contessa adored him, knowing only a saviour and a source of unfailing support – Darius told her nothing of himself. It was not unusual for men, such as one he pretended to be, to have committed appalling acts during military careers. Confessions, had he been inclined to make them, would not have altered her loyalty, and at length he decided not to bother.

One night she seduced him – a brave act for a virgin of that time, but one she consummated exquisitely well. Darius was not an expert in that field, most of his previous encounters with women having taken place in circumstances best not mentioned or compared. He was transfixed by her exuberance and needed no persuasion to commence regular visits to Contessa's tower.

It was during icy autumn that he noticed the glow of her skin, and Darius smiled at the irony of this recollection through a curtain of pain. For many human lifetimes he will remember a single, fleeting moment – a young woman standing on the crumbling parapet in pallid sunshine, auburn hair blown by the rising mountain wind.

Her face looked as if it radiated light. She looked at him and smiled.

He stared without understanding, still puzzled when she walked towards him, placed her palms on his shoulders and leaned into him, gently kissing the notch just above the breastbone. He smiled uncertainly and cradled the top of her head with his arms, then she looked up, encircled by blue velvet of his sleeves – in those days he only wore blue – and she told him.

He feigned elation, but it took him some days to accept what happened and to accept it. The winter went fast, then came a mild a day in April when new leaves began to burst from buds towards the still-distant sun, and on that day he heard her scream.

As was custom, he had to wait outside for many tense hours, the village midwife scurrying in and out of the tower. At dawn of the next day the screams became louder and more desperate, then suddenly stopped.

Darius stood still, staring at the top of the tower. He dared not breathe until silence was ended by another cry, a sound that was not the weak, mewling complaint of newborn humans. A low growl came from the tower to warn the cowering world: its new lord had torn a bloody path into daylight.

Darius saw the baby, freshly washed, wrapped in linen and greedily sucking at Contessa's breast as he burst into a room that reeked of sweat and pain. Darius dropped on his knees at her side, took her hand and held it to his pounding heart. She smiled weakly and fell back on the pillows, exhausted.

The baby finished feeding, and the midwife came forward, pushing Darius away. She picked up the baby and covered the sleeping Contessa with blankets, then Darius took the baby from her arms. She tried to squawk something in objection, but he merely turned away, his elbow thrown at her body to fling her hard against the wall. She limped from the room in terrified silence.

The baby opened his coal-black eyes and fixed his father with a bottomless stare, which Darius returned. There was an exchange that said everything that needed to be said, and Darius knew that the connection was now complete.

He sat on the stone floor all day, cradling his son in his arms. Both mother and baby slept until evening, then the baby woke up and was put on the mother's breast without her awakening. He fed and went back to sleep, Darius returning him to the cradle of his blue tunic and falling asleep himself, his brain craving leave to catch up with recent events.

He awoke the next morning with his son's urine tricking down his stomach. He called in the servants, gently awoke the Contessa and held her for a while, kissing the damp forehead.

Somehow she survived the crude ravage of that birth, although whatever happened made her reluctant to sleep with him. One day, she said, and she would not speak of it further. He quickly let go of his need, allowing it to wither as only his kind can.

She limped for many weeks after giving birth, but he thought nothing of this defect. For the rest of his unimaginably long life whenever he saw her or thought of her, he would always see a woman with glowing skin on the parapet of a decrepit castle.

But the baby was fine and strong, feeding lustily and growing fast. The dense black hair that covered his body was beginning to thin out, and the misshapen lump at the bottom of the spine started to flatten.

He began to make speech-like noises at two months of age. By four months he was able to understand most of what his parents said – and mouth a few simple words in reply.

One day Darius came back from riding around the estates. Satisfied with their appearance, he walked up the spiral staircase to his living quarters and began to undress for a hot bath – a distinct innovation at that place and time, using a pulley system to deliver firewood to the top of his tower and burning it to heat water from a stone cistern he constructed on the roof.

He immersed himself in hot water, closing his eyes and leaning back against warm stone. Eyes remaining shut, he merely smiled when he heard someone enter the water and felt her press against him, caressing his genitals with a soft hand.

He gasped with that hand's progress, and his eyes were still shut when the woman sat astride him, moaning softly as she slid all the way down. Then he realized that her action was impossible with Contessa's damaged hip, and he opened his eyes with a start.

Darius jerked awake in the dim light, pain from the shoulder surging through his torso like lightning. He savoured the bitter tide that washed over him, studying the sensation of that hurt as he may have studied a new arrowhead he extracted from a chink in his armour.

He moaned as the throbbing from his shoulder overcame him. The cop outside heard it and called the night nurses, who crowded into the room.

A few minutes later Darius had his pulse, blood pressure, oxygen saturation and temperature taken, sweat mopped from his face, ice cubes put into his parched mouth and pupils checked for response to light. Above all, the rate at which his pain medication was infused into the vein was adjusted to the maximum prescribed setting.

"Herr Schtampfler," one of the nurses tried her school

German on him. "Hau ist das… der schmertz?"

"It'z okey," replied Darius, his tongue heavy but still producing a good imitation of a South German accent. "I speek Inglish."

"Do you need more medication for the pain?" asked one of the nurses clearly, pointing to the infusion pump."

"Nein," said Darius, sounding obtunded. "It iss gutt now."

"Do you know where you are?" asked the nurse.

"I think diz iss a hospital," said Darius. "Why iz dis? Did I have an accident?"

"You did," confirmed the nurse. "You will be all right."

"Ach," said Darius, sounding weak. "Am I badly hurt?"

"You have a wound in your left shoulder," said the nurse. "You had an operation to fix it. It was a success."

"Grüss Gott," said Darius. "How long have I been here?"
"Three days," said the nurse immediately. Everyone knew about this case.

"Ach," said Darius slowly.

"Listen," said the nurse, leaning closer to him. "Is there anyone we should notify?"

Darius looked at her in consternation.
"Family?" repeated the nurse.

"Ach," Darius smiled feebly in recognition. "Nein. No family."

"If they are in Germany, I am sure our government would help out with transport," said the nurse, placing her hand over his forearm. She was on solid ground, her ward having recently hosted to a busload of German tourists who went over an embankment on the way to the ocean.

"No, it'z okey" said Darius, experiencing a comfort he hadn't felt for a long time at her touch. "I do not have family."

He smiled as she stared back with concern.

"It'z okey," he repeated. "Believe me."

***

Maggie and Turner lay entwined in the back of a brand-new station wagon, whose acquaintance with its first owner was now inevitably delayed by a lengthy appointment with a steam cleaner.

Maggie joked that the car lost its virginity too but couldn't have liked it nearly as much. Turner laughed, knowing that a similar comment would have earned him an elbow in his aching ribs.

Dawn was creeping from the east, where a blood-red line opened between the black sky and the ragged edge of the horizon.

A few minutes later the clouds turned crimson all over the eastern sky, then the light crept over the silent earth still shrouded in rising wisps of mist.

Maggie and Turner looked at each other and looked around the car.

"Oh dear," said Maggie.

"Yeah," replied Turner laconically. "That's what happens."

"No wonder parents warn you about sex," said Maggie. Then her expression collapsed, and she sobbed on Turner's shoulder. He kept his mouth tightly shut and held her supportively. That was a lesson he learned in combat – grief must be allowed all the space it needs.

A while later they dressed, Turner climbing out of the car to give Maggie some space. They concealed the remains of their presence by throwing a spare wheel over the highly suggestive marks and raising the rear seats upright. Just to be on the safe side, Turner went over all of the surfaces systematically with his T-shirt, wiping all fingerprints they might have left.

"There's still a lot of DNA," said Maggie sceptically, pointing at the stain.

"By the time they get the results, we'll either be very far…" Turner stopped himself mid-sentence.

"Or dead?" asked Maggie defiantly.

"Yes," said Turner.

***

"Mr Schtampfler," said Carson with mock exuberance. "Nice to have you back with us."

"Thank you," said Darius simply. "I am grateful for what you did."

"Oh, that's all right," said Carson with a poignant smile. He was about to add that he would do this for any good Aryan but checked himself. Carson was half-Jewish.

"You are doing well, Mr Schtampfler," he said in a more businesslike manner. "I think you have a bit of an infection in that bullet wound, but you will get over it. In fact, you nearly have. Your fever has settled."

Carson had many questions, most related to

satisfaction of his intellectual curiosity. He learned that his patient is a reasonably prominent German ornithologist, who was taking his sabbatical in Australia to enjoy observing native birds, which were not his usual speciality. In youth Herr Doktor was a successful trapeze artist, which was how he earned a living whilst studying at university. Hence the huge muscles, which circus performers tend to keep for life.

Neither Carson nor anyone else had raised the subject of enormous genitals, which would stretch cross-cultural camaraderie beyond reasonable bounds.

The haematologists came back to collect a lot more blood, which Darius allowed to occur. Such a thing happened to him once before, but a wayward Russian shell soon took care of his problem. It landed on a tent where his blood sample was being enthusiastically studied by a young army doctor, instantly vaporizing both. Darius spent the rest of that war telling people that he once had syphilis, which made them less inclined to collect his blood to save wounded comrades.

His haemoglobin had dropped in response to the illness, which he knew it would. The doctors put the initial reading down to severe dehydration after the injury, and that controversy was defused.

But that still left what they saw when his blood was smeared on a glass slide and stained with dye for viewing under microscope. He had no idea what he was going to do about that.

The police found nothing to contradict his story and concluded that he was in a very wrong place at the wrong time. One of those who attacked Turner must have made their escape, which took him past a silly foreigner sitting on a hilltop looking at nightingales instead of drinking and whoring like a good tourist should.

Apart from the blood business, it all looked good. Darius allowed himself to relax and respond to the excellent care he was receiving.

Somewhere on this earth there is another girl like her, he thought to himself through a fog of pain killers, which suddenly cleared to reveal the woman on the parapet, her skin glowing in cold sunshine.
Somehow I will find her. No, he corrected himself. Not her but one like her. Before humanity toyed with another philosophy which made them resistant to subversive ideas.

The only problem, in his extensive experience, is that there was never a shortage of radical philosophies. In a tinder-dry climate of widespread and undeserved misery they caught alight and spread faster than fire in a drought-ravaged forest.

He remembered the last such fire all too well. He did not have a hope of being heard, let alone being listened to, over the racket whipped up by the frenzied corporal. Darius just came along for the ride, to see if he could broaden his experience in that whirlwind cataclysm, most of which he spent in an experimental commando unit, which operated beyond the limits of known human capabilities. It was the closest, he thought, he came to being in a company of equals.

There was some reason, he reflected, that he never bothered to analyse why he was now using a German identity. He told himself it was his admiration of the Germanic way, a tradition of not going to bed until nothing was left to chance. That was a kindred spirit to his.

It could be a stepping stone towards my heritage, thought Darius. That culture is the closest the tired old world comes to the future. Setting that ethos to rid the world of it putrescence would crown thirty thousand years of back-breaking effort and unending sacrifice, an endurance of hardship human marauders would find impossible to fathom.

He leaned back on the pillows, knowing that nothing can get in the way of such unstoppable force. With so much on his side, he could never lose.

Then he opened his eyes with a start, just as he opened them in the castle tower, but instead of the senescent hospital décor he saw oil lamps flickering against blackened sandstone, and in that dim light he saw one of the castle's servants. She straddled him in ecstasy, head rolled back, long dark hair swaying with her motion behind sweaty shoulders.

He raised both hands and grasped her neck to strangle, but the pressure only made her more frantic, and she thrust on his lap so fast that he too began to lose control, his hands dropping back into warm water.

As next morning dawned she burst into his room as Darius slowly came awake in his bed. When he asked what was wrong she struggled onto the bed, moaning with pain, and she stood astride him, raising her skirts.

He saw that her genitals were bright red, swollen and covered with weeping scratches, inner thighs streaked with bloody fluid. She screamed that he gave her the Spanish disease, and she would now die.

He laughed, knowing that she was merely suffering a reaction to his seed. But something made him wish to hurt her, and he said she may not have much time, so she must see a priest and make a final confession right away since he suspected, he added with a poisonous smile, that her sins may take some time to recount.

She cursed him and hobbled out of the room. He never saw her again.

***

They jumped off the train as it reached inner Sydney and stopped at a red signal. That was a dangerous move, running across many lines of tracks in broad daylight and climbing the tall wire fence under the curious looks of the kids playing basketball in an empty car park. But this was Sydney, and observers had a way of becoming very forgetful when it came to answering police inquiries.

They walked to the nearest shopping centre and caught a bus to the city. Turner found a cheap hotel and asked Maggie to join him later.

Wearing large sunglasses to hide his black eye, he walked into the fly-blown lobby. He was confronted by a clerk behind a tall counter, a sallow-looking middle-aged man with a paunch over his dirty jeans. His T-shirt advertised a motorcycle gang made infamous a few years ago by a shoot-out with police.

"I need a room for one night, please," said Turner.

"Single?" asked the clerk contemptuously.

"Never for long," replied Turner with a mischievous wink.

The clerk looked up with a sour expression, correctly assessing the last comment to be a deadpan insult to his, eternally single, status.

"Overnight or by the hour?" he asked without a change of tone.

"Overnight," said Turner.

"Seventy five, payable in advance. Will it be cash or credit card?"

"Cash," Turner counted out the money. "Don't worry about a receipt."

That earned him another acidic scowl, but the clerk tossed across the key with less hostility.

"One-four-three. Up the lift on the fourth floor and turn left," he said curtly, turning away.

Turner nodded and walked away. A few other comments came to his mind, but he decided not to needle the man and mark his memory any further.

Maggie heard the entire exchange from the street. She crossed the road to talk to the greengrocer, who was about to finish hosing down the pavement outside his tiny shop.

She borrowed the hose to wash her face and to smooth her hair. She gave it a few minutes to dry and walked into the hotel, smiling at the clerk.

"Yeah?" he asked sourly.

"I'm here to see a man, darling," said Maggie, still smiling sweetly. "Are we fucking blind or what?"

"Jesus," muttered the clerk. "Who?"

"Calls himself Arthur," said Maggie. "Said he only just checked in. Guess he was quick with the Bible."

The clerk shook his head in disgust. He knew this to refer to the practice of prostitutes leaving their mobile numbers in the saucier chapters of Gideon's Bible.

He picked up the phone and dialled Turner.

"Arthur," replied Turner on the first ring.

"Your lady is here," said the clerk with hatred. "If I were you, I'd check her age and wear three layers of rubber."

"Yes, sir," said Turner jovially. "Show her up, will you?"

The clerk hung up.

"Up yours, honey," said Maggie after receiving the directions. "You I wouldn't fuck at all, no matter how many layers you wore."

She turned regally and ascended to the fourth floor.

***

Darius was very pleased with his recovery. His wound looked just as ragged outside, but he felt as if its interior healed. He still had relatively little power in the left arm, but this was not a problem given his operational status.

The police switched from the role of suspicious investigators to that of authorities bending over backwards to help a visitor in distress. They organized for the Mercedes to be cleaned by a service often used by victims of violent crime. Bereaved relatives frequently needed to separate bits of their loved ones from property redeemable for cold hard cash, the latter being the pre-requisite for the grieving period to commence in earnest.

The detective in charge of the investigation called a local car dealer with a complex past and told him how much police would appreciate a timely resolution of all loose bits to do with this case. The dealer appraised the Mercedes and gave Darius an excellent quote, which was immediately accepted.

Darius even made a small profit despite the miles he's driven. It was a small point for someone who accumulated resources for such a long time, but he liked each detail to stand up on its own.

The police even delivered his well-searched belongings to the hospital, and, for the first time since stopping a full metal jacket round, Darius was reunited with all his travel kit and in charge of his situation.

He didn't plan the next move until later that week, when he was watching a midday news program with sound turned down whilst scanning local newspapers for clues to Fraser's fate. There were none – as per his plan, Fraser appeared to have borne the brunt of the blame, not a single detail becoming public information.

Out of the corner of his eye Darius suddenly saw bones being removed by gloved hands from what looked like a shallow mass grave. He knew it wasn't Bosnia because lush palm trees towered in the background.

As he turned his full attention to the screen, a skull was brought close to the camera to display an appalling depressed fracture of the parietal bone, which looked like it was made by a heavy axe.

Darius fumbled for the remote control with his right hand and turned up the sound. He learned that a once popular leader of an uprising in a Central American country was now its hated dictator and struggling to remain in power.

The opposition was headed by his brother, a Catholic priest-turned-dissident. The brother was interviewed, belabouring the question of people who seemed to disappear after questioning the regime, especially in regard to any possible connection with the mass graves which seemed to be turning up all over the country.

The dictator was having some trouble, having found himself afoul of the politically correct world powers. This didn't prevent their oil companies from busily pumping natural gas out of his sea and paying a large royalty into the dictator's Swiss bank account.

But US intelligence was recently ordered by the sharing and caring US president to target its satellites on that wretched country. The world policeman applied twenty-first century technology to image the sites of recently disturbed earth, where evidence of primaeval morality awaited in abundance.

Darius watched the report carefully. That afternoon he made his way downstairs to the ground floor of the hospital, where the gift shop was selling a good range of newspapers and magazines and came back with a heavy bag of recent publications.

He climbed back into bed with a pile of newsprint and began to read relevant articles whilst his wound healed. Later that afternoon he looked out into the car park, processing what he just read. It was an article about mass arrests in another happy part of Central America, where paramilitary police developed a habit of surrounding the homes of opposition figures, arresting them and making them disappear. The rumour said they were loaded into helicopters and taken out to sea, where they were dropped from considerable height, thus sparing United Nations investigators the effort of digging up the evidence later.

He savoured that image – a blindfolded man prodded out of his seat inside a thundering helicopter, made to take a few steps only to realize, at the last moment, what the rush of cold air means for his career, struggling against the cable ties around his wrists and vainly trying to push his head into the machine's roof, only to be kicked in the stomach by a spit-polished boot, double over – then the tapering scream as he falls towards a churning sea.

But the image began to drift, and Darius was unable to check it in time. What he saw next was her fall from the tower's window, auburn hair spraying in the rush of air.

Darius crouched, castle wall against his back and a line of crossbowmen surrounding him in a semicircle.

Pursuing soldiers leaned out of that window as if to follow, and they watched Contessa hit the distant earth with a loud, sickening thud.

Darius let the axe drop to the ground as soon as he heard the sound of her death.

***

"So what the hell was this charade?" demanded Maggie, marching into a room.

"It's simple…" started Turner, standing by the window with a beer.

"And what a flea pit," interrupted Maggie, looking at faded furniture and dusty windows with disgust. "Just thought I'd mention it."

"At least the mattress is new," replied Turner suggestively.

"You were saying?" asked Maggie sternly.

"See, the authorities will be looking for two people, a man in the prime of his powers and a young lady," explained Turner enthusiastically. "If we came in as such, the clerk would rat on us."

"And he won't now?" asked Maggie curtly.

"Er, no. In a place like this, men who hire under-age prostitutes are ordinary customers. Start telling on them, and business goes bad. So the operators and the police learn to live with each other. As long as the hotel is not protecting wanted criminals, nobody wants to ask them what they really know."

"I am not under-age," said Maggie indignantly.

"No, but you could be."

"I see," replied Maggie in her schoolmistress voice. "Very well. Strip."

Turner smiled widely and obeyed. He stood in front of her naked, his arousal increasingly difficult to ignore.

Maggie threw off her clothes and dumped them over his. She nodded approval at his lean muscular physique and bent down abruptly, picking up the clothes from the floor.

"Laundry day," she said, heading towards the shower.

"Oh, good," said Turner meekly and went back to his beer.

Maggie washed everything and had a long soaking shower, returning to hang the wet clothes over the furniture.

"Hand washing," she said disgustedly. "That's worse than any prostitution. Wherever we are going, there better be a good washing machine."

Turner nodded, somewhat speechless.

"The shower is free now," added Maggie. "You know, cleanliness is next to godliness?"

"Yes, ma'am," replied Turner.

He went into the shower, smiling to himself. The hot water smelled of some chemical, but it was a very welcome addition to his recent life.

He was rinsing his hair, face looking up into the stream of water with eyes closed, when a pair of arms enclosed him in a tight embrace.

The last of the soap banished from his hair, Turner returned the embrace and closed his mouth around Maggie's. Their bodies met as the stream of warm water cascaded around them, washing away the dirt, the pain, the damage and the fear.

Later they slept into the balmy afternoon of Sydney autumn, their clothes drying quickly around them. At four Turner woke up and shifted in bed, Maggie's arm gripping him tighter in her sleep.

In the bright seaside sunlight her auburn hair was laced with copper strands. The dark eyebrows frowned in her sleep, a reflection of the last days. Her arms and ribs were covered with large bruises of varying colours, but the rest of the skin glowed a healthy pink.

Turner put his hand over her side, feeling her deep breaths, interrupted by an occasional shudder. He was drifting back to sleep when she suddenly startled under his hand and sat up.

"Hi," said Turner tenderly, caressing her sweaty forehead with his palm.

She reciprocated his caress and fell back on his chest.

"I had a nightmare," she said. "About them. The chase."

He held her tightly with both arms.

"We're safe now," he said. "It's over."

"How do we know?" sobbed Maggie into his chest. "How can we be sure of anything?"

"We are alive," said Turner, gently moving his fingers down Maggie's back. "I know that much."

Their bodies again caught fire, and afterwards they spent a long time laying still, listening to each other's breath as the sun sank behind tall buildings.

They went out to eat after dark, Maggie sneaking past the front desk unseen. Turner suggested Chinatown.

They walked along the darkened street full of people from all walks of life – tourists, drug dealers and everything in between. Every now and again an armoured police car would cruise the street, its side-mounted spotlight crawling along the pavement, engine growling in low gear, tall antennae swinging with the rhythm of bitumen's potholes.

Maggie walked a little in front of Turner in case one of them was identified. Turner thought that she was one tough girl, just marching through the crowd after what she just lived through without so much as turning back to confirm his presence.

Suddenly her head snapped to the left, and she darted into a narrow alley off the main street, her spine curving into a crouch.

Turner followed her immediately without a change in his demeanour. He strode quickly into the alley without becoming conspicuous, his eyes adjusting to a dimmer level of light.

He saw the cause of Maggie's movement all too quickly. A young Vietnamese girl was cornered by a gang of toughs in the cul-de-sac, her eyes wide with terror.

Maggie barely broke her stride to swing a sidekick into the nearest youth, felling him motionless to the ground. The boy standing next to him flicked around, only to accelerate the blow of Maggie's elbow across his mouth, which drove him backwards into his pals.

When they rounded on her, Maggie expertly used one of them for cover, raining blows on his nose with her fists, following up with a knee to his groin. As he slid to the pavement she parried a kick, twisting the foot which was aimed at her to drop the assailant to the ground.

The next gang member leaped over him, only to be knocked out cold by a punch that loosened all of his front teeth. The rest retreated to the wall and pulled knives from the pockets, the air coming alive with the clicks of blades springing open from the handles.

Maggie grunted contemptuously and leaped back, landing with the gun already in her hands. Turner chuckled, seeing instant terror on the faces distorted with homicidal fury only a moment before. He pulled his gun out too and stepped next to Maggie.

"Police," he said, waving the gun in the dim light. "Fuck off."

The youths did not need a second invitation to start running. They left their wounded comrades behind, completely secure about their silence. A few seconds later Turner nodded at the girl, who ran off as well.

"Very chivalrous," said Turner gruffly, putting away his gun. Maggie followed suit.

He was about to say something else, but she held up her hand, admonishing him to silence, her body dead still. Then she threaded her arm around his, and they walked out of the alley in search of a crowded restaurant.

***

The day of discharge was finally upon Darius. Carson removed the stitches and gave instructions for the rest of recuperation. Darius thanked him profusely, meaning every word.

The cops did their last duty by driving him to the airport. A tall constable turned up and asked for his luggage – then simply bundled all of it under one arm, operating the lift with the other.

They walked the long corridor on the ground floor to the entrance, where a police cruiser was left parked against all regulations. The constable unlocked the boot and placed the luggage inside, still only using one hand.

He drove to the airport at a sedate rate, only exceeding the speed limit by a fraction. He helped Darius secure a trolley, loaded it with bags and left without saying anything.

Darius wheeled his luggage into the airport, using right hand only. He walked to a row of counters and awaited his turn in the queue of backpackers and businessmen.

"I am trying to get to Monte De Libertad," he explained pleasantly to a girl at Aerolinas Argentinas counter.

She dropped her gaze, tapping the keyboard furiously. A few minutes later she looked up.

"I can get you a flight to Santiago and a connection," she said with consternation. "But only in business class."

"No problem," said Darius reassuringly. "My company will reimburse me."

A short time later he crossed the metal detector, which remained silent at his passing. He slowly made his way to the VIP lounge and sat down in the corner, stewards falling over each other to make a fuss over a wounded guest. He accepted an offer of drink, choosing a rich Shiraz which he savoured for the first time since being shot.

Unfortunately, he stared at it a moment too long, and its lavish colour became the robe of a small man with a greying goatee, his voice droning in passable Latin.

Darius was lying on the rack, his cord-like arms enclosed in solid metal restraints. The droning emanated from a senior official of the Holy Inquisition, who revelled in not only being the first man in history to capture an incubus, but to have a conversation with one.

The evidence spoke for itself – a specimen of apparent male perfection, complete with an impossibly long phallus, totally insensitive to pain and mocking his torturers as they tried to damage him. He reminded them that they were prohibited from drawing his blood by Inquisition's own rules, all in scholarly Latin, not the bastard version spoken by many priests.
The incubus laughed as they broke a gear on the rack attempting to stretch his spine, and his crushed fingers appeared to belong to another body, for all his reaction to their mutilation.

Darius learned that the servant's discussion with the priest was recorded in lurid detail, after which the whore made a miraculous recovery from her affliction, deciding, instantly, to become a nun. This expression of spiritual rapture also happened to end her dealings with Inquisition, which would otherwise be required to purge her of sin by various inconvenient means.

It was the mangy village priest who understood the significance of a woman being burned by her lover's seed. It made instant sense in the light of his lord's legendary physical strength and contemptuous refusal to baptise his son.

When the broken body of that child was recovered from the moat, investigators made careful note of copious body hair and the rudimentary tail visible at the base of the spine, an obvious mark of the child's infernal parentage.

Contessa's body was tied to a stake and burned in the main square, after being sprayed with enough holy water to make the wood reluctant to ignite.

Some distance away there was a smaller pile for her son. The wood was green, and it took a long time for flames to bring the awful scene to conclusion. Darius forced himself to watch from the window of his cell.

As embers died at the end of that vile day and the last of the onlookers drifted from the plaza, he twisted the chain that bound his wrists until he could get enough leverage, and one link broke along a weak forge. He did the same with his ankles, and when they came for him through the narrow entrance to the cell, he rammed the door from inside, throwing them backwards.

He burst from his cell and rushed headlong, killing the entire detail with blows delivered with fragments of heavy manacles, swung like mace from both wrists. He was grateful for that chain – his fingers were too damaged to use in a meaningful manner. Darius ran through the prison, starting fires along the way and escaping among the throng of men running from the burning building.

He was crudely disguised in the helmet and cloak of a guard, whose neck he broke not far from the exit, and no one saw him dissolve into the deepening dusk. In those dangerous times few cared that the abbot who presided over the capture of his incubus soon disappeared during a rain-soaked journey to a nearby village.

There were whispers about his guards being found massacred, their bodies dismembered by what looked like a giant axe and gnawed by animals of the forest. But Inquisition heard every whisper, and it had ways of silencing rumours.

As for the abbot, or what little was left of him, being found in a large hole filled with hundreds of rats, with whom he apparently shared more than the last few days of his life bound to a heavy log hand and foot – that rumour was too awful to be believed.

***

Turner and Maggie awoke the next morning and caught the train to the commercial port. They walked along the quay until they found the berth whose number he wrote down after calling the port authority.

The boat they sought was an ageing ocean-going trawler. A huge Maori man slept on a blow-up mattress, barring the gangplank. Turner woke him up politely and asked to see Frankie.

The sentry ambled up the gangplank and soon came back with another Maori man who was only slightly smaller. His face broke into exuberant smile at the sight of Turner.

"Jack!" he nimbly ran down the gangplank and threw his arms around Turner, nearly knocking him off his feet.

"Good to see you, Frankie," replied Turner, returning the embrace to the best of his size and strength.

"Let's go on board," said Frankie. He looked at Maggie uncertainly.

"This is Maggie," said Turner, extending one arm around her.

"Hi, Maggie," said Frankie. "Kia Ora. That means 'welcome' in my language."

"Thank you," said Maggie with instinctive warmth.

They were soon on board and in the captain's quarters, Frankie pouring whiskey into coffee mugs.

"Fucking good to see you, man," he said to Turner.

"You too," answered Turner. "You been okay?"

"Oh, you know," said Frankie vaguely. He handed them their cups. "A false charge here and there. A bit of a bankruptcy. Wife's fat. Kids growing. Doing good."

"Great," answered Turner. "Cheers."

They toasted and sipped the single malt.

"Need help?" asked Frankie.

"Yeah," said Turner. "We'd like to get over to Aoteoroa. Real quiet, like."

"Ah," said Frankie. "You kill too many bastards?"

"Something like that," replied Turner.

"You both going?"

"Yeah."

Frankie nodded slowly. "You in real trouble?"

"Yeah, we are."
"All right." The Maori skipper went through a few

things in his head, counting them off on his fingers in silence. "We sail tomorrow night. Can't leave sooner – our engines are being serviced. The contractor's pulled the top off one motor, otherwise I would put out now."

"Tomorrow is fine," said Turner reassuringly. "We'll come back at midday."

Frankie swigged more of his whiskey.

"About time, Turner," he said.

"What do you mean?" asked Maggie, breaking her silence for the first time.

"Oh," Frankie looked at her as if he just saw her. "See, dear, what you have here is a real man. About time he went to live where real men belong."

He hugged Turner with one arm and emphatically drained his mug with the other.

***

Turner walked along a busy street, the traffic snarled through the long stretch of shops. He wore mirror sunglasses which completely obscured his face, but just to be sure he added a false grey moustache and also shaved his hair, wearing a stylish pork pie hat over his raw scalp.

He strolled around his intended destination until he saw what he wanted.

A large semi-trailer was trapped in the one-way street, the driver tapping his hands on the steering wheel to music no one else could hear.

The lights changed to red just ahead of the truck. The driver leaned back and shut his eyes.

Turner walked across the road abruptly. As he passed the vast grille of the semi trailer's bonnet, he grasped the pistol grip in his pocket.

He kept the sawn-off shotgun he used on the bulldozer in the police headquarters, along with a box of the solid slug cartridges. He now aimed the cut barrels through the lining of his coat.

As he passed the truck, he pulled both triggers. The roar of the shotgun was disconcertingly loud, even in peak hour traffic, but there were few pedestrians to hear it at that particular moment.

Two solid projectiles shattered the first cylinder, and the engine seized. The prime mover rocked on its suspension and came to a dead halt as the lights turned green, the traffic immediately building up behind it.

Turner completed the road crossing and walked quickly for the next five hundred yards until he was well in the middle of the traffic jam. He then entered a bank with an envelope in his hand and joined the teller queue to await his turn.

"Next please," he heard at last. Turner marched to the indicated window and passed over his envelope.

"Just this, thanks," he said pleasantly.

The clerk opened his envelope and studied the single sheet of paper within. Her face turned pale.

"No sudden moves," reminded Turner calmly. "Call the manager."

The manager, an older man with a suit stretched over a bulging paunch, joined her instantly, looking at Turner with fear.

"Here's the deal, pop," said Turner, opening his coat to show the manager a glimpse of the double barrels. "These can blast through the whole counter. Now, all I want is money, okay? There is no need for anyone to get hurt."

The manager nodded eagerly.

"I want three hundred thousand in bills of fifty and hundred," said Turner. "If you don't come back with it, this lady will die."

"Don't do that, mister," said the manager hastily. "You can have what you want."

"Fill your briefcase with the money and bring it out here," said Turner. "Don't close it. If there is a dye bomb, you die first."

"Right," said the manager breathlessly. "Give me a minute."

He left hurriedly. Turner smiled at the clerk pleasantly then turned away from her, looking like a man patiently awaiting resolution of a bureaucratic misunderstanding.

A few minutes later the manager came out of his side office with a large vinyl briefcase and stood next to the door. Turner nodded at the clerk and walked over to look inside the briefcase.

At this point the guard standing outside the bank entrance turned and ran inside.

Turner had his pistol out before the guard made it past the glass doors, but the young man didn't look up in time and pulled his revolver out of the holster.

Turner fired a single round in his direction, and the guard fell back against the wall, gun clattering from his grip to the floor.

Turner pushed the manager away and briefly checked the contents of the briefcase. He snapped it closed after rifling through bundles of cash, put it under his arm and walked out of the bank past the body sitting against the wall in a spreading puddle of blood.

The traffic was still stuck behind the stranded semi trailer. Turner heard the police sirens in the distance, but they had half of a mile to go to the scene of his crime and only if they were able to run that far. He walked briskly, one hand sweating around the pistol in his coat pocket.

He swung into an alley off the shopping precinct, which led to the nearby train station. Stepping into an alcove half-filled with smelly rubbish bins, he stripped off his hat, glasses, moustache and coat. He transferred the contents of the briefcase into a day pack worn on his shoulders under the coat and distributed his discarded gear between different rubbish bins.

The sawn-off shotgun was wrapped into smelly newspaper from one of the bins and thrown onto the roof of the building behind him. He heard it slide into the gutter noisily and dumped the remaining shells into a storm drain filled with filthy water.

He walked out of the alley less than two minutes later, an athletic-looking tourist from New Zealand who had a passport to say so in his pocket – just so long as nobody looked inside the heavy backpack or wondered why he hid an automatic pistol in his stylish track suit. He managed to arrive at the rail station just as a city-bound express was approaching the platform.

As the train pulled away, Turner watched police cars cordon off the shopping precinct with collegial approval.

***

They approached the coast in damp darkness of an early morning, its strong surf buffeting the trawler. As the light crept over the mountainous horizon, Turner and Frankie embraced.

"I am glad, man," said Frankie. "All that shit back in Timor. I don't think we are even, but at least I could pay back a little."

"Oh, we are even, all right," replied Turner, slapping his hands around the skipper's large shoulders. "Look me up any time you need a vasectomy."

Slightly unbalanced by his backpack, he climbed down into an inflatable boat Frankie's men winched into the turbid West Coast surf.

"So long, Jack," yelled Frankie, bathed in pink morning light. Turner saluted him lightly and clipped the backpack to the side of the boat before he did anything else.

Maggie made it down, and Turner started the engine. He tossed the line back to the deckhand and pointed the inflatable towards distant shore, just visible in the dim light of dawn.

Their boat rocked on two-foot waves as it closed the

distance to dry land. Turner looked back to see the trawler head out to sea, its engines struggling against incoming tide.

They ran the last few hundred meters at high speed, engine cut only at the last minute. The inflatable shot over the last of the surf to land on the pale sand shadowed by lush vegetation. It stopped as the propeller ploughed a long track in New Zealand's soil.

They sat still for some minutes, taking in the new reality. Then Turner stood up and vaulted over the side into the sand.

"Here we come," he announced quietly.

***

Darius smiled at the young shop assistant benignly.

"I need to check something over a telephone line," he said, proffering her a few banknotes. "It won't take long."

She studied the banknotes and shook her head.

"Sorry," she said uncertainly. "I don't think we are allowed to let the customers use the phone."

Darius peeled off some more notes and put them on the counter.

"It'll only take ten minutes," he said. "Really. After that you can cut me off yourself."

She looked around in a furtive gesture.

"Can you do it out here?" she asked quickly.

"Oh yes," replied Darius. He picked up the telephone and pulled out the line. "All I need is this."

She pocketed the notes, turning away from him. Darius fired up his laptop and dialled the hospital's pathology mainframe.

It took him no time to log in with administrator's privileges, using a pirate program he downloaded from the Internet after finding out the brand of the hospital's database server.

He found his blood results and read them with some amusement. Then he changed the hospital number for all of them, linking them to the identity of a drunk with recurrent liver failure, whose file he spied in the nurses' station on one of his walks.

Just to be sure, he corrupted the entries, replacing them with what looked like gibberish from one of his laptop's system files. Then he logged out.

He closed the laptop and repacked it, reconnecting the shop's telephone. The entire operation took just seven minutes.

He bowed politely to the shop assistant and wheeled his trolley towards the nearest bookshop.

By the time his plane was boarding, Darius knew a lot about Central America and its ugly politics. His head was full of facts and figures about banana plantations and underwater oil drilling.

He left the books he just read on a coffee table in the departure lounge, taking with him only the Spanish dictionary, which he intended to memorize on the flight. It was some years since he spoke Spanish. Indeed, Spain was still in charge of both Americas at that time.

***

Maggie and Turner dragged the boat into bushes and deflated it, hiding the engine inside the collapsed craft. They covered the lot with branches and other detritus from the floor of the lush tropical forest that came within a few metres of the beach.

Frankie said that if all went well, one of his crew would dispatch a cousin to collect it in a few days.

They walked down the beach in search of access to the seaside highway.

"Aw, fuck," screamed Maggie. "What are these?"

Turner flicked around on his heels, gun in hand. Then his face spread into a sly grin.

"Sand flies," he said gleefully. "Welcome to Aotearoa. Now roll down your sleeves like I told you to do in the boat."

Maggie stuck out her tongue, but complied immediately. They started walking again.

"How long do these itch for?" asked Maggie sullenly.

"Oh, about ten days," replied Turner helpfully. "But it's only bad at night."

"Fuck," said Maggie soulfully. "I'd rather have snakes. Maybe New Zealand isn't such a good idea."

"Oh, never mind," said Turner. "It's only in summer. Too cold for insects the rest of the year."

"Great," answered Maggie. "Just great. Any other surprises?"

"Yes," said Turner. "We are still alive."

"Right," acknowledged Maggie. "But for how long?"

"I don't know," replied Turner neutrally.

"Right," said Maggie.

"Well," Turner stopped to look at her. His loose shirt was whipped by the stiff breeze coming off the surf, and Maggie suddenly realized that even domed by his stubbled scalp, he was a very handsome man. "How long does anyone have, anyway?"

Maggie nodded in acknowledgement of this point. She put her arms about Turner's neck and kissed him for a little while. He kissed back.

Rather than bash uphill through dense vegetation, they walked nearly a mile until the road came close to the beach and climbed the embankment. A friendly tow truck driver gave them a lift into town where they found a cheap motel, scored some delicious fish and chips at the local grease outlet and fell into bed.

Turner warded off sex. He needed his energy for the next day, when he planned to use a backpack full of false documents and real money to start a new life.

Epilogue

Turner gratefully sank onto veranda steps and poured Chardonnay from an unlabelled bottle. As befitted his new profession, he carefully studied the colour, sniffed and sipped the fruity liquid before imbibing it for its true purpose – reduction of anxiety and inducement of euphoria.

An icy gust blew across mountains into the valley. He took another sip of wine and pulled the unzipped jacket closer to his body.

He did very well to snap up this long, narrow block of land wedged between two jagged ridge lines that ran straight into the sea. It was completely suited for its present purpose, the growing of excellent grape, whose juice was gratefully purchased and bottled by nearby wineries.

However, that was not Turner's concern when he bought it – he was far more impressed with lack of access into the valley. The only way in was from the coast, unless one had access to aircraft or enthusiasm for mountaineering with the added weight of firearms.

From his porch he could see the entire valley, now denuded of lush native forest and covered with rows of vines, their leaves bright yellow in the tentative afternoon light of late autumn.

Years took their toll, joints creaking and backs hurting. But hard labour slowly relieved the sleep deprivation of those who suffer frequent nightmares and awaken at the slightest noise.

They worked it to a point where it was realistic to feel safe. The entire valley was covered by infrared sensors, solar-powered and transmitting all night. They weren't too good to begin with, going off at little more than birds and rats, but they now had them tuned to the point where even with dogs false alarms were rare.

The dogs patrolled the valley each and every night and were only allowed to stay in the sheds when the valley was snowed in, which usually happened for a few weeks every year.

A row of piercing spotlights with bulletproof shields could reach to the mouth of the valley. Turner wired them to trip the generator, as they could drain the house batteries within one hour.

The good news was about guns. New Zealand turned out to be a gun freak's paradise, with all manner of legal and illegal weapons selling for next to nothing, and ammunition for them to be had with no questions asked.

After a number of discrete shopping trips and given just a little warning, they could hold off a whole battalion with what was stored behind a false kitchen cupboard. The battalion would be much smaller by the time they finished – Maggie turned out to be a superb shot who could give Turner a run for his money.

She got back from town when Turner was into his third glass, almost recovered from the day's exertions. Maggie swung the truck around and climbed down from the cabin, carrying a few plastic bags.

She was now a startlingly beautiful woman, whose looks would have caused her a major problem in a larger community. Her auburn hair was streaked with blond from the deadly New Zealand sun, and lines formed at the corners of her eyes, where most locals had permanent wrinkles from squinting.

Her skin was not yet harmed by this light but glowed a perfect colour of honey. The figure was now more mature, with wider hips and larger breasts, but she was still as taut as a wire, her posture strong and sure.

The other door of the truck cabin suddenly sprang open, then Turner heard it slam. A boy of five with Turner's tall forehead and Maggie's eyes ran towards him, firing a new water pistol from the hip. He was not without success, Turner hurrying to put his hand over his wine glass but copping the rest on his face.

"Oh, you little devil," he said proudly. "Stop, ratbag. Go do it to your mother."

The boy ran up and collided with him at full speed, throwing his arms around his father's neck. Turner saved the glass just in time and put it down, clasping his son in a bear hug.

"Ouch, daddy," said little James.

"Oh, sorry," Turner released him and rubbed the boy's ribs where they dug into the gun in his holster.

But his son already forgot about pain, bringing up the water pistol to aim at Maggie, who was walking up to them with her shopping.

"No!" she cried with mock anger. "You promised, remember?"

"Oh, yeah," said James. He pretended to safe the water pistol, thumbing the replica of a safety catch and tucked it into the waistband of his pants.

Turner sighed inwardly at this display of expertise and stood up, lifting James out of his mother's way. They each took a bag out of her arms and walked her to the kitchen. Turner returned to the porch whilst they unpacked.

With his son inside, he whistled curtly. Five blue heelers raced up from the shed where they lead a rather indolent life by day. They fanned out into the vine rows for their nightly patrol.

Maggie came out with James and a fresh glass. She poured herself some wine and let James sniff it. They touched their glasses in a toast, James extracting the water pistol from his pants and toasting with it instead of a glass.

As they drank, he put the muzzle in his mouth and sucked out some water. That didn't work well, so he pumped the trigger. Turner cringed.

"Now, that's not a good thing to do with a gun," said Maggie.

"No," the boy conceded. "But this isn't a real gun, Mummy. When I grow up and carry a real gun, I would never put it in my mouth. You know that!"

Turner shook his head in sadness, his expression downcast.

Maggie sat close to him and put her head on his arm. James climbed up his father's back and sat on his shoulders, sipping water from his pistol out of parents' sight.

They drank and gazed at the mouth of the valley, visualizing an attack as it would come.

They willed the cold wind to blow down mountain ridges.

They commanded the sun to let earth descend into winter.
They yearned for snow that falls softly through the night, disconnecting the world from their shelter.

They craved just a few blissful weeks of safety that would last until the snow melted again, laying them bare to their past.

IBE
2000 – 2005